imagination series #14

Cleveland State University Poetry Center

Acknowledgments

An earlier version of Ruthanne Wiley's novella was published as her Master's thesis by the Cleveland State University Department of English in 1998.

Thanks to Sheila Schwartz for conceiving of the contest and for her on-going support.

Thanks to Michelle Herman for judging the inaugural contest.

Special thanks to Eli Epstein and Adam Epstein for their help and support.

Thanks also to Will Wells for proofreading and Jessica Schantz for type-setting.

ISBN: 978-1-880834-75-6
Library of Congress Catalog Card Number: 2006939997

Ohio Arts Council
A STATE AGENCY
THAT SUPPORTS PUBLIC
PROGRAMS IN THE ARTS

Duo: Novellas

Volume 1

Nothing and Two
by Ruthanne Wiley

Isn't That Just Like You?
by Eric Anderson
Winner of the Inaugural Ruthanne Wiley
Memorial Novella Contest

Contents

Series Introduction

by Sheila Schwartz

When I first began teaching novella writing courses in 1983, the required anthology advised that this form of fiction was anywhere from 60-120 pages.

"That's a pretty big range," my students complained.

Even worse, the anthology contained a novella which was 45 pages long, and one which was 128 pages.

"What does this mean?" the students clamored. "Does this definition have any meaning?"

The editor's introduction continued with a description of novella qualities that was like a smorgasbord, a list nearly as long as a novella: The novella has the single-minded focus of the short story. The novella is decorated with a series of unified images, like the short story. The novella takes a deep, deep point of view like the short story, it often includes rants by madmen—or madwomen.

"Do we need to include all of these?" my students asked. I threw up my hands. I had never written a novella. I was as close to the edge of not knowing as they were. All I knew was that I loved this form. All I knew was that I knew one when I saw one.

One like the novella included here, *Nothing and Two* by Ruthanne Wiley. Her story of a girl imbued with the spirit of rebellion inspired this contest. Ruthanne worked on this novella in graduate school. She was putting the final touches on her story when she died suddenly in 2003. Her son Adam's tribute describes her memorable voice and personality, the liveliness that was in her and in her writing. We wanted to bring this work of fiction to light, bring light to our contest, start it off on the right foot.

The same is true of the second novella included here, which is our contest winner, *Isn't That Just Like You?* by Eric Anderson. It is a lovely and elegant example of how to weave a series of events together through a unified point of view. The way in which Rona interprets her world enlivens the story with humor, drama, and irony.

Both of these novellas illustrate the discoveries I made about the form as I continued to teach it. I began to see what the possibilities were, what I enjoyed most about this particular length fiction. There are effects which seem to work best at a certain length: the focus on a single plot, a single point of view, a single theme or subject, the sheer intensity of the novella, like a short story, but even more so. It has an arc that stands out. It often ends the way a short story does with a unifying epiphany. Events are interconnected. They build upon one another to a climactic turning point, as in a short story. Like a short story, it is best read in one sitting.

Then there are its novel-like qualities, which also delight. The novella may have many episodes. It may cover a great deal of time. It may include many characters. It may philosophize. It may give you the impression of an entire world or historical era.

I have my own thoughts on the PERFECT novella: *Sula* by Toni Morrison, *Goodbye Columbus* by Philip Roth (a textbook example if you want to call it that. Learn how this novella works and you understand the essence of Novella). Most recently there is Michael Chabon's breathtaking work, *The Final Solution*, and *Caroline's Wedding*, by Edwidge Danticat, one of the very briefest of novellas. (Richard Ford includes it in his wonderful anthology, *The Long Story*).

Like other editors who have tried to articulate the joys of novell-as, I'm well on my way here to producing another definition-fest. I now understand that the strength of the novella is to produce so many dazzling effects.

Justifiably, the novella has had a resurgence in the past few years. Novella contests. Collections of novellas published by one author. Reviews of novellas. New anthologies.

We hope that our annual contest will contribute to the continued exploration and popularity of this form. The novellas we're publishing this year bode well.

—Shiela Schwartz

Nothing and Two
by Ruthanne Wiley

Preface
Adam Epstein

Voices. My mother had a beautiful voice.

I suppose many children find their mothers' voices soothing, but more than just the sound of her voice lingers in my mind. What stands out is rather the generosity with which she expressed her love for me and her genuine delight in speaking to me, whether I was two or twelve. For instance, I can vividly recall many evenings of my mom giving me a bath in the porcelain clawed tub in my parent's bathroom in our old, six-bedroom house. I don't know many children who look forward to their bath, but as a young boy I took great joy in this nightly ritual.

My mother would tell me fantastic bath-time stories. They were usually participatory, totally engaging, and always funny. I remember the classic one she used to tell me about the boy who never cut his fingernails. There was so much dirt and space underneath that tomato plants began growing under his nails (we tended tomato plants in our garden). This story was as entertaining as it was a ploy to convince me to submit to the nail-clipping scissors after the bath. It usually worked. Other narratives starred me in extraordinary stories with the pterodactyls, brontosauruses, or T-rexes that I'd seen at the Cleveland Natural History Museum. Other stories were full of Carrollian nonsense and often I got to fill in the details. She completely improvised all these stories, and they were different every time.

Sometimes during my bath, waiting for the shampoo to take effect before I dunked my head to rinse, mom and I would play speaking games, for lack of a better term. We played this one game called "Junior Mosquito" (pronounced mo-skwee-toe), in which I would play a boy mosquito named Junior and mom would play my cockney-accented insect mother. Every time we played, I (as Junior Mosquito) would be in trouble for biting a human and my mother would read me the riot act for what I had done. Pausing in her lecture, she would say, "And what do you have to say for yourself, Junior Mo-skwee-toe?" I would attempt to explain myself, saying, "um, well, uh…", but before I could say anything of substance, mom would interrupt, "Don't speak, Junior Mo-skwee-toe, you are in far too much trouble already," in her nasal cockney voice. I giggled every time. This continued for a few rounds until she couldn't go on anymore and I had laughed to my satisfaction, though I was always ready for "one more time."

Then there were the story games that involved my bath toys. It is these parts of my baths that I remember the best. Our favorite was the continuing adventures of Cecil, a small, rubber Dragon with wings who would constantly get tired flying across the vast ocean of the bathtub on her way to her aunt's house or a family reunion or something. Mom played Cecil and would adopt the perfect raspy voice of a fatigued and slightly pathetic aging, female dragon. While the particulars of Cecil's travels were different every time we played, it was always the case that Cecil would land on the snout of my mostly submerged killer whale toy, mistaking it for a nice rock to rest on and sun herself. She would say, "Oh god, this is nice, I'm so exhaaaausted." Inevitably, I, playing the otherwise tacit killer whale, would thrust the toy upwards in an attempt to eat Cecil. In a flurry of flapping wings, Cecil would jump to the other end of the bathtub. Panting on her side, she would say her famous line, "Oh God, how awful." I belly-laughed madly and asked for it again if I didn't yet have "chicken fingers"—what we called the water-logged, wrinkly skin of a very long bath.

After my bath, mom would race me to see who could get their PJs on the fastest. I would quickly get into bed, and she would read me a bedtime story, usually Goodnight Moon, Dr. Seuss, or a Babar book. She always read these with funny voices suited to every character. I would often chime in to identify the mouse in Goodnight Moon or the party hats in Go, Dog, Go! The sweet melody of her voice singing lullabies about pirate ships brought me to sleep on these nights.

In retrospect, it was a bittersweet loss for me when I began to take showers and read myself to sleep.

Still, my mother's voice was always present as I grew up. As during bath time, she was always talking to me and encouraging me to talk. Coming home from school, I would have long conversations with her about my day—what I had learned, which kids were nice, who the bullies were, etc. This even continued into my teen years; I genuinely enjoyed talking with her about whatever. I especially liked all the imitations she did. From teachers, friends, and family, to the world's fastest talker and other colorful, but fictitious characters, she always had a great "voice" to share. I remember going on road trips with her on the Ohio and Pennsylvania Turnpikes, when she would pretend to be a dim-witted woman with a Southern drawl every time we had to pay a toll. To the attendant in the booth, she would say things like, "Now I've been working with this for a few hours [the toll ticket], and I can't make head nor tail of it. Do we owe the $1.43 or the $72.50?" Another favorite was, "Can I keep this card? We've been using it to play bingo." Nine times out of ten, the toll takers would take her completely seriously and impatiently answer her absurd questions. I enjoyed pretending too, even though I laughed way too hard to be remotely plausible.

She could convince anyone that the voice she adopted was completely authentic. One particularly memorable time was when she called up the National Football League to protest Art Model's moving of the Cleveland Browns to Baltimore. A die-hard sports fan of all the Cleveland teams, she could not let this pass unheard. She called up the NFL about twenty times in a row, each time adopting a different voice, matching accents from different regions of the country, sometimes using a man's voice. From toll booths to telephones, mom knew how to have a good gag.

I do not want to make it seem that my mother used her voice in only humorous ways. A Unitarian church school director, she had a clear, patient manner with all of the children. She also spoke against violent toys at Church, organizing an innovative and well-attended Toy Gun Buyback event. In all these endeavors, she was very eloquent and always completed whatever she put her mind to.

And so it was with writing. From all these anecdotes about my mother, it is obvious that she was a gifted storyteller. In fact, when she first met with Sheila Schwartz at Cleveland State University about the Master's program in Creative Writing in the late nineties, she made a point to mention her narrative abilities during my baths. Later in her writing career, she wrote a short piece called "Bathtime Story," a tale that I like to read once in a while to remind me of my baths. I can hear her voice very clearly when I read those words of that wacky tale about Kitchen Utensils gossiping.

But it was not until my mother began to write Nothing and Two that she began to hear other voices. As a kind of literary schizophrenia that all writers must suffer from to a certain extent, my mother was haunted by her characters. She would wake up in the middle of the night to Billy Ray's voice, who was saying, "You better get out of bed and write this down, 'cuz I ain't gonna tell you this in the mornin'."

He would then narrate her next passage or reveal a new detail as my mom wrote away. The few times she didn't get up, Billy Ray was right.

My mother threw her whole self into her passions, a trait which she happily passed on to me. She worked feverishly on her novella for hours on our old, boxy Mac Color Classic, constantly backing up her latest revisions on a floppy disk. Often, she would read her latest paragraphs to my dad and me. When reading, she would always take on a sort of authoritative narrator's voice—quite different from her mothering voice—yet giving a special accent or manner to her characters. She was constantly searching for the authentic voices of her characters. As a rule, mom began a story with ideas for her characters, and she would fit a plot around them, just as she did in the stories of my childhood.

I believe that in her search for her characters' voices, my mother was really looking for her own voice, deeply desiring to share it with others. Her imitations, her lullabies, her piano and violin playing, her dreams of Billy Ray, her singing, her bathtime stories, and her fictions—these and so much more were all her true voice, all aspects of a beautiful expressive self that was shining out to share with others. I think that her writing was the next step in her lifelong career of creative expression. In truth, all of these voices were authentically hers.

How lucky was I that I got to be her son, with her in the flesh for nearly fifteen years. Always telling me stories, asking me questions, engaging me, encouraging me to talk—I feel that my voice is so much a legacy of hers. She taught me that much of life was about sharing it with others in a loving and truthful way.

Nearly six years ago, my mother was quickly silenced by a sudden heart trauma that none of her doctors anticipated. She had been trying to publish her novel and had just begun another. At her funeral, my dad read the opening passage from her novel, and we played a video tape of her talking to me as a two-year old from behind the camera. Though we could not see her face, her voice filled the room with her still very lively spirit. It is such a comfort to hear her voice on that tape every time I watch it, for it is often easy to forget that sound, even one so familiar, and all the feelings associated with it.

For me, the publishing of this volume is a remembrance and an affirmation of my mother's voice. I feel so grateful for this opportunity for my mother to share her voice with others, even in her afterlife. Their voices echoing in their writings and the memories of those they knew, people as lively as my mother do not die so quickly.

Many thanks to Sheila Schwartz, Neal Chandler, the CSU English Department, The CSU Poetry Center, Whiskey Island Magazine, my dad, my dog Elvis, and the late Robert Lauretig for making this book possible. And thanks to you, the reader, for listening to a bit of my mother's voice. May you feel as engaged and involved in her yarns as I did when I took my baths. May you, too, receive some beauty from her stories.

I love you, mommy. Thank you for sharing your voice with me and so many others. You totally deserve this.

—Adam Epstein
   1 September 2006
   Mussoorie, Uttaranchal, India.

Nothing and Two

Prologue

It is just there, beyond the shining grass, beckoning like a tune he remembers but can't sing, returning to him from long before; and Virgil is almost ready. He can almost believe. But now he feels Billy Ray's voice, near, reaching for him, pulling him back to the beginning, telling him again to remember, to write it down: It was a game. . . . It was a game. . . .

I.

Fontana Lake Retirement Home
Near Bryson City, North Carolina
Present Day

"It was a game like any other," Billy Ray began.

"Top of the eighth. We're ahead, 9-8, but they got runners on second and third, no outs, with their big lumber coming up. I look over at Diz, and he's doing what Diz done best—figuring. He looks like he's about to make a move, and when Diz is about to make a move, you just leave him alone. That much I knew.

"The moon looks like a giant hanging curve ball as it rides the awesome blackness of night in June. I have a mind to snatch that moon down and throw it over the plate. I keep thinking the moon's watching the game, waiting to see what move old Diz is going to make.

"Moon like that reminds me of my mama, on account of her love for the sky and anything in it. I used to sit on her lap at games from the time I was born. When somebody hit one deep, she'd say, 'There goes another one. The sky burns with home runs. See how they all stick up there? That's where they go to live. The sky is the only place that can hold their heat.'

"She believed in such a thing as that. She believed the night sky to be guardian of the fire, a fire so hot it burned white rings around the eyes of the owl who tried to capture it. She was part Cherokee, on her mother's side. That's where my mama learned those things, sir. From those who still believe them.

"Her Cherokee name was Digu-Lanahita. It means One Having Long Ears. Yes, her ears were big, like mine, but her ears were long in memory, in what she'd heard and remembered. The Cherokee called her Lanahita. Everyone else called her Lana Poole, even her children.

"Lana Poole loved the game. She loved it any way she could get it. The Cherokee way, with sticks and a rolling ball and a dance before and after suited her just fine. But she could lift a bat through the air too. She played for Ralph's Diner in Bryson City and before that, played catcher for a Bloomer Girls Team over in Knoxville. Caught a great game. Now some folks say that a woman, if she's going to play, shouldn't play catcher—it's unladylike. But Lana Poole said that playing catcher was the most ladylike thing she ever did. Had great knees. Even after seven babies, had knees like steel coils.

"Lana Poole was at the game that night, sir. But even she, with all her intuition, did not know what was about to happen, or so she claimed later.

"So anyway, we're all waiting for Diz to make his move. Then Joey Asper, the bat boy, comes out of the clubhouse looking like a scared rabbit. He says 'Diz, there's a delivery for you.' Now everybody in the whole state knew that you don't bother Diz when he's figuring and Joey knew it too. I remind Joey that we got us a situation here and he should shut up. Diz just ignores him.

"I see that Diz is ready. He moves like he's underwater. He strolls out to the mound. He whispers to the pitcher, King Presley, for a bit, kicking dirt, his back to the crowd. Then he takes the ball from King and waves to the bullpen real slow, like a snail in syrup. Jesus 'The Savior Carpenter has been ready for two innings, revved up like a corvette on cement blocks with the engine running. King crawls back to the dugout, head bowed, and The Savior comes out of the pen like he's been finally set free. I saw this dance a thousand times. I could've seen it with my eyes closed.

"Diz comes back to the dugout with that moonshine following him like a puppy in love. He sits down and Joey starts yammering again. 'Diz, there's a package for you out back.' Jesus is still throwing warm up pitches and Joey goes into the clubhouse and directly brings out a basket, all covered up with a torn blanket and a note on it that plainly says 'Diz.' Now I knew that Diz could read his name but had trouble with big words. He opens the note, studies it a little, crumples it up real gentle and puts it in his pocket. The moon's just shining on him like he's an angel or something. It fairly takes my breath.

"I didn't know what was in the basket, but I didn't ask, 'cause if Diz wanted you to know something, he'd tell you. And besides, I thought it was probably just a load of corn muffins from some widow lady or maybe even a mess of new flies from one of Diz's fishing partners. Diz had many admirers. But Joey should've known better than to bother Diz with any of that during a game.

"Meanwhile, Jesus must have left the engine running too long 'cause his first pitch goes out of the park and the next three batters all reach. Now they're ahead, 11—9, and Diz goes back to figuring. The basket's right next to him and he kind of fusses with the blanket a little. Then he does his dance to the mound and makes the call for Mongoose McCoy. Kid threw about two hundred miles an hour, everywhere but over the plate.

"While Diz is out on the mound I hear it for the first time. Just a crumb of a wail. Then the basket shakes a little and starts screaming like it's possessed by the devil. All the guys in the dugout, including me, freeze. We just sit there like we're stuck up to our asses in swamp mud.

"Diz comes back from the mound like everything is as usual. He sits down, looks at the basket and uncovers it. That moonshine is leaking all over and Diz says, 'Hush now, honey. Mongoose'll pitch all right, you'll see.' Then he brings up a little tobacco to the edge of his tongue and lets it go. Now I'd been watching Diz for years and I knew that when he hit that spot, he'd made up his mind on something."

Billy Ray straightened his bow tie and leaned close to Virgil.

"It was a baby. A tiny, shiny baby. And when Diz tells it to hush, it just hushed up real fast. And it shut up for the rest of the game.

"Lana Poole breezed by and looked into the dugout and saw the baby and said 'Is it ball-sticks or bread?', meaning, in the old Cherokee way, is it a boy or a girl. 'It's bread,' I told her, and she seemed pleased."

Billy Ray leaned back in his rocker. He rested his hands on his knees and spread his eyes over Fontana Lake.

"Game went sixteen innings that night. We won, 19—18. Mongoose pitched ok, better than usual. Only hit five batters. That baby lay there in her basket and never so much as peeped. But I thought I could hear her breathing, slow and measured, like Diz when he's figuring. She watched Diz the whole time, as did the moon.

"When I was a child Lana Poole told me that long ago, the moon was a ball that was thrown against the sky in a Cherokee game. Two tribes were playing each other. One of the tribes had the best runners and had almost won the game, but then their leader picked up the ball with his hand—a thing that is forbidden in Cherokee ball play—and tried to throw it through the goal; but the ball, which knew it had been unfairly touched, struck against the hard vault of sky. It fastened itself there as a warning to all players to respect the rules of the game."

Virgil nodded and wrote in his notebook. He didn't look up. He tried not to grunt. Cherokees and owls and Bloomer Girls and moons and babies in the dugout. What an assignment, he thought. Just great. "Okay, got it. What next?"

Billy Ray leaned forward in his rocker and pushed himself up to stand. "Next, I go inside and get some fresh cigars. You sit here and wait. When I come back, we'll have us a little chat."

Something about the way Billy Ray looked when he said that made
Virgil feel a little nervous, as though the teacher had just told him to stay
after school.

II.

The Fontana Lake Retirement Home was a Grecian style century house with wide porches hugging all sides and thick, gracious
white columns supporting the second floor balconies. It slumbered at
the eastern end of Fontana Lake between the Smoky and Blue Ridge
Mountains, and though it needed some minor repairs and a good paint
job, one thing it did not lack was rockers. Rockers crowded the porches
like gulls on a beach and were at least twice as noisy. The house was
surrounded by overgrown gardens that sagged with robust lavendar
lilacs, hanging like ripe grapes on bent branches as though in a suspended curtsy; and though the tulips were long past, Virgil could still
see soft bits of burnt red and yellow scattered under the headless
stalks. Below, at the bottom of a long slope, Fontana Lake proclaimed
its ancient blueness. Virgil thought if you had to be parked somewhere when you were old, this might be a tolerable place for some,
although he didn't think that personally he could take the charm of it
for more than a day or two. For him it was just too sweet, like too
much cake.

Virgil Alcover wrote for a small sports weekly and had been on
the minor league beat for twenty-three years, mostly on the road, eating bad food at rural diners and listening to prospects lie about how
great it was to play in the minors. The knowledge Virgil had attained
over the years bored him, sickened him, made him wonder sometimes
why he'd chosen this path, for he couldn't truly remember the reason.
It wasn't so much that baseball had become boring, though there were
things about the game that bothered him. It was the stories that irritated him. He didn't know if he could stand to hear any more stories.
Lately he felt that there was no way to tell if the people he interviewed
told him the truth or not. After all, they could say anything to Virgil
and he'd write it down without question. Most people, Virgil had decided, had one goal when they were interviewed, and that was to make
themselves look as good as possible. So they might lie about how old
they were when they started to play, or lie about having won some little

league award or what their ERA was in high school. But it didn't matter anyway, Virgil thought. The readers don't care. They just want something to read and believe and they'll never remember it anyway. Virgil certainly didn't. He listened to their stories, wrote them down, and tried to forgot them. The only reliable and marginally useful information Virgil had acquired over the years were things like the seating capacities and dimensions of every minor league stadium in every league, and which ones had the best nachos and the worst corn dogs.

His latest assignment was a story about the first regular female pitcher in the minors, playing Class A ball in Watertown, New York. Virgil's boss at the paper had been contacted anonymously about an angle to the story. According to the source, there was a vague (and silly, Virgil thought) minor league legend surrounding the girl's mother, that she was the baby girl delivered to Diz Durant that night in 1947. The source further stated that the baby girl became quite a ballplayer herself. Virgil's boss suggested that it might be good background material for the piece on the girl pitcher. In fact, his boss told him, make a vacation of it. "Take all the time you need. A week or even two. Do a little fishing. Beautiful country up there," he'd said. "It's on us." Just what they'd told Ned Silfiss before they gave him the boot, Virgil recalled. You can't exactly say no to an assignment, he thought. At least Virgil never had. But even Ned didn't have to chase down something like this, something so offensive and so obscure.

When phoned, the girl pitcher refused to talk about her mother, refused to even say whether her mother was the baby girl or even if she was alive or dead. She'd only talk about the game, she said, and nothing more. Mother and daughter had different last names and Virgil's paper hadn't been able to locate the mother. Virgil didn't much care one way or the other and thought that if they were going to let girls in the game they'd have to expect the hard-to-get treatment, but he was sent anyway to talk with Billy Ray Poole, an assistant coach who'd worked with Diz Durant. Billy Ray was the only known person still living who had both knowledge of the tale and a willingness to share it, according to the anonymous caller, anyway.

It was probably Billy Ray Poole who'd phoned in the tip, Virgil thought as he waited on the porch. An old man with tales to tell and no one to tell them to, that's what he is, Virgil concluded. Just looking for an audience.

Virgil himself wasn't that old, really, but he felt old, like he'd never been young at all, like he'd been born aged and unbelieving. Everything seemed false to him and sometimes, when he let himself think about it, he wondered if this was all his life would be, just this string of stories end to end, like a game of dominoes waiting to fall. But he tried not to think about that. He kept his mind on his gas gauge and on what he needed to accomplish at his next motel stop, like doing laundry or mailing bills and maybe phoning his boss at the paper, just staying busy until he was too tired to think at all; then he'd lie on his bed in the motel room with a beer on his stomach and loosen his tie and turn on the remote, and whatever show or game someone else was in, he'd just watch.

Virgil didn't like mountains, either. On the drive up to the retirement home he'd felt more and more enclosed as the mountains circled around him, as though watching. Virgil didn't like to feel watched. He wondered what those mountains were keeping out or keeping in and felt for a moment that it was himself. He checked in to a little motel called the Cool Waters on Route 19 in Cherokee, about a half hour's drive from the home. It was clean and quiet. Virgil liked clean and quiet.

When Billy Ray came back there was a shiny row of aromatic cigars with golden bands lined up across his vest pocket. Virgil examined his subject for the first time since the interview began. Billy Ray Poole. He looked young somehow, thought Virgil, especially young for ninety-one. In fact, Virgil thought, Billy Ray seemed absurdly baby-like in features and expressions, as the elderly sometimes do. He wore an old cream colored cotton suit with suspenders and a bow tie. His hands were wide and thin, and magnified behind his dense glasses were blue eyes that knew things, Virgil thought, that had seen a lot. Wisps of white hair like little clouds floated around his ears, his most striking features. His ears stuck almost straight out at right angles and the lobes were thick and supple, like sugar cookie dough. The deep lines of his face, carved over nearly a century, traced the paths of his life. He was full of brightness and Virgil wondered how Billy Ray managed to seem so young and so worn all at once.

"Ever been married, sir?" asked Billy Ray as he sat. Virgil was startled by this question.

"No, no, not me." He began nervously rummaging through his briefcase for an empty note pad, though the one on his lap was barely filled. "You know how it is on the road. Hard to keep family ties." Maybe this was all the "little chat" was about, thought Virgil hopefully, just small talk.

Billy Ray sat nodding and released the first cigar from the row. He stroked its smooth body and held it under his nose, breathing deeply.

"Good cigar reminds me of Lana Poole," he whispered dreamily as he rocked. "She loved a good smoke, yes sir."

Virgil rolled his eyes, making sure Billy Ray couldn't see him do it. "Your mother must have been some woman," he said flatly.

"Oh, yes, remarkable, she was," Billy said. "Raised us kids on her own since Pa took off drunk and never was seen again. Lana Poole said she didn't mind much, he was starting to annoy her. Never wore a watch in her life. She considered it a sin to press something as made up as time against her flesh. When you asked her what time it was she'd say 'Same time it always is—now.'

"In the evening, after all the chores were done, Lana Poole would gather us under her and tell us about how she played for the Bloomer Girls. There were teams all over. Chicago, New York, Boston, Indianapolis. There used to be girl's teams everywhere, but they've gone out of fashion, you might say. And she told us the old tales, the ones about Itagu nahi, also called John Axe, the great Cherokee mythkeeper. Maybe you've heard of him, sir?"

"No. Never heard of him. But why don't you tell me about--"

"That's a shame. Itagu nahi was Lana Poole's uncle," Billy Ray continued. Virgil's shoulders fell. He closed his notebook. "Born in 1800 and lived a hundred years, to see the change from horse to machine, to see the Cherokee ways drained from the mountains. Lana Poole didn't grow up with him in the tribe, since her daddy was a fellow named Zegel. They lived in town. But my grandmother was mostly Cherokee and saw to it that her children, including Lana Poole, knew the ways of John Axe. It was John Axe who named my mother Digu-lanahita and who told her about Cherokee ball-play, that he called the Anetsa, played with sticks and rattles. In his youth he was a great player of the game and still carried his ball stick with him in his old age, used it to lean him through the rest of his days. It was John Axe who first told Lana Poole that the invisible spirit people were strong with her. He taught her to be still and listen for them. Maybe, he used to tell her, you'll be lucky enough to see them someday, though they rarely show themselves to women.

"Lana Poole would say 'This is what Itagu nahi, John Axe, told me when I was girl. At first, when the gods created the world, all was blackness. And so the gods took nine pieces of fire from their world and threw them hard into the darkness. And then the light came and made the water that cooled the fire, and creatures came out of the water to look for land to live on. But there was too little land to hold them all, so a beetle offered to dive down into the deep part of the waters to see what he could find. The beetle returned with soft mud and the mud grew into an island they called earth. And the great buzzards flew over the earth and their wings began to flap and strike the soft ground and their flapping made valleys and the great mountains themselves and the mountains pushed out from its chest the spruce and cedar and holly and pine for medicine. Still, there was no ruling light. There were only the nine fires, each one spinning on its own in the blackness. And so the gods made a big circle of fire, using a small flame from each of the original nine, and hurled it into the center and called it sun. And it rules over all the others."

Billy Ray sat and puffed his cigar. Virgil wondered if he'd be able to stay awake.

"Don't take to tale telling, sir?"

"We should be getting on with the interview, I think."

"Sure, sure." Billy Ray touched a cigar in his pocket. "Would you like one?" asked Billy. "I always have extras for fellow rockers."

"I really shouldn't," Virgil said. "Thanks anyway."

"Not at all. It's there if you change your mind. Diz and me, we smoked them end to end, sir. But never in the dugout. Only chewing tobacco there. Cigars are for rocking and relaxing, never for figuring."

Virgil hoped the stories were over. I'll never get out of here, he thought: this guy is crackers. He opened his notes and found a page with a list of questions he'd prepared. "So tell me. When did you see this girl play, the one who you say was left in the dugout?" He wasn't looking at Billy Ray and didn't notice that Billy was eyeing him curiously.

"I've read some of your work sir," Billy said quietly. "Read two articles just last week that you wrote about that new manager up in Richmond."

Virgil nodded.

"Seem like a nice fellow to you?"

Virgil shrugged. "I guess." He checked his watch as covertly as possible. "May we get on with the interview now?"

Billy Ray narrowed his eyes and held the cigar between his teeth. "Don't think much of the game, do you, sir?"

Virgil looked up from his notes. "Sorry?"

"I said don't think much of the game, is that it?"

Virgil had not often been in the position of being asked what he thought about anything, a prospect which both confused and irritated him. He sat back in the rocker and shrugged again, shaking his head. "I like it, I like the game."

"You like the game."

"Sure, sure I like it. I mean like anything else, as time passes--"

"Time doesn't pass," Billy Ray interrupted. "It wears. When something passes you, it doesn't leave marks. But time leaves its marks. It comes with you. Are you writing this down, Mr. Alcover?"

Virgil's head was cocked to one side and his mouth hung open slightly. "Well, no, not yet—"

"This is exactly what you should be writing down. This is what folks in the game need to know. Not just batting averages and where you were born and who your heroes were. Like all that stuff you wrote about that fellow up in Richmond."

Virgil felt a little hurt, something he'd rarely experienced as a reporter. Even when his subjects ignored or insulted him, he'd never felt hurt, and Virgil realized suddenly that he wanted Billy Ray to like him.

"So you didn't like my articles, I take it?"

Billy Ray smiled and patted Virgil on the shoulder. "I liked them all right. Don't listen to me too much. But after I read them I thought, fellah who wrote these just doesn't like the game. Can't feel it anymore. Maybe he could once, but not now."

Virgil sat up to defend himself. "The game has changed, you know, Mr. Poole. Not like it was in your day. It's all about money now. All about TV rights and free agency and endorsements."

Billy Ray sat nodding. "Game's still in there, sir. Seems to me you should know that." He pulled back to rocking position and Virgil waited to see what would happen next. "So you want to know about Honey Durant, the baby I told you about? You say her daughter can throw? Let me ask you something. Why should I tell you this story?"

Virgil sagged. He began to wonder if he'd driven all this way into these suffocating mountains for nothing. "My paper sent me here because they'd said you'd agreed to talk to me."

"And that's what I'm doing. Talking. But this story is just a story to you. Part of your job. To me, it's something else. I'm its keeper and at my age there's not much left to part with. So tell me, why should I tell you this story?"

Virgil winced with irritation. "You've told me the beginning of it, why not continue? Why did you even start if you didn't intend to finish?"

"Now there's something I agree with," Billy said. "There's a good thought. Write that down. Completion. Keep that close. But don't answer my question with a question. Just tell me, other than it's your job or your duty, why should I tell you this story?"

Virgil folded his hands on his lap. In all the hundreds of interviews he'd conducted over the years, no one had ever made him justify his existence as a reporter. No one had ever really asked him anything more than *How are you?* Or *Are we done yet?* And though he did not feel terribly comfortable about it, there was something he did not recognize stirring in him, something he felt drawn to, and yet no answer came to him.

"Can't think of a thing, can you sir?" said Billy. "What is it you're after, anyhow?"

"I don't know. Whatever you want to tell me, I guess."

"Whatever?"

"Yeah, you know——" Virgil suddenly brightened, as though he'd remembered something familiar, like an old book he hadn't opened in years.

"The truth. Just tell me the truth."

"That's an interesting idea. And how do you know it will be the truth? The truth that you're after, anyway?"

Virgil shut the notebook. "This isn't going to work. I've made a mistake. I'm a busy man and I've got places to go." He stood and realized that wasn't true, but he thought it sounded good and besides, he kept thinking, this guy is crackers.

Billy Ray scratched his chin and laughed a little. "Sit down, sir. I'm old and when you're old you think you can say whatever you want. You find someone who has to listen and suddenly you have something to say. Ask me anything you like. Write it down. Make sure you get the important parts."

Virgil sat. He carefully opened his notebook again and pressed the page flat. "Tell me about the girl, the baby, I mean. Where exactly did she come from?"

Billy Ray was busy re-lighting his cigar. It wove smoky clouds around his head and its orange ember faded in and out like a search light in the fog. "Where does anybody come from? Seems to me that's something we can never really know." He got the cigar going again and leaned back a bit. "I can tell you about Diz Durant, the man who raised her. We'll see where that takes us. How would that be?"

Virgil felt relieved. "Fine, just fine." He poised himself over the white page. He fixed his eyes on the blankness.

"Old Diz was the manager of the Bryson City Bombers for more than twenty years. He was the flat out best manager I ever saw. 'Course he was my best friend too, though I hardly knew nothing about him. Except I knew he could smell a rainout three days before it happened and call a game better than anybody. Now he wasn't what some folks would call handsome, at least when you first met him, but his looks grew on you.

"I met Diz over in Winston-Salem, when we were both starting out. Diz was a catcher, and me, I fancied myself a pitcher in those days. Didn't have the patience for it though, and blew my arm out throwing too much heat. I stayed away from the game for awhile, tried to make a life without it. Lana Poole said I'd be called back when the time was right, when the invisible spirits had softened towards me. Make sure you write that down.

"So one day the phone rings and it's Diz. Just been made manager of the Bombers and wants to know if I'll come be his pitching coach. So I packed up and went, and Lana Poole came with me. She was glad to be coming back to the mountains, closer to her people.

"There's lots of ruby mines in the Cowee Valley, yonder." He waved his cigar towards the south. "Diz and me, we used to go ruby hunting once in a while and talk about dreams. I don't mean daydreams, like playing in the Bigs or anything like that. I mean real dreams.

"Once in a while Diz would say 'I had that dream again last night, the one where I'm a sailor and I live on an old wood boat and I can tie all those knots like sailors do, and while I'm dreaming I try to pay attention so I'll remember how to tie the knots but when I wake up I can't remember. I can still feel the rope in my hands, as though I've always held it, but I can't tie the knots when I'm awake.' It's funny, you know, 'cause Diz was never on a boat in his life." Billy paused and scratched his head.

"Diz had his chance to make it to the Bigs once, as a coach, but for some reason it fell through. Me, I never got close. I thought it would just about break his heart, coming that close, but he surprised me. Diz was a man who could kind of trick you.

"Take this baby thing. I was the most surprised person in the universe when that baby showed up. But Diz, he acted like he kind of expected it. Now I knew Diz for many years and I never knew of any gal or sister or aunt that could've produced Honey. That's what he called her, you know, Honey.

"Anyway, every time somebody asked Diz about her he'd say 'She's mine.' Well, she had to come from somewhere, that's what everybody said. It was rumored that she was the bastard child of someone on the team who wanted her close, wanted her around the game. Others said that Diz had a girl down in Asheville. Maybe, but I never saw her."

Billy Ray's cigar resembled a firefly in the darkening evening. Its glow throbbed rhythmically and he shook it a few times, to release some ash, then returned it to the blackened dent on his lip. Virgil admired that dent, though he hardly knew why.

"The baby's mama just up and disappeared. Daddy too, I guess," he continued. "People disappear all the time, even when they don't ever leave. Better write that down. You see what I mean, don't you?"

Virgil shook his head. He found himself listening, which surprised him.

"Take my younger cousin Lurlene, for instance. Now Lurlene Chatelain was a fine looking woman, smart and kind, too. Her people were French, from down New Orleans. Had mysterious ways, Lurlene did. Lana Poole used to look at her with one eye closed. Shook gansetis at her, Cherokee rattles made from dried gourds, to banish the troubled spirits. Said there was a curse around her. Lots of folks thought so. But not me. She just had bad luck. A fine woman.

"Lurlene hooked up with McGinn Wicks, a local businessman in Bryson City. They were seen all over together. Now McGinn was older than Lurlene and married to boot, but everyone said it was Lurlene's evil charms that led him to it. I never knew exactly what Lurlene saw in him that the rest of us missed, but it must have been something. Lurlene was warned from every pulpit in the county to stay away from McGinn, but that didn't matter, since she never went to church anyway. Every night she and McGinn were out drinking and dancing and carrying on. They loved the ballpark, too, and were big fans of Diz, just like everybody else in town. They rarely missed a game.

"McGinn up and died, and folks blamed Lurlene for that too. After that she was just gone. Some said they saw her cast herself into the Nantahala River. Others swore she hitched a ride out of town. But Lana

Poole said that Lurlene had gone to live with her true tribe, the Nunnehi, the invisible spirit people, who can appear whenever they like and disappear too. The Nunnehi lived on low bend in the Tuckasegee River, a few miles north of Bryson City. Lana Poole said she'd seen the Nunnehi herself, washing their clothes in the river and hanging them out upon the bank to dry. The name of the place is the Gisehunyi, Lana Poole said, which means Where the Female Lives.

"After that I didn't see Lurlene no more. Never saw her around here, anyway, though some, including Lana Poole, say they've seen her at night, when the Nunnehi are known to go about dancing. I wished that I could have seen Lurlene too. But she stayed with me." He was whispering now. He gently rocked. His hands were folded across his chest. "My, just look at that sunset. Like warm tea and honey sliding down your throat. Just slick as you please."

Virgil had stopped even the pretense of writing. He'd gotten a little information on Diz Durant, at least, but he wondered what the rest of it had to do with anything. So the old man loved someone, he thought. After a bit Virgil cleared his throat and said, quietly, "But what about the baby? Where did she come from?"

Billy Ray blinked and seemed to awaken.

"Beats all hell out of me. Could be she came out of the river, like the child of Selu, the first Cherokee woman. Selu was washing some freshly killed game and spilled too much blood into the cold, fast waters of the Nantahala. Soon a boy rose from the redness and Selu captured him and washed the river and the blood off him and tried to tame him, but he was always in trouble, always causing mischief and using his magical powers to get his way. 'He Who Grew Up Wild,' that's what they called him. He could not be tamed because he was made of dirt and blood and wind and the river and all the secrets they hold. Maybe that's where Honey came from, too."

Billy Ray looked up. In the distance, a pale moon was grazing the edge of the Cowee Valley. "Who knows where that baby came from? Maybe she fell off the moon and landed on Diz."

III.

Pearl Harpham's Boarding House
Bryson City, N.C.
June 1947

In her darkening front parlor, Pearl Harpham sat knitting a pair of gray socks on a large, overstuffed crimson sofa, the one her Aunt Ella had left her. At her feet slept an old whitish mutt with long silky ears and two inch legs. Pearl lived just down the block from the ballpark, and through her front window, she could hear the noises of a late game this very night. The house boasted a cozy front porch with gingerbread railings painted blue, and would have been a cool, comfortable place to sit and knit on this unseasonably warm, clear night. But Pearl held firmly that front porches were only for early evening sittings, right after supper, never ever for late nights such as this.

The parlor was crammed with heavy mahogany antiques and faded embroidered rugs. Much of the furniture, including the crimson sofa, was bathed in creamy lace delicate as a spider's web, stitched by Pearl's own hands and the hands of her ancestors. Around the sofa's lower edge strummed a thick, braided fringe which Pearl lovingly and dutifully combed each Tuesday to keep it clean and straight. When one sat on the sofa one had a clear view into the adjoining dining room which held the heart of the house; the ancient, thick-legged walnut china cupboard, with glass doors that clicked like a scolding tongue when opened or closed. Inside was Pearl's all: her blue and white hand painted inherited Bavarian china, perfectly and precisely displayed, shining like smiling sisters.

Above the parlor fireplace on the plain oak mantle stood two porcelain ballerinas, identical except for the colors of their stiff tutus. One was a soft pink, almost rosy; the other, a deep jade, a bit faded now. A third, the yellow one, had somehow been lost. Pearl's grandmother had promised the trio of ballerinas and other treasures to Pearl, and when her grandmother died and the box of items arrived, everything that Pearl was expecting to be in it was there, except for the yellow ballerina. Pearl made some inquiries and although she never did find out what happened to the yellow ballerina (and couldn't prove anything, she was always quick to point out), she always suspected it was her Aunt Patsy who'd swiped it. After all, thought Pearl, Patsy had helped pack up Grandma's things and everyone in the whole family knew how Patsy coveted those ballerinas. But not a word about it ever bent between Pearl and Patsy. The set of ballerinas was the only thing Pearl owned that was not complete.

Pearl herself was a compact woman, taking up exactly the space she needed and no more. Her rich brown hair held streaks of dark cherry and, here and there, a line of silver. She wore her hair loyally in a bun at the back of her head, not so tight as to pull at the edges of her eyes but not so loose as to be a source of constant annoyance to her. A stern kindness sat on the edges of her angular face, highlighted by her long, some said elegant, nose. For clothing she chose simple home spun dresses of dull blues and grays, believing that fanciness was fine for furniture and china, but to adorn one's self in such a manner was to be a fool.

She measured the days of her life by the opening and closing of her living room shades, ivory lace shades, as though the opening and closing were all that mattered. It was like breathing to her, the most important of all her many rituals, and in the evening when she closed them, she always said, out loud, "Another day gone."

In front of her house Pearl grew white lilacs, but she never allowed them to be trimmed, nor did she ever allow the blooms to be cut for the vase; to her that was a sin. It was the only part of her garden that she let grow wild.

She'd been made a widow while still rather young and used all her reliable senses to raise her five children on her own. When Frank Elmer, her husband, died, Pearl fell into an even more orderly life than before, lining up her children like recipe cards in a box and assigning each one their daily chores. The first two children she'd named George and Georgina, and Pearl found it difficult to break the habit afterwards, naming the next three Georgella, Georgetta, and the youngest, born after Frank Elmer passed, Frank Jr. She said it was easier to remember their names if they all had about the same one.

Pearl had married Frank Elmer Harpham not for love but for something she felt was stronger: compatibility. It wasn't so much that they had a lot in common or came from the same kind of family or anything like that. It was that he seemed to just let her be. He didn't fuss about which dress she should wear or how her hair should look or what she should cook for supper, as her sister's husband did. In fact, Frank didn't fuss much about anything. As long as there was beer in the fridge he was easy and quiet. He wore bright colored wide ties that Pearl's mother was suspicious of. "Man who wears such things is hiding something," that's what her mother said each time Frank came up the walk when he was courting Pearl. At their wedding, Pearl encouraged Frank to wear the widest, biggest, most colorful tie he owned.

He wasn't at all the type she'd imagined she'd marry, but he was someone, after all. Lots of her friends had fancied him on account of his charmed looks and he could have had any one of them, thought Pearl, but he'd chosen her; he said he liked the way she handled things, so she tried to handle things as best she could. Frank Elmer didn't seem to care how many children they had, so Pearl just kept on having them.

Pearl was known as a sucker for babies, mostly because they couldn't talk back. One thing she could not abide in a child was sass. In raising her own children, she believed in taking the hard line when necessary, to make sure they learned respect. "Otherwise," Pearl was fond of saying when she met folks in town, "they'll walk all over you and get into trouble. Child needs someone to take after. Look what happened to Lurlene Chatelain. Never had no strict mama to keep her on the right road."

Though Pearl had inherited the house and some money from her mother, after Frank died and the children were grown, the house seemed suddenly empty and grim and Pearl decided to board out a room or two, for company, for someone to take care of. This decision was met with stern opposition from Bryson City. A woman simply did not own her own business, surely not a woman of her age. Her children were expected to care for her. In fact, the eldest daughter was expected to live with her and then inherit the house herself eventually. This was the proper passing on of things. But Pearl's eldest daughter, Georgina, was dead; she'd died at seventeen, from wildness and "untamability," according to Pearl, and none of the other children had ever demonstrated even the slightest breath of desire to live at home. In fact, her children had moved away, Frank Jr. to California and the other girls and George to the big city, to Atlanta. Pearl saw them twice a year at most, always in Bryson City. Pearl herself did not travel, though she owned a Chevrolet that was kept out of sight in the garage. Grown children, she always believed, should come to their mothers for visits, not the other way around.

Pearl was aware of what was expected of her, that she should simply live out her life alone with her old dog and her things around her and make lemoncake and attend church socials while others shook their heads and said what ungrateful children she had to leave her alone like this. But Pearl could not see this as her life for the rest of her days, so in her mind she merely amended the local code to read: "A woman shall not own a business on her own unless her husband up and dies out of his own stupidity (such as being hit by a beer truck when he's dead drunk walking home on the highway all alone in the middle of the night) and her children have grown up and hardly ever call and, thenceforth, she may do what she sees fit to provide for her own well being, within reason of course."

"Within reason" to Pearl meant renting out rooms in her maze-like Victorian home, and Diz Durant, an old friend of Frank Elmer's, was her first and sole long-term tenant.

And so it was that on this late June night, while the moon poured like milk through the front windows and dusted its glow onto Pearl's knitting needles, Diz Durant walked into the house with a baby in his arms.

"Late game, was it Diz?" asked Pearl. She did not look up. The pale dog lifted his head and squinted dimly at Diz and the baby.

"It's all right, Robert E, just Diz," said Pearl loudly. He dropped back to sleep. "Poor blind thing." She looked up and abruptly stopped her knitting. The needles were crossed, frozen in the air. "Why, who's that you got there, Diz?"

Diz stood by the front screen. His short, stout legs were twitching slightly. He held the baby in one arm and took off his ball cap with the other, revealing a shiny, nearly bald head speckled with sweat.

"Pearl," he said flatly, "I've been living here for going on fourteen years. Before that I watched you raise up some of your own kids. You seem to have a knack for it.

"This baby girl is mine. Now I know it's asking a lot, seeing as how you're done with your own, but I'm asking you to help me raise her proper. If it can't work out, if you don't want her, I'll understand, Pearl. Me and the baby will be gone tomorrow."

Pearl nodded but began her knitting again and felt an old stirring inside that made her hold the gray socks a little closer. A baby in the house again, she thought; a baby's just the thing. She remembered everything. The feedings, the first steps, the little clothes, the closeness, the pale smells and soft helplessness of a new baby. It swirled around her like the bluebirds on the edges of her china.

The town would talk, she knew. The town was always talking. They'd talked when Diz, a man of the game, had moved in with Pearl. Most said it would never last, the odd union between them. Diz hadn't always been easy to live with, Pearl thought. Tracked sand into the house and kept strange hours and never seemed to ever really need anything except dinner and his clothes washed. Secretive too, sometimes, but that was due to shyness, Pearl had decided. He was more to her than a boarder now, though that fact had never been exchanged out loud from her mouth to his ears. Boarders come and go and you don't really care about them, Pearl thought. You feed them and give them clean sheets and then they pay you. Diz still paid Pearl each month but it felt more like shared expenses than board. That's how it is when someone stays, Pearl thought. Things take hold between you. Things don't have to be said. It didn't occur to Pearl, then, to wonder or to ask if the child was truly Diz's daughter. She liked this feeling of a connection between herself and Diz, something other than sharing dinner or sitting in the parlor on winter nights, Pearl with her knitting and Diz asleep sitting up. He needed her on this. Let the town talk all it wants to, Pearl told herself. Let them laugh if it makes them feel better. The noise of all that didn't penetrate her, not this night. Funny how age takes the jolt out of things, thought Pearl.

Diz was standing there pressing the baby close to his chest. The little gray hair he had sparkled in the dim light of the parlor.

"Hold up her head, Diz," Pearl said. She put her knitting aside. "You'll smother her in your shirt. And stop all this fool talk. Where do you think you'd be going, anyway?" She rose and took the baby from him. "This is where you live. We'll do right by her. What's her name?"

Diz stood awkwardly next to Pearl as the child began to fuss. He stroked her nose, and she quieted. "She doesn't have a name yet. What do you think?"

"I used up all the names I could think of with my own kids. Just keep it simple, Diz. You don't want to be forgetting her name all the time, stammering like a darn fool. Child can't respect its daddy if he can't remember her name."

Diz tilted his head and looked at the baby. "I just been calling her Honey, but I guess that's not a proper name at all."

"Why not? You're the daddy. You can do whatever you want to. Now go on up to the attic and fetch down the crib. Put it in the front bedroom."

Diz smiled and nodded once at Pearl and then did as he was told.

The acceptance of the infant into their lives was as simple as all the trans-actions between them.

Pearl examined the child. About six weeks old, Pearl thought, maybe more. Old enough to have been somewhere else for a while, to have been held and rocked and changed by another's hand, to have been given another name, to have been loved or unloved. Honey seemed all in disarray to Pearl; part baby girl and part something else that Pearl didn't want to see. A fierceness in the eyes, eyes that still hadn't settled on a color yet, Pearl noticed. There was dirt from the ballpark on the baby's face and on the torn blanket that limply hung about her, but the dirt seemed to suit the child, and that's what worried Pearl. "She's just confused, is all," thought Pearl. "The ballpark is no place for a baby girl, after all. Some of it got on her and it's turned her all upside down." Pearl believed in the possibility of a place rub-bing off and settling in. It only makes sense, she thought. A child absorbs its surroundings like a damp sponge absorbs dirt. It must be wrung out and peeled away, Pearl knew. She removed the yellowed blanket from Honey. She tried to wipe the dirt from Honey's face with a finger and some spit. Honey resisted by wiggling. "Hold still now," Pearl said. "In this house, you'll be a proper young lady." But even as Pearl was speaking the baby slit her eyes as though in contradiction, as though she understood Pearl's meaning.

Pearl held the baby carefully and walked to the corner mahogany high-boy. She opened the top drawer and pulled out a crocheted pink blanket, folded in quarters and tied with a white ribbon; the very wool that had once wrapped Georgina and all of Pearl's daughters. Pearl released the blanket with one tug of the ribbon and wound it around Honey. Then she fetched a damp towel from the kitchen and rubbed the dirt from Honey's face. "That's better," said Pearl. "I'm starting to see the girl in you now." She sat down to rock Honey. The awkward noises of Diz, fumbling with pieces of crib, twisted down the stairs.

Honey stared up at Pearl with a look of untamed knowledge that frightened Pearl for a moment. It was as though Honey knew some shameful secret that would lay heavy upon them all, and it made Pearl hesitate. It made the tips of her fingers go cold and made her neck tighten and made her remember for a moment that Georgina used to look that way sometimes too, but then the moment passed. Then she saw that Honey was smiling a little at her, that she was liking the pink blanket, that it was softening her and comforting her as pink blankets are bound to do with baby girls. Then everything seemed all right. Everything seemed as it should. Then it was just Pearl and the infant and the pink wool and the rocker, all gliding in the same direction, as if lassoed by an invisible force of gentle strength.

"Honey girl, all clean and bright," Pearl sang. The baby reached for something to hold and found Pearl's index finger. She held it so tightly that Pearl felt the child's fingernails slice into her skin.

❖ ❖ ❖

The next morning, Pearl walked to the market to get some supplies for Honey. Diz stayed home practicing diaper changes. That was the day when Pearl first heard the whispers.

At the Bryson City Grocery the butcher, Fletcher Pulgram, stood slicing a pound of fresh cured ham while May Hetrick yapped at him. Pearl had known May for years, May having been one of Frank Elmer's earliest and most fervent admirers. Pearl listened distrustfully around the corner.

"I hear she was just left in the dugout, Fletcher," said May. "A filthy baseball dugout." She looked over her shoulder and lowered her voice a little. "Now you know, Fletcher, that I would never disclose information of a personal nature without having it properly confirmed. I heard the whole thing just now from a well-known source of reliability over in the frozen food aisle."

"That's a pound, even," said Fletcher.

"It does look so fresh and pink, Fletcher. Better cut me an extra pound. And I'll need a pound and a half of swiss, too."

"What kind?" It was the question Fletcher was best known for.

"The kind with the holes in it." Fletcher shook his head and May continued.

"Child with no mama is the child of a curse, as you well know. A lost child. Just like Lurlene Chatelain," she added, as though inspired, "and look what happened to her." She checked behind her. "I even heard whispers that she came from coloreds. The baby, I mean. Maybe even from a Cherokee Indian. I don't know which is worse. I'll tell you, Fletcher, Pearl Harpham has finally lost her sense and I mean all of it if she means to take that child into her home. She's had no business letting that man live with her under her roof all these years, anyway. Why would anyone leave a baby with Diz Durant? He's old. He's unmarried. He's a ballplayer for goodness sake."

"Diz is a good man," said Fletcher. He held an oily pound of ham in one hand.

"Well of course he is!" said May. "We Hetricks have always been followers of the game. I know, of course, what a fine man he is. I only meant to say that-"

"Hi May. Hi Fletcher." Pearl pretended to be eyeing the specials.

"Pearl! I haven't seen you in ages. I was just getting some ham." May began fussing through her purse. "Now where is that list? I have a million and one things to do today." She dropped some lipstick and some coins and nervously began picking them up.

"Something wrong, May?" said Pearl.

"Oh no! Everything's fine. I'm late is all. Really got to run."

"May, did I hear you mention Diz?"

"Diz? You mean Diz Durant?"

"That's the one."

"No. I didn't say a thing about Diz. I mean I guess I heard a thing or two is all." May closed the metal lip of her purse and then took the wrapped ham from the counter. She looked in Pearl's cart. There were several jars of baby food and some cans of formula and May's eyes passed over these things. Their presence seemed to grant her a new confidence. She relaxed her shoulders. She cocked her head. "How is Diz, anyway, Pearl?"

"Fine, fine."

"Anything new?"

"Nope. Everything is as usual. You?"

"Same old same old." Fletcher was wrapping the swiss. Pearl and May stood with their carts nose to nose. Fletcher's knife glistened on the counter between them. May took the cheese and threw it in her cart.

"You're sure nothing is new, Pearl?"

"What are you getting at, May?"

"Now look, Pearl. Just spit it out. After all, everyone knows anyway. You don't have to pretend with me. Where did that baby come from?"

"What baby?"

"The baby Diz got at the game! You know the very one."

"Oh. You mean his daughter."

"His daughter? I doubt that. And even if it's true it's positively shameful. Come on, Pearl. You can tell me. And Fletcher here barely speaks so you know he won't repeat anything. It's only fair, Pearl. I told you about that awful thing with my cousin Dolores and that man from Nashville, didn't I?"

Pearl smiled. "Fletcher, I'll be needing about three pounds of your best flank steak. Wrap it for me and I'll pick it up later, ok?" Fletcher nodded and rolled his eyes in May's direction and then went out back.

"All right, Pearl. We're alone now. You don't have to tell me, of course. It's your choice. But the rumors are flying. Wouldn't you rather have us know the truth? Wouldn't that be better? You're not seriously thinking of keeping that curse in the house, I hope. This town has seen its share of girls like that. Remember Lurlene Chatelain?" May came close and whispered. "My goodness, you poor thing, you've been through it yourself already, with poor Georgina."

Pearl had been enjoying this up to now. "Fletcher better mind where he leaves that knife," said Pearl steadily. "Someone might get hurt." She turned to go.

May stood with her fists riveted to her hips. She spoke to Pearl's back as it moved away from her. "You're too old to raise a baby, Pearl. You got no earthly idea what you're doing."

Pearl pushed her cart away and pressed her lips tight. It wasn't so much that May had accused her of being too old. After all, that was probably true, Pearl thought. It wasn't even that May had been railing on Diz. Everyone in town, after all, knew what a gossip May was. May had a nerve and a half to refer to Georgina that way, but Pearl didn't permit herself to dwell on that. Her mind rested on the cruelty of it for an instant but then yanked itself elsewhere. Pearl had become quite skilled at changing the subject with herself when need be, whenever thoughts or events turned to her dead daughter. It was something else that chewed on Pearl as she made her way passed the canned goods, something that May Hetrick had said about Lurlene Chatelain.

That name made Pearl remember something that sent an electric shiver down her backbone.

IV.

There were two separate, incompatible seasons in Bryson City—baseball season, and a gray, mild kind of almost-fall, when leaves seemed unsure of whether to cling to life or just give it up and jump off. Grass stopped growing but didn't die altogether, and as the days grew shorter, the town slowly curled up and in and didn't so much sleep, really, but quietly napped. Of course there were patches of winter from time to time, due mostly to disobedient children and too much gossip amongst the women; but those were thankfully rare. Nothing ever happened in the almost-fall.

But baseball season, well, that was the time. Folks in Bryson City said that spring officially arrived when Diz Durant made his first pitching change. It was never the exact same day each year, and the weather may have been warm for almost a month already, but folks swore that their tulips would not bloom until Diz had made that first call. And so it was, Pearl recalled after she'd seen May Hetrick and was walking home from the market, that Lurlene Chatelain's troubles began early that year, shortly after the baseball season had started.

Around Bryson City, Lurlene was known as a "wild woman with a capital Wild." She had been orphaned as a child in New Orleans, floated around the family, and ended up, as a teenager, in Bryson City at the home of Billy Ray and Lana Poole, Lurlene's aunt. She was oddly pretty, folks said; her features were proud, even robust, resolute. Her hair was the color of just churned butter but was coarse and not easily tamed into the styles of the day, and her upper lip was somewhat off center. Something about her eyes suggested a toughness, a kind of sad caution, as though she was perpetually expecting to be disappointed.

The talk was that Billy Ray had a crush on Lurlene. He acted like a giddy school boy around her, though he was twenty years her senior. Over at Pearl's, dressed in his best Sunday suit and heavily doused in drug store cologne, he'd say "Let me get you some more tea and cakes, Lurlene dear. Pearl, Lurlene must be the best dancer in the county. You should have seen her! Prettiest girl there, too."

"Oh, cousin Billy, stop. Pearl's not interested in that."

Pearl saw that Lurlene smiled kindly at Billy Ray. She also noticed that Lurlene always referred to him as "Cousin Billy" and never sat close to him. "She's got that wild look," thought Pearl as she poured more tea, peeking sideways at Lurlene's green eyes. "I saw that look in my

Georgina and Georgella. I lost one to her willfulness, but I tamed the other with good mothering. This poor child has no such guidance."

After a while, Lurlene stopped seeing Billy Ray and moved out on her own, having finally gotten a job as a cashier at the Five and Ten over in Cherokee. Pearl heard that Lana Poole was unwilling to bless the relationship, but Pearl knew that wasn't the only reason.

Lurlene's stint at the Five and Ten was short lived. She took up with The Reverend Mister Palanker's son when she was nineteen and ran off with him to New Orleans for a few months. There was a terrific scandal and when Lurlene came back she was seen wearing tight silk dresses slit way up and red high heeled shoes with silver glitter that were the main topic of conversation everywhere for weeks. Most folks said she'd finally let her wildness get the better of her, but Pearl understood otherwise.

Lurlene was often seen at Bombers games, chatting over the fence with Billy Ray or Diz between innings. It seemed the place where she was most content, where her challenge to the world softened. But she had no such ease in the town; Bryson City simply had a certain way of doing things, and Lurlene could not be made to live within their code. Folks were as bound and staid as the thick white columns in front of the county courthouse. Those sparkling red shoes of Lurlene's were like sweet, forbidden candy they would never taste.

It was during this time, Pearl recalled, that Lurlene caught the eye of McGinn Wicks, thirty-five years older than Lurlene and the owner of Ralph's Diner and Pete's Used Cars. McGinn had married late in life and had six young children and a small, pretty wife who stayed home and stayed quiet.

News of the affair with McGinn was juicier than Fletcher's best flank steak. Tongues wagged like puppy's tails before dinner. There were scattered whispers that Lurlene had a black lover over in Knoxville, and though no one ever saw them together, Lurlene and McGinn fought publicly about the man once when they were at a bar in Cherokee. Those who were lucky enough to overhear any argument between them became instantly popular at the local bowling alley and beauty parlors.

The Reverend Mister Palanker, still stung, perhaps, by his son Jepson's quick exit to New Orleans with Lurlene, delivered a fiery sermon entitled "Save Yourself McGinn." It was very well attended. Children composed jump rope rhymes such as "L-U-R-L-E-N-E, is as bad as she can be." Parents were heard telling their teenagers: "You be on time now, youngin. I will not tolerate any Lurlene-in' in my house."

Though McGinn had been famous for his dalliances (Pearl needed both hands to count the women who'd been McGinn's rumored lovers), everyone in town talked like it was all Lurlene's doing. Pearl wondered why it was so. McGinn was, after all, the one who was married, the one who had children, the one who'd been with so many others; and he was so much older than Lurlene. McGinn wasn't handsome and Pearl was certain he was not a passionate romantic, but he had a sly charm and he had money and most folks in town had neither. McGinn took whatever he liked. He didn't seem to care a thing for what anyone thought. And he probably knew how to make promises, too, Pearl thought, the kind of promises that a shunned young woman such as Lurlene might want to believe. Or maybe, Pearl reasoned, Lurlene was using McGinn as much as he used her. Maybe she did it to make someone else jealous, or just for the company. Whatever her motive, Lurlene was the one who was condemned. Though her looks obscured it, Lurlene was part Cherokee and the Cherokee women could not be trusted, that's what folks said. It was one of those things that just *was,* thought Pearl. It's the way things are set up so everyone will know who to blame when things go wrong. Pearl knew that folks blamed her after her own daughter had died, knew they thought it was because she didn't do her job as a mother. No one ever said anything to her directly, of course, but it was in their eyes and in their looks. And Pearl knew that if someone was going to blame you, you'd better just learn to take it.

It was a warm night in early October, Pearl recalled, when McGinn and Lurlene were out at the Cue Ball Lounge in Bryson City. Somebody clanked a nickel into the juke box and Billie Holiday started singing "God Bless the Child." Lurlene, who had a few drinks in her, peeled off her beaded pink dress, revealing a lacy slip. She then climbed up onto the pool table. She was still wearing her red heels. She started dancing, holding up her yellow hair with one hand and singing along with Miss Holiday. It wasn't a bump and grind, just a slow, sadly elegant dance, her eyes closed, her singing soft. The male customers began to gather around with their drinks, and McGinn starting yelling at her. Sweat waxed his comb-over.

"Lurlene, you get down here right now! Get offa there! Or I'll come up there and—"

"Shut up, Wicks. I'm dancing. This is how the girls in Asheville dance, ain't it? You sure seem to like it when they do it. You don't own me, anyway."

McGinn, by all accounts, thought otherwise. He bristled as the men around him laughed. He lunged at Lurlene and tried to drag her down, but she kicked him and got free.

"Don't you kick me, you whore! I said get down! I'll slap you good for this."

"Shut your mouth. I'm busy."

The men in the bar were getting into it, shouting and whistling, throwing money at her. "Go at it Lurlene! Strut it, sugar! That's some woman you got there, McGinn." A drunk customer wobbling nearby said "Do you rent her out on the weekends?"

Pretty loaded himself, McGinn swung at the man but missed and the men laughed again. McGinn then turned the color of red licorice and reached again to try and pull Lurlene off the table. "I order you to get down right now! You are my woman and no woman of mine will make a fool—"

"Shut up, Bryson City!" Lurlene bent and removed both of her glittering red shoes and threw them hard. They sailed over the men's heads to the back wall of the lounge, where they hit with a thud, leaving two deep red marks. She could have taken out someone's eye if she'd aimed lower. The men whistled and clapped louder than before. Some started to roll pool balls between her legs.

"You all think you're so much better than old Lurlene, don't you! Talking about me like I'm some kind of filthy stray dog that you can kick and swear at! But you'll come here and whistle at my body and then go home to your stuck up, swallowed up fat wives and tell them what a whore Lurlene is. Ain't that right? I've had enough of it! You don't even know me, any of you. You never even look at me, never look at Lurlene." No one seemed to really hear. Her voice was just part of the cacophony. "This is Lurlene talking now! Get it right so you can repeat it with confidence tomorrow at the barber shop!"

The song was off the juke box now and the room had quieted a bit. In one corner some of the drunker men were singing, their arms joined around the shoulders.

"And you, McGinn." She raised her pinky finger and carefully aimed it at McGinn. The dim light bounced off her red nail polish. "You were supposed to love me. Always lying that you're going to leave that thing you call a wife and make a respectable woman out of me. I'm tired of waiting. I got someone else to think about now. I know what love is, but I didn't learn it from you! You can die, Wicks." Her voice was clear and flat. "The world would be better off without you. I want you gone."

And then, as then men turned laughing to face him, McGinn Wicks dropped dead. Right there in the Cue Ball Lounge. Just kind of deflated in the smoky haze with Lurlene Chatelain's frozen pinky still riveted on him. Suddenly the men were silent, still, like stone markers in a graveyard. They looked as though they had witnessed a religious miracle. Later on the doctor said that McGinn had a massive heart attack. McGinn was not young, and was living way beyond his years, but folks who were there said it was Lurlene who killed him. It was plain. The Curse of Lurlene.

Lurlene hadn't been seen for weeks. In the meantime, McGinn was laid to rest in one of the biggest funerals Bryson City had seen in a while. McGinn's best friend, Skiff Hoskins, delivered a tearful eulogy, praising McGinn for his skills as a businessman and father. "The poor man, tired from his long day at work to support his six children, stopped at a local tavern to refresh himself. And there he found his destiny." McGinn's wife stood by the open grave holding her youngest child in her arms. She did not, as others did, throw a fresh flower on the coffin. Diz went over to Skiff to offer his condolences. Pearl overheard Skiff tell Diz to pray for protection from The Curse, which made Pearl roll her eyes and click her tongue. Diz just patted Skiff on the back. After the funeral, someone painted "Beware Lurlene's Curse" in sloppy red paint on the front door of the Cue Ball, which became a shrine to McGinn's memory.

The Legend of Lurlene had begun. It rose quick and hot as steam from boiling water. No one knew where she'd gone. Some said the devil himself had taken her to where she truly belonged. After all, she was from New Orleans, they all said. Voo-doo and black magic are rampant down there. Word spread around that those red shoes had been painted by the fires of hell. As summer turned to almost-fall and the air began to cool, folks said it was the cold breath of Lurlene that blew across the trees.

On a cool evening a month or so after the funeral, Pearl happened to be taking some of her neighbor's children, who she watched sometimes, for a walk to the park. The air was musky gray and most people were home, lighting fires and retrieving sweaters from their cedar chests. Pearl was quite surprised to see Lurlene sitting alone on a bench in the park, sipping pop through a paper straw, her shoulders wrapped in a white crocheted shawl. She had a ghostly appearance and Pearl did feel a little afraid. "Now stop that, you old fool," she said to herself. "This is just a poor lost soul. She would've been all right if only she'd had a reliable mama to straighten her out. Nothing to be scared of." Pearl set the kids loose on the playground and sat down beside Lurlene.

"Hey Lurlene," said Pearl nonchalantly. "How's it going? I haven't seen you in ages."

Lurlene nodded a bit and continued to sip her pop. After a few minutes she said, "Say, Pearl, you've had lots of babies, right?"

"Raised up five kids all alone."

"Babies aren't so bad, are they?" Lurlene touched her hand lightly on Pearl's arm. "I mean, some folks say that they're a heap of trouble and nothing more, but that's not true, is it?"

"Hey there, Jacob," Pearl yelled to one of the children. "You just stop yanking on your sister's hair or I'll be yanking on you!" Pearl knew she'd never actually lay her hands on someone else's child; it was the threat that counted, that would teach. She shook her head and turned to Lurlene.

"So you want to know about babies, do you? Well, I'll tell you. They are a heap of trouble, but a good kind of trouble, mostly, Except when they get older and start to sass you. Some can never be tamed. And then you got yourself a whole bucket load of trouble. But babies? They're nice. Folks who say they aren't are folks who should never have them."

Lurlene smiled slightly and finished her pop. She stood up, closed her shawl tightly around herself and shook Pearl's hand. Then she leaned down and kissed her softly on the cheek.

"Goodbye, Pearl." She turned and walked into the evening.

And so, while Pearl was coming home from the market, she wondered about Lurlene Chatelain and the baby that Diz brought home and added up the months in her head and she knew, knew what the truth must be, and felt the curse shiver within herself to know such a thing all on her own.

Maybe she should give this more thought. Maybe raising a girl who everyone believes to be cursed, whose own mama had killed a man with her pinky finger, wasn't such a good idea. It's not easy to tame those who are naturally wild, Pearl knew. She'd been through it once before and though Pearl had survived it, her daughter Georgina hadn't. Diz would understand.

Of course, Pearl mused, a baby knows nothing of curses and

rumors. And besides, the only curses are the ones we make up, aren't they? Pearl had always thought it ridiculous that Lurlene had been labeled as cursed, when it was McGinn Wicks who was dead and buried. Lurlene, Pearl thought, was powerful, not cursed. She could do with her smallest finger what most women couldn't do with a weapon. She'd gotten rid of her lying lover. But it didn't matter what Pearl thought, and she knew it. It was the town that would collectively decide who Honey was or wasn't. And the town, led by May Hetrick, had already decided she was cursed, even if they hadn't guessed who her mother was. And Honey would grow, and the curse, made up or not, would grow with her, unless Pearl could stave it off, trick it, you might say. Pearl saw that now, understood that she had been appointed by someone or something to protect Honey from the curse. Pearl had been given another chance. After all, whoever left that baby with Diz must have known that she'd be raised by Pearl too. It only made sense to think so. May Hetrick had been right about one thing. Why *would* anyone leave a baby with Diz? Pearl was the experienced parent, after all. It made her smile, to think she had been hand picked, maybe by Lurlene herself. She must keep the secret. She must be vigilant in case Lurlene came back to claim the child. This was to be her penance, thought Pearl. This time she'd get it right.

Then another thought crept in which made Pearl walk slower and bite her lip. Did Diz know anything about Honey's true mother? Would he tell? Who was the father? Would the evil spawn of McGinn Wicks be living in Pearl's house? What about Billy Ray? Or could Diz himself be the true father? No, that didn't seem right. If Diz wanted to do something like have a child he'd do it right out in the open, Pearl thought, just like he did everything else. So then what was in it for him, wondered Pearl? She had not been accustomed to questioning Diz about much. His life was so quiet and routine there was never anything to really ask him about. But maybe, she thought, it was time to start.

When Pearl walked into the house Diz was sitting on Aunt Ella's sofa. He was holding Honey. Robert E was curled up against the crimson fringe.

"Pearl, I want to tell you something."

Pearl nodded.

"Could be there's talk around town about this baby, Honey. You might hear things. You might have already heard things."

Diz stopped talking and looked straight at Pearl, who was still standing by the door with the groceries in her arms.

"This baby is mine," he said flatly, "She's as much mine as anybody ever was. And she needs a good woman like you to fill in as her mama. That's all I got to say."

Pearl took the bags and went into the kitchen. Then she tied on her yellow apron, the one with the little roses on it, put the groceries in the cupboard, and started to heat some baby formula.

V.

Present Day

Virgil arrived back at his room at the Cool Waters a little after eleven. What a night, he thought. I'm going to look like some fool with this story. The only thing to do is to try and extract as many of the facts as possible, Virgil decided. Trouble was, so far there weren't too many facts. But whatever. Let the old fellow ramble all he wants. I don't have to use any of that. Virgil felt this could well be his last assignment, and he wanted to do it right, to do it his way.

He'd managed to get the end room of the one story, sprawling Cool Waters. Virgil liked end rooms. There was only one neighbor to contend with and the noise from the motel office was filtered and obscure. Virgil could park his car directly in front of his room and not have to look at or deal with anyone. Sometimes the maids will try to befriend you if you stay longer than a day or two, Virgil thought to himself. They try to get more familiar than they should, probably because they want a tip when you leave. But Virgil never tipped and he rarely spoke to the maids either unless there was something wrong with the room. After all, no one ever tipped Virgil after an interview. And besides, making beds and changing sheets wasn't so hard. Try talking to crazy old men who can't answer a simple question without telling you the whole history of the Cherokee tribe. That's hard.

The name of the maid for Virgil's room was Maria. Virgil knew because when he'd checked in there was a little card on the bed with her name on it that said Virgil should contact her at any time if there was anything he needed and that she hoped he'd have a nice stay. The writing was carefully printed, as though written by a child for school. Some of it looked like it had been erased and done over. Virgil felt a pang of humiliation for Maria, having to place a note just like this on every bed in every room, but his sympathy quickly hardened to irritation. They only do this so you'll feel sorry for them and give them a bigger tip or something. That's what he told himself as he crumpled the note and threw it in the trash.

Virgil was a little drunk when he got back to the room. After seeing Billy Ray he'd had a couple of beers at a bar in Cherokee. He hadn't eaten dinner and wasn't really a drinker anyway, so the beer had whistled quickly through him. The room was dark. He'd forgotten to leave a light on and he made a fuzzy mental note to himself to remember to leave a light on next time. He hated entering dark rooms and this one had no light switch by the door.

He turned on the television to break the silence. It droned in the background as he changed into his pajamas and sleepily gargled. When he came out of the bathroom he noticed a small, thin book on his pillow. He hadn't seen it when he first came in. Maybe Maria found it somewhere in the room when she'd cleaned and thought it was Virgil's and left it there for him. (They do that to get more tips, he reminded himself.) The book was just lying there and Virgil felt it was watching him, sizing him up. It seemed to waken him. Silly, he thought. It's only a book.

It was old. The cover was torn and silvery threads wept from the binding and when Virgil looked closely he could see no title. He sat down on the bed and opened the book. Many pages, including the title page, had been ripped out. In front of him was a story that had no title but that Virgil started to read without really meaning to. It's only natural, he thought, to be interested in something you've found in your motel room. It's almost like having easy entrance to someone else's life. Virgil enjoyed finding things that others had left behind. It was a sort of hobby of his, since he spent so much time in motels. The things he discovered somehow made Virgil feel connected without actually having to face anyone in particular. Once, Virgil found a letter in the bottom drawer of a white-washed dresser in Bellefield, Georgia. It was from a man to someone named Emily, and there was no envelope and no date or signature, just the name Emily. Virgil kept the letter folded in his wallet and had memorized the words of it and often he said them out loud while driving down some southern road: *Promise to wait, I'll be home soon and everything will be settled, don't leave until I get there, promise.* Virgil wondered why the man never mailed the letter and wondered if Emily had waited anyway and the words taunted Virgil, made him feel alone, but for some

reason he kept the letter with him. He thought of that letter for a moment as he began reading from the book that he'd found on his pillow.
The television was still humming low but Virgil relaxed into his elbow
and read, bowing over the pages and squinting to make out the faded
print:

"In ancient times the animals challenged the birds to a great ball
play. The leaders fixed upon a day and place, and so it was all arranged.
The Great Bear went about boasting for many days about his strength
and how he would tear down all who got in his way at the game. The
Terrapin bragged that his shell was so hard that even the heaviest of
blows would not dent him in the least. The Deer, too, rambled on
about how fast he was, how he could outrun any other animal. All
together they felt it was a fine company.

"The Eagle was the captain of the birds. He had with him the
Great Tla-nu-wa, the ancient Hawk, who was mighty of wing and
swift as the Eagle; and yet they were a little afraid of the animals, who
had bragged so much.

"They all gathered on the smooth grass near the river and began
the dance of the ball-play. When it was over, a mouse the size of a
small fist whisked up the tree in which perched the Eagle, pruning his
feathers for the game. The mouse asked the Eagle if he might join the
birds' team.

"'Why do you not ask the Bear? For you are four-footed as he is,'
replied the Eagle. 'I have asked,' said the mouse. 'But he laughed at me
and said I am too small and weak.'

"The Eagle, annoyed by the Bear's swollen pride, pitied the poor
mouse and allowed him to join his team.

"'But how,' the Great Hawk asked, 'can this mouse join our team
when he has no wings? The animals will not allow it.'

"The bird leaders decided that they would make wings for their
new teammate. They took the hard skin of a drum used in the dancing, and cut it into wings. They then fastened them to the mouse. In
this way the first bat was created — Tlameha. When they threw the
ball at the Bat, he dodged it and circled it and always kept it in the air.
The birds knew they had found one of their best players."

Virgil closed the book. The affects of the beer had left him and he
felt somehow that this story was meant for him, that someone was trying
to tell him something. After everything Billy Ray had said, this seemed too
much of a coincidence. He suspected that Billy Ray himself had planted

the story, except that was impossible. Billy Ray was spry, but not *that* spry. And he didn't own a car. Still, Virgil imagined Billy Ray sneaking into his room and leaving the book, smiling his baby-faced smile, twinkly smile, and this annoyed him.

The things to do is just get rid of it, Virgil decided. It's all silliness anyway. If Billy Ray has something to say he should tell it to me straight. He thought he'd take it down to the motel office and drop it off there, but it was late and he was ready for bed.

He could just throw it away, but for some reason he didn't. He opened his front door and placed the book outside, leaning it against the wall where he thought maybe a night janitor might discover it. All he knew was that he didn't want it in the room with him, though he couldn't think why.

He switched off the lamp and the television too and got into bed. Right away he noticed that the lights were on in the adjoining room. He could see a long, fluorescent slice oozing from underneath the door and hoped that whoever was in there wouldn't keep long hours. Virgil was bothered by odd lights in motel rooms. He thought he heard voices weaving next door, followed by the sounds of some-one shushing someone else. Virgil grunted and rose again, twisted a bath towel and was about to stuff it into the crack when the light vanished. There were no more voices, either. Virgil smiled. At least one thing has gone right today, he thought. He bent himself into the bed and went to sleep.

Virgil woke with plenty on his mind. It was Sunday morning and he was scheduled to meet Billy Ray for a brunch at the home to continue the interview. If one could call it that. Virgil had heard, at least, that the food was wonderful, and so it might be worth it just for that. He'd eaten at so many diners that every meal seemed exactly the same. Nothing tasted different anymore.

While he dressed Virgil remembered a dream he'd had the night before. He dreamt he was a gardener, a gardener who could grow any-thing. Whatever he planted thrived and became abundant, even if he didn't tend it that well. It was almost like magic. His gardens were fa-mous and people came from all over to admire the red and white striped lilies and the purple peonies and to inhale the perfume of peach roses and blinding yellow sunflowers and in the dream Virgil noticed that the colors were like flavors, like something you could taste and smell, a garden of candy. The garden's visitors were pulling up the flowers and eating them and offering a taste to Virgil but he didn't eat.

He finished dressing and tried to stop thinking about the dream, though he could still smell the melon-sweet aroma of the orange and green striped tulips and wished for a moment that he'd tasted one. He remembered to turn on a lamp in case he returned late. He thought of writing a note to Maria to tell her not to turn the light off but then realized that was silly, that she might think he was afraid of the dark or something, and besides, he hadn't even met her. He gathered his briefcase and keys and headed out.

When Virgil opened the door he remembered the book and looked down, but the book was gone. A sadness tinged with shame washed through him for an instant. That didn't make sense and he knew it; it was only a book. Thankfully the feeling passed quickly and Virgil threw his stuff into the back seat of his Civic and slid himself in and began driving up to Fontana Lake.

Just as he pulled out of the lot, in the near shadows amongst a crowd of pines, Virgil thought he saw an enormous eagle with white wings and a great gleaming gold beak eyeing him from the blackness of a dark spruce. Virgil turned to look, but nothing was there.

VI.

Bryson City, 1951

Time passed and Honey grew to be about four years old. The gossip in Bryson City had died down considerably, but the relative silence was born more of collective confusion than of folks minding their own business. One belief which they'd always held close was that Diz Durant was a man to be revered and trusted. Folks didn't ever question Diz on anything. They didn't second guess him when he'd change pitchers in the eighth inning with two outs and a shut out going, they just trusted that he knew what he was doing.

But this baby thing was different. After all, this just wasn't done. Maybe in the big city, where people didn't have the slightest idea of how to behave. But not here. Someone whom they greatly respected and held up as a long standing symbol of their community had gone and taken an abandoned baby, calling her his own and giving her his name. Few if any of them seemed to believe that Honey was Diz's real daughter; she looked nothing like him and besides, Diz never seemed at all interested in the kind of relations that could bring about such a disaster. But why would he take her if she wasn't his own child? Many wondered to themselves and to each other, especially at bowling leagues and the Elks Lodge, just on what one could count now that a puzzle such as this had presented itself.

At the boarding house, Pearl, Diz and Honey had settled into a routine, though not a particularly comfortable one as far as Pearl was concerned. Pearl called Honey her gypsy baby, for Honey had olive skin and brown curls. Her ears were so close to her face that one had to turn sideways so one could see them, and her wide set, dark blue eyes sailed resolutely above her cheeks. Her skin looked as though it had been tinted from another, hotter sun, as though she'd spent a lifetime in that skin already.

To Pearl's curious dismay, Lana Poole was a frequent visitor of Honey's, though Lana and Pearl were hardly friends. Lana Poole brought gifts of rattles and sticks with bizarre markings on them that horrified Pearl but that Diz accepted graciously. Lana Poole would hold the child and whisper to her about the invisible spirit people or some such hogwash, as Pearl called it. Pearl always felt that Lana Poole was intruding on Pearl's work, that there would be much to erase when Honey was old enough, that one should not visit so often unless one has been asked to come.

There were days when Honey was pliant and soft as warm clay, when she minded Pearl well. She'd learned to use her own cup and could feed herself without much mess and was a fine, careful walker and took her naps without any fuss when Pearl laid her down. But then there were those other days, the ones when something else seemed to emerge from Honey, the something that Pearl had seen that first night. An anger, or an old secret, Pearl thought, that's what drives her on the bad days. Something left over from Lurlene. On those days Honey would want only Diz. She couldn't bear it when he went away. Her screaming was like that of a goat at the slaughter, Pearl thought. Chilling screams, like something was being ripped from her skin. And when Diz would return home late, after a game, he'd find Honey still desperately awake, exhausted, refusing to be lulled by Pearl's stories, songs and threats. Then he'd take Honey out to the front porch and slowly rock. The porch seemed to comfort her, Pearl thought. It was more outside than in. Pearl would spy through a crack in the ivory shades. "She'll get used to me," Pearl would say to herself. "She'll let me comfort her too, even on the bad days. Takes time for a child to adjust to its surroundings, sometimes." But Pearl would feel relief too, relief that Diz was home and could quiet this demon who had captured Honey for a while.

Pearl saw the strange bond between Diz and Honey, those two who shared not an ounce of the same blood. She wondered how someone as calm and quiet and polite and steady as Diz could abide the presence of one who at times was so chaotic and wild. How was it that he loved this child? Pearl herself felt an odd love for Honey, on the good days. Then it all felt familiar and correct and Pearl felt that Honey loved her too. She'd sit on Pearl's lap and watch her knit and put her hands over Pearl's and laugh at the clicking motion of the needles. The world made sense to Pearl on those days. But the bad days, Pearl felt as though she were raising someone else.

It had started slowly, Pearl thought, the appearance of this other Honey. At first the tantrums were scattered, rare, not as violent. It was when Pearl started adorning Honey in Georgina's old dresses that Honey's wildness began leaking out. It was as though, Pearl felt, there was some leftover rebellion on those dresses, passed down from Georgina herself; that Honey was absorbing, through cotton and silk, Georgina's proud disregard for authority and structure. Can such a thing as that be carried in the dress of a dead daughter, Pearl wondered?

Pearl's other daughters had worn those dresses, but they didn't seem to inherit anything from them. They only complained that they wanted their own clothes, not hand-me-downs from Georgina, who never appreciated those dresses anyway (Pearl had made them herself, stitch by stitch) and didn't care for them properly, according to her sisters.

As Honey's looks took hold of her, Pearl allowed herself only once to wonder if the child was half black or Indian. She'd heard the rumors that scribbled around about Honey's supposed parentage, but Pearl paid little attention to rumors. It was facts by which Pearl lived, what she could smell and see and touch. She told herself that Honey was simply dark. After all, lots of folks are dark, like Pearl's own cousin Ermingarde, who'd raised some eyebrows in her time, so what? McGinn Wicks himself had been darker than average, Pearl reminded herself. Sometimes dark things come out of light ones and vice versa. Besides, it didn't really matter. This baby needs a mama, needs a strong hand to guide her, and fate has seen fit to give her to me, thought Pearl. She told herself all these things in an instant, and in the next instant she banished all such thoughts from her mind; and when Pearl banished a thought, it stayed away.

The season started as usual that late spring, the time of year when everything happened, on a cloudy, pleasantly cool day in early June. Diz ate his breakfast, kissed Honey goodbye, and walked to the ballpark. Pearl put Honey, kicking and screaming as was her routine, into the playpen. At four years old Honey had strong, wide legs and was big for her age and certainly too big for the tiny, rickety playpen. (Pearl's own children had been put into the playpen until they were six or so, since Pearl believed in keeping them contained and in sight as much as possible.) The front screen door let in a nice breeze and Robert E, blind in one eye and mostly deaf, lay quietly snoozing on the old green hooked rug next to the sofa. Fat black flies circled his head.

"Diz went to the ballyard, Honey, but he'll be back." Pearl crossed her arms. "That's how it is. I hope you can get used to it sometime, girl. You and I will have a fine time together. Now I'll be in the kitchen for a while. Don't be chewing on that fringe, Robert E," she warned. She twisted a bony finger at the ancient canine. "You know the rules." Robert E barely flinched. Most of his teeth were gone and he hadn't chewed on anything in years.

Honey continued crying and Pearl went into the kitchen. She tied on her apron, turned up the radio volume to drown out the crying and sang "Why Don't You Love Me" along with Hank Williams while she peeled three pounds of potatoes and two carrots. Then she turned down the radio to see if things had quieted in the next room. "That little girl is getting the idea at last," thought Pearl happily. "She's finally learning when to give up. It's about time." She creased open the kitchen door to check on Honey. The playpen was empty.

Pearl roared into the living room. "Where'd that child get to? Some watch dog you are! Which way did she go?" Robert E lifted his head, looked around the room and sniffed a couple of times. That was the apparent extent of his search and he dropped off again.

"Useless old hound." Pearl began to search the room. "Honey! Honey, now, come on out! Where are you? She must be around here somewhere."

She looked upstairs, under all the beds, in all the closets, behind all the chairs in the parlor, and called to her over and over. Georgina had been a climber too, Pearl recalled with brief dismay, and Pearl checked all her old hiding places. Honey was just plain gone.

Now Pearl started to worry. Her head filled with crazy thoughts of Lurlene. Maybe she had sneaked into the house and taken the baby. *My* baby! Maybe they were already half way to god-knows-where and Pearl would have to tell Diz that she'd lost their little girl.

Pearl went outside. Her neighbor, Caleb Henniss, was sitting on his porch. "What's all the fuss about, Pearl? I heard you howling like a coyote for Honey. What's she done this time?"

"Climbed out of her pen and I can't find her anywhere."

"I sure ain't seen her out here."

"That so? I wasn't fixing to ask you, Caleb. You're blinder than Robert E."

She couldn't see Honey anywhere in the yard. Then she started to walk quickly to the ballpark. Maybe Diz had an idea of where Honey might be. Diz was the one who knew how to handle Honey on the bad days. Pearl would rather not call the police until absolutely necessary. They'd look at her with disgust, she thought. They'd be thinking, "You lost another one, Pearl?" She could hear May Hetrick's laugh spilling all over town about this. In her mid she saw Lurlene speeding away in a dirty blue pick-up, laughing, Honey on her lap.

The ballpark was only two blocks away but Pearl had walked fast and was out of breath when she got there. She sat down on a bench to settle herself and waved to Billy Ray to come over.

"What's the matter, Pearl? Are you sick?"

"No—it's Honey—can't find her—climbed out of her pen—where's Diz?"

Billy Ray put his hands on his legs and laughed.

"I don't think a lost baby is so amusing! I'm about to have a heart attack here! Now where's Diz?"

"Right over there." He pointed towards the dugout.

Diz was watching batting practice, holding Honey in his arms. Honey was smiling and holding a ball. Pearl put her hand over her heart and exhaled loudly, but her shoulders fell when she saw the two of them together.

"We sent Joey over to tell you that Honey was here. I guess he hasn't got around to it yet," said Billy. "I'm sorry for laughing, Pearl. But she's ok. You know she's been here before with Diz. He likes having her around."

"It's no place for a little girl." Pearl stood and walked over to Diz and Honey. She stretched out her arms. "You come on home with me now, baby girl."

Honey smiled, but shook her head.

"This isn't a game, Honey," said Pearl. "Now come on home. Your daddy has work to do."

"Honey can stay, Pearl. She misses me is all. I'll watch her all right," said Diz.

"She could get hit in the eye or worse! Let me take her home. It always worries me when you bring her here. Come on Honey, come with Pearl now." Pearl came close and tried to take the child from Diz.

Honey stopped smiling and shoved Pearl with fierce strength and Pearl suddenly felt punished, banished; she felt that something was slipping by, just beyond her grasp. She remembered feeling that way before, with Georgina sometimes. Honey had never pushed Pearl so meanly, not in the house. The ballpark seemed to strengthen Honey. It was the place she came from, Pearl remembered, and some of it is still on her. Pearl dropped her arms. She waited for Diz to chide Honey but he didn't. He was far too soft on her, Pearl thought.

"Don't worry, Pearl. We'll see you at home later," said Diz. "Enjoy some time to yourself for a change." He turned and walked away towards the outfield. Honey's chin was resting on his shoulder.

Pearl walked slowly back home, shaking her head and talking out loud to quiet her thoughts. "That child climbed out of her pen, went out the front door and walked to the ballpark alone. I don't know where she gets such ideas. Sassing me already and only four years old." But it wasn't the sass that bothered Pearl so much as the feeling that she was being slowly brushed aside in favor of something she could not understand or share; but she buried those thoughts. She knew how to do it.

Later, when Diz and Honey came home, Pearl revisited the event. "I don't think it's such a great idea, rewarding her wicked behavior that way, letting her stay with you. I got to have some rules around here, after all. You let her get away with too much and she's never going to learn respect or learn to be a lady if you don't harden a little, Diz."

Diz gently lowered a sleeping Honey into the playpen. "I'm sorry Pearl. But she's only four years old and just loves the ballpark. Got plenty of time to learn how to be a lady, seems to me. It's not hurting anything when she comes with me."

"But I counted on having her with me today, Diz. I had plans."

"She can stay home with you tomorrow, I promise. You'll have plenty of time with her," he whispered.

Honey did not stay home the next day or the day after that. She went to the ballpark with Diz, but Pearl kept quiet. She did not intervene, though it was hard for her. The only thing to do, she thought, was wait it out. There will be times when Diz goes on the road and then you can get back to the work of taming her wildness, Pearl reassured herself. And when the season is over, then Honey will be home again all the time. There won't be any ballpark to escape to. Things will get back to normal. Honey will let me read to her and help make cookies and wear the dresses I made. You can only do so much, Pearl reminded herself. You've got to share her with Diz. It's only natural that Honey would want to be with him. She is not your own child, after all. She is his. No one can blame you for it if things go bad, not this time.

And so Pearl filled her summer with mending and knitting and playing bridge and on the good days, when Honey allowed Pearl to lift her into the enormous, hooded carriage, she'd wheel Honey around town and tell herself that Honey was getting used to her, that when the season was over, all would be well.

Summer crept on until the middle of August, when Diz left for the longest road trip of the season. Pearl was relieved. This was a chance for Pearl to have some real time alone with Honey, to show Honey what it was like to have a real mama, someone to sing to you and read to you when you were tired and fussy, as Pearl's Aunt Ella had done for her. Yes, Pearl thought, Diz sang to Honey and read to her and was able to soothe her, but he was a man, and a child needs a woman to do those things. She needs me, Pearl thought.

Pearl's own mother had been a wonderful woman, Pearl recalled, so vibrant and capable and so busy, what with her clubs and parties and all the children. She never did sing to Pearl or read to her or play with her, because she was just so busy, but so what? Who would have had time for such things with all those children and all those responsibilities?

Everything had gone fairly well so far. Diz had been gone for six days and though Honey was quiet and more distant than Pearl had hoped, at least she was minding Pearl. At least she was eating and washing and wearing the clothes that Pearl chose for her each morning. The child hadn't slept well and seemed frightened at night, but had allowed Pearl to comfort her somewhat.

On the seventh day, Lana Poole came to the house early, before breakfast. When Pearl saw who was at the door (and so early, without an invitation, the very idea) she quickly latched the screen. "What is it, Lana Poole? Honey is just waking up."

Lana Poole wore a long, plain gown of thin leather. She carried a basket covered with a cotton cloth on her elbow. Pearl couldn't quite see what was inside but Pearl smelled corn meal and something else she didn't recognize. "I've come to see the child," Lana Poole said.

"She's not even up and dressed yet."

"I'll only be a minute, Pearl."

Pearl sighed. If Diz were home, she knew she'd have to let Lana Poole come in. But Diz wasn't home. This was Pearl's time to share with Honey and things were at least tolerable. Pearl certainly didn't want to share Honey with some crazy ball-playing Indian lady who only wanted to shake rattles at the child.

"Come back later, Lana Poole. Come back next Friday, when Diz is home."

"I must see the child today. I've made some muffins for her."

Pearl was noticing, then, how much Honey resembled Lana Poole. It was more than the tanned skin and the dark wavy hair. It was a power, an odd energy that rumbled from each of them, that threatened to swallow anything that got in its way. It made Pearl feel inadequate, small and pale in comparison. It made her feel left out. Of course, Pearl reminded herself, Lana Poole was most likely Honey's great-aunt, so some family resemblance and similarities of nature are expected. It occurred to Pearl then that Lana Poole must know of her relation to Honey. Why else would she care to see Honey at all? Lana had never made even the whisper of a claim on Honey and her visits were thankfully rare, so Pearl had not considered this possibility before. But after all, thought Pearl, Lurlene could have bequeathed Honey to Lana Poole, and she hadn't done that. She'd left her to Diz and therefore to Pearl. So Lana Poole would just have to get used to it. And as kind as Billy Ray Poole was, Pearl believed him to be somewhat of a crank. Pearl realized that she must carefully tend the space between Honey and the Pooles, to make certain that their influence did not infiltrate the child's upbringing. She must stand firm. Pearl knew she must also make certain that she didn't anger Lana Poole.

"You can leave the basket for her if you want to Lana Poole," Pearl said as kindly as she could. "I'd be happy to give it to her. Why don't you come back some other time?"

Lana Poole smiled a little. "All right, Pearl."

Pearl cracked the screen door and reached out her hand to take the basket. Her fingers brushed against Lana Poole's for a moment. Pearl felt a quick sting, as though she'd been bitten, but she didn't falter. One must not show any sign of weakness, thought Pearl. She took hold of the basket and folded it through the opening and shut the screen and the front door too, with Lana Poole still standing there.

Once inside, Pearl examined her aching finger. There was a slight redness and it itched. "Probably just scraped it on the wicker," Pearl said out loud.

Honey was at the top of the stairs. "Lana Poole," Honey said.

"Yes, Lana Poole was here. She brought some muffins. We'll have them when Diz gets home. Time for breakfast now, Honey. Come on down."

Honey wove slowly down the stairs and came into the kitchen and sat on her chair. Pearl was gathering breakfast items and looked at Honey out of the corner of one eye. She knew something was off this morning. She's probably just tired is all, Pearl thought as she mixed oatmeal and applesauce for Honey's breakfast. Maybe she had another bad dream.

But when Pearl looked squarely at the child, she saw more than fear and fatigue rubbing on Honey's face; she saw the old wildness struggling to free itself, the look Pearl had seen the very first night she'd met the child, the look she'd just seen glowering on Lana Poole, the look she'd seen so many times in the eyes of Georgina. Pearl steadied herself for the eruption she knew was coming.

Pearl began a spirited attempt to feed Honey the applesauce and oatmeal. Now Honey was old enough to feed herself but Pearl had decided that even the slightest breath of wildness must be threatened. Honey wanted one of Lana Poole's corn muffins but Pearl had refused. "Those are for a special occasion, when Diz gets back," Pearl told her as she put the basket on the highest shelf of the pantry. She really meant that the muffins would be tossed as soon as Pearl got the chance. Pearl was hoping that Honey would forget all about them in the meantime. No telling what was in them, anyway. "Now come on, Honey. Eat your breakfast."

The battle had begun. Pearl kept trying to shove the food into Honey's mouth and Honey kept spitting it out and yelling "Diz! Diz!" Pearl's red apron was soon fertilized with applesauce and oats and drool.

"Diz isn't here. You can yell for him all you want and it won't make a lick of difference, girl." Pearl's face had a new line on it for each minute of the morning. "Now look here. You got to eat. And you got to get used to the fact that I'm the one who's in charge when Diz is away. Here, it's good! It's just so yummy! See, even I like it." Pearl pretended to taste the mixture and while the spoon was near Pearl's mouth, Honey leaned close and yanked the spoon hard. The applesauce landed mostly on Pearl's face, dripping off her chin. Honey opened her mouth to laugh.

Pearl was mad and saw her chance and picked up the spoon and shoved a messy puddle into Honey's mouth. "Ha! Gotcha! Now what's so funny, missie!" Pearl felt a wash of victory.

Honey's blue-black eyes burned as she sat silently with the spoon protruding from her mouth like a steel cigar. Then she screeched so loudly that even Robert E apparently heard her, for he lifted his ears and left the room. Honey then snarled the spoon onto the floor and grabbed Pearl's hair.

"Now you stop that right this instant, you naughty thing!" Pearl freed herself from Honey's sticky grip. Even this was extreme behavior for Honey and Pearl let it all out. "When are you going to learn to accept things the way they are? Is that so hard to do? Diz is away and there's nothing you can do about it. You got to mind me. You got to let me take care of you. One minute you're sweet as cherries and the next, you won't sleep, won't eat, making a mess, acting like a wicked boy. I've never seen your equal and I've seen some bad ones. That curse will not be allowed to flourish in this house. It's going to stop or you'll have me to contend with!" She sighed loudly and then Pearl, still muttering to herself, began to clean off her own face with a damp towel.

Honey sat still for a moment or two, twisting her brown curls between her fingers. Then, staring at Pearl with the look of a hawk about to land its supper, she stood up in the chair, picked up the little jar of applesauce and hurled it hard and fast. For an instant, as it whizzed past her face, Pearl felt the sticky glass against her cheek and her mind flashed on Lurlene. The power to get mad and throw hard seemed to run in the family. The speeding glass hit the wall in the next room, shattering applesauce and shredded glass onto Pearl's good embroidered carpet. Pearl's face would surely have been cut fiercely had Honey hit her mark. That's what Pearl thought.

Honey stood there grinning, like she'd won. Pearl's mouth hung open. Both of them were swabbed in spit up oatmeal and applesauce. Robert E blinked, rolled over, and went back to sleep.

Pearl shut her mouth and squinted at the child. The redness on Pearl's finger swelled and she felt it burn and in that moment, for the first time, Pearl calmly understood exactly what she was up against; and her resolve to tame this strange, savage thing hardened to stone.

VII.

Pearl is sleeping on Aunt Ella's crimson sofa and she feels the cool, crimson smoothness of a clothes pin in her hand, holds it in her mouth and begins to hang a wet linen tablecloth and the rope sags. And now someone is next to her and Pearl thinks it's Honey but she turns and there is Georgina holding a clothespin but she won't give it to Pearl. Georgina laughs and hides it behind her back and runs in a tight, perfect circle around Pearl who watches with horror and delight. She has come back. She has never left me. Pearl catches her but she is not Georgina anymore. She is Honey. Pearl instructs Honey to sit on the grass and she obeys. And now Lana Poole taps Pearl on the shoulder and says "She is here." But Pearl can't see anyone. "Who is here?" asks Pearl. "The true mother," Lana Poole says and now Pearl thinks she sees her, out of the corner of her eye, sees the blond hair and red shoes and now she comes fully close and Pearl says "You can't have her back. She's mine now, babies are nice." But the true mother doesn't answer. Now Pearl sees the woman bend and take something from the laundry basket, something that belongs to Pearl but it's not a dress or sheets or towels. It's something else. Something Pearl thought she'd lost. The woman brings forth the yellow ballerina, polished and perfect, and Pearl reaches for it. "Give it back. It's mine. It was promised to me." The woman shakes the ballerina and it makes a slight rattling sound and now the woman says "I'll trade you. I'll trade you this for her." And Pearl knows she means the child, who is waiting so silent and dark, and Pearl does not hesitate. She knows she must hurry for she feels herself waking and so she quickly says "Take it then. Take the porcelain and leave the child to me." And now the woman is gone. Pearl feels she has banished her, for a time; only the basket remains, the empty wicker basket and the clothes pins, lying like long teeth, glistening in the grass, just beneath the crimson fringe.

VIII.

Fontana Lake Home

Billy Ray looked wide awake and freshly scrubbed. He sported a red and white polka dot bow tie, the kind that Virgil thought only bad comedians or clowns wore. The Sunday Brunch was in full swing and visitors were everywhere, chewing muffins and sipping coffee. Some had even rented small sail boats which brushed Fontana Lake like cotton puffs on dark glass. Long tables draped in white linen reclined on the porches and balconies, while the aroma of fresh strawberries and watermelon dusted the breeze. It had been a while, Virgil thought, since muffins and coffee and linens had tasted and smelled and felt so fine. He was eating his second helping of blueberry pancakes. Billy Ray's plate held sausage, waffles, shrimp salad and a huge cranberry muffin. Between bites Billy Ray nursed his coffee and rocked.

Virgil, too, rocked as he ate and suddenly began to wonder about all who had sat in the rocker before him. Its blue paint was faded and had been rubbed off almost entirely where former inhabitants rested their hands on its arms, but it felt altogether comfortable and comforting, and Virgil liked the wear on it. It's always a good thing in life, thought Virgil, to have such a rocker, one that bends with you, welcomes you; one that, no matter how many have called it theirs, always makes you feel like it's only yours. He couldn't remember ever having had such thoughts before, thoughts of rockers and paint and longevity; he'd held his life closely, carefully, and always thought he would know what he'd be thinking about every minute of every day. It must be this place, the slowness of a Sunday, he thought. And that book in my room, too, the one with the story about the ball game. It's got me thinking about crazy stuff, stuff that doesn't matter. He looked sideways at Billy Ray, wondering if Billy Ray approved of him, wondering why he cared.

The late morning sun splashed over the porch rails and lit up Billy Ray's bow tie and suddenly Billy was talking.

"Honey Durant watched the team practice from the time she was two years old," he said. Virgil reached for his notebook. "Went on the road with us, sometimes, when Pearl would let her. Did I mention that she lived at Pearl Harpham's, with Diz?

"Anyway, Diz made a little bat for Honey when she was three or so. I remember him leaning behind Honey at the plate, his arms wrapped around her, showing her how to swing. She never played like no giggly girl, neither. She'd take an inside pitch to the chin and charge the mound like a bull in heat. We'd laugh our heads off and that made her madder. Truth be told, the ball found *her* when she was at the plate. That's the way it looked to me, anyway. Had a nose for the zone like I rarely seen. When she was just a little bit of a thing, Diz gave her a mitt with her name scratched on it. But as she grew, she didn't get much of a chance to play, not even at school.

"In fact, I ran into Diz and Pearl when they were taking Honey to school for the first time. Asked if I could tag along and they said ok. Honey's about six years old and Pearl has her all dolled up in some hand-me-down from one her own kids. It's a little faded pink and white number, all frills, and Honey keeps tugging on it around the neckline, complaining that it itches her."

"'Young ladies do not scratch at themselves,' says Pearl.

"'You do it all the time,' says Honey.

"'You hush now.'

"Honey holds onto Diz's hand tight as he leans down to kiss her goodbye. He looks like he's going to bust out crying any minute. Like he couldn't bear to leave her there. But Honey looks ok to me, and Pearl yanks on Diz, saying, 'She'll be all right' and 'You got to let go sometime.' Stuff like that.

"So me and Diz go on down to the ballpark and he's sitting at his desk pretending to be working and all, and then we have a meeting with the general manager, then we go out to lunch, then he pretends to be working again. But he keeps looking up at the clock on the wall. I can tell it's a long day for him.

"Around 2:30 or so he gets up and so do I and he says 'Might as well get there a little early' and I ask if I can come along, kind of curious to see how it went. So we walk on down to the school and there's Honey sitting out front alone. Her dress is torn a little and she's holding onto a note addressed to Diz.

"Diz looks almost relieved. Not surprised or worried, just relieved. He gives Honey his hand and she takes it and we start to walk home. Honey hands the note to Diz but he doesn't look at it, he doesn't ask her what happened or anything. He just slides it in his shirt pocket like he already knows what it says, and I'm thinking, I've seen this before. This child always has a note for Diz.

"I start asking Honey if she had a fine day at school, and isn't that a nice teacher she has, my cousin Valma had her too, but Honey doesn't say anything. So then I ask her, what did she learn today? She looks up at Diz and says, 'I got me the curse.'

"Diz doesn't answer. I say, 'Honey, that isn't so! You don't have any such a thing.'

She says it again. 'I got me this curse, and no one else has it, just me. It's all mine. I heard about it before, at the ballpark. Everyone says I have it. Even the teacher says so.' Honey says it just that like, almost like she's proud, like she knew it all along, but not like she's scared.

"Diz is just walking along, nodding a bit. I wait for him to tell her it's not true, that there isn't such a thing as a curse, but he doesn't.

"Things eventually settled down at the school, I heard later. They got the stains off the walls and out of the teacher's dress and someone donated a new hamster to the class. Honey didn't go to school much after that. Pearl taught her reading and writing at home and everyone seemed to accept it."

Virgil was making notes, writing down some of the details that seemed relevant but he was thinking about that story, the one with the animals and the ball play, though he didn't know why. Billy Ray was chewing on the remnants of waffles and then slid back into his tale.

"I used to walk into town with Honey once in a while, buy her a chocolate soda. One time we're sitting at the counter of a little diner. Ralph's Diner. Some little girls come in the place. They seem about Honey's age, maybe six or seven. They stand by the door with their hands cupped over their mouths, pointing at Honey, who can't see since she's sitting with her back to them. They're looking at Honey like she's a movie star or an Indian princess or something, like they want to get near so some of her will rub off onto them. I can hear their little whisperings. 'You ask her.' 'No, you.' Seems to me they aren't saying mean things or anything like that. And I'm wondering why I never see Honey with other little girls. She seemed to only exist at the ballpark and at Pearl's.

"Then I'm thinking, maybe Honey thinks they don't like her. So

I say 'Those little girls yonder seem like they want to play with you. Why don't you run and play with them?'

"'That's what Pearl always says.' Then Honey gets this flat look on her face. 'Don't look at them.'

"Seems like an odd thing to say. 'What do you mean, don't look? They're standing right there! Hard not to look. Pearl wants you to have fun with other children. Go on and play.'

"'Don't look at them. They'll leave if you don't look.' The girls whisper a while longer. Then one of them buys a licorice whip, a long thin snake of a thing, and the four of them walk away, each with a piece of the licorice whip in their mouths. They're like horses all bridled on the same post. I remember looking at Honey and thinking, they seem the same. That's what was funny about it.

"I noticed, after that, how other children kept their distance from Honey, how she made sure of it. Once at a game, Honey's sitting on the edge of the dugout, up on top. She's swinging her legs and leaning back on her hands. I'm standing nearby, talking to her. Some kids in the stands start pelting her with peanuts. They're laughing but not saying anything to her. She doesn't turn around to see who it is or anything. She just sits, still as stone, while the peanuts are hitting her. I go and shoo the kids away. Then I see Honey start to pick up the peanuts one by one and put them in her pockets. Looks like she has balloons in her pockets. Then she starts swinging her legs again, watching the game.

"Diz was there the whole time, and I know he saw what happened. But he didn't say anything, didn't even go over to see if she was ok. That's how it was between them."

IX.

"It was the year of Honey's tenth birthday when Delancey Cooper, biggest ump in the league, dropped dead on opening day. Two calls into the game, count is two strikes, and Delancey looks over at Diz like he wants to tell him something. Then he shuts his eyes and dies, right there sprawled over home plate, all four hundred pounds of him. When I told Mama about it she squinted her eyes tight and said something was mighty wrong and that the spirits of the game were giving us a sign, giving us a chance to fix it. Could be, I thought. Or maybe old Delancey just ate one too many hot dogs with chili and onions. I always did wonder, though, what he wanted to tell Diz.

"Anyway, it was that same summer, and Honey was always after me to take her out for a catch, show her the different pitches. So one day, I take her over to the Bryson City playground, where there was a nice grassy spot.

"Me and Honey start to throw the ball around, and we're having a pretty good time. She's asking me all kinds of questions, and telling me stuff like, 'You know Slap Morgan? They been pitching him outside a lot lately. He should open up his stance some.' Now I knew she was right. I figure she must've heard that from Diz.

"Then a gang of boys arrives. They're about Honey's age, and they all got bats and gloves with them.

"'Hey mister, we want to get a game going here,' says the big one with the freckles. I mean a lot of freckles, sir. He was more freckle than face. 'How about you and the girl go over there by the bushes to have your little catch?'

"I start to answer but Honey jumps in. 'Cause we were here first,' says she, arms folded. 'You all will just have to wait till we're done.'

"Come on!' says Freckles. 'You're right in the middle of the infield. Why can't you go yonder? It's just a catch. Not like it's a real game you're playing. You don't need all this room.'

"'Don't matter how much room we need,' Honey says, throwing the ball back to me. 'Only matters that we got it and you don't. We were here first and I'm working on my pitching today.'

"Freckles and his gang bust out laughing. 'Yeah, right! Like a girl can pitch a ball.'

"Honey catches the ball I throw her and yanks down the lid of her cap. 'I'll give you the field if I can be in the game.'

"Freckles frowns. 'I say we don't let her in. Let's just go over to School Hill and play there. I'm not playing with no girl. Especially this girl.' I see the flame light in Honey's eyes.

"'Oh come on,' says a little guy with a ripped Yankee cap. 'School Hill is too small. Let's just let her play so we can get the field. It's not that big a deal.'

"Freckles shakes his head. 'If we give in, you wait and see. She'll be back here every day expecting to play with us. It's not right.'

"'It's just one game.' says the Yankee. 'We'll hardly know she's here. Come on, let's play.'

"The boys all look to Freckles, saying, 'Yeah, it's just one game.' and 'We'll show her how the game is played.' stuff like that. Honey and me are just throwing the ball back and forth, waiting.

"'I know who she is. You all can play with this here cursed half-breed if you want to, but I'm not.' Then Freckles throws his mitt down and goes and sits under a maple and starts grabbing at the grass around him.

"'Ok,' says the little Yankee. 'I'll take Pete and Sam and the girl. Let's play. Mister, can you be catcher?' So I say ok.

"The Yankee's side is up first. Pete and Sam both get on base, on errors, and now it's the little Yankee's turn. He swings through the first two pitches and swears.

"Honey comes up to him and says, 'Shorten your swing some, and don't hug the plate so much.' Good advice, I thought.

"Little guy says 'I don't need any help from a girl,' but he says it real polite, quiet, not looking at her. Then he swings through strike three and sits down.

"Honey picks up the bat and strolls to the plate, which is an old piece of cardboard. She takes a practice swing or two, and then nods at the pitcher. I always had to laugh when I saw her nod like that.

"The fellow who's pitching is a little older than the rest, a tall kid with long arms. He's got a pretty fair curve ball for his age, and when he's getting the curve in a good spot, the other kids can't hit him.

"He throws Honey a curve that she gets way ahead of. Freckles, under the maple, is muttering about a curse. Honey sticks out her tongue at him.

"Next pitch is the kid's heat, which wasn't too bad neither. Honey gets a good cut at it but misses. Sam and Pete are on base, yelling, 'Come on, girlie! Hit me home!' Honey practice swings a couple times again, then nods.

"Next pitch is the curve, and this time she waits on it good, but fouls it. 'We're gonna be here forever waiting for her to hit something!' shouts Sam. 'Just pitch it to her easy, Dickie.'

"'What, so you can score? I don't pitch easy to nobody,' says Dickie, and he gets ready to throw.

"Now she's down in the count, nothing and two, and Honey digs in, bends her knees more and brings back her left shoulder some. I can see that she understands.

"Pitcher throws his fastest stuff. Honey lifts up her right foot and swings, more balanced this time, but she let the bat head drop too soon. Ball just does graze the stick, but they call her out. I could see that she was trying too hard, trying to show off, and it got in her way. She never expected to fail, not even a little. So I says, 'Everybody strikes out, Honey. It's not that big a deal. Just don't try so hard. You got to try easier, not harder, you got to let it come out of you easy, but she tells me to shut up and then she starts yelling at Dickie.

"'I tipped it! It was foul and you know it. You can't call me out!'

"'You're out, missy!' says Dickie. Then Freckles, smiling, picks up his mitt and comes into the game. 'Take a seat or get lost,' he says as he passes her.

"Honey throws down the bat, puts her fists to her hips and spreads her feet apart and I remember thinking how much she looked like Pearl. 'I won't do neither, you'll see!' She starts to walk out towards Freckles, like she's going to jump him, but I get in between them and hold her back.

"'Settle down, Honey,' I says. 'Just get your mitt and play in the outfield. Stay in the game.'

"She shakes me off. 'You all think you know so much! Just a bunch of dumb asses. Nothing new here. Just scared to see if I can really beat you!' The she grabs my arm and says, 'Come on, Billy Ray. We don't even want to play with no cheaters. Let's go over the ballpark and find us some real ballplayers.'

"'I don't have to cheat to beat no girl,' says Dickie, as Honey and me walk away. They start playing again, but when I look back I notice that the little Yankee is just sitting, quiet, drawing with a stick in the grass."

Billy Ray paused and sipped his coffee. "Coffee could be stronger," he yelled to one of the nurses. "I like my coffee strong," he said to Virgil, who nodded. Billy dabbed his mouth with a white linen napkin and then folded it neatly on his lap.

"She practiced more after that," he continued, "and she got better, you know, more patient. Paid more attention to the game. I'd come to the park at noon, and she'd already be there, in the batting cage since morning. She must have spent hours there, all alone. By the way, have you tried these tiny shrimps?"

Billy Ray held up his plate to display the shrimp salad he was currently devouring. "I just love these little things."

He sat rocking, licking his fingers, chewing the shrimp with small, tight little bites, and washed it all down with a huge gulp of coffee.

"Every year, Diz and me, we'd take Honey to the beach." He took out a fresh cigar. "You know, kind of a vacation, after the season was over. Now Honey loved the beach. Couldn't wait to get there. We'd go fishing, swimming, and play ball too, every day. She hit more balls into the ocean than I care to remember. Probably knocked out her share of fish. Folks would stand around with their eyes popping out of their heads, watching this child hit hard liners all over the place, playing ball like other folks sing. It was her one chance every year to really play. She liked the beach, she said, on account of the sand."

He paused to bite off the cigar tip and spit it out. "Good cigar keeps you young." He puffed on it eight or nine times to get it going, then sat back and rocked, slowly.

"It was the year after that, when she was eleven, that Diz and me took her on such a trip to the beach. Now one morning Diz wants to sleep in a little on account of he was up late making out the rookie wish list for the next spring. So me and Honey, we go on down to the beach together. I'm feeling tired myself so I tell Honey to play in the sand for a bit, then I'll help her with her curve ball. I start reading the sports pages while I'm laying on the towel.

"So she starts building a sand castle or something and I'm still reading the paper. She left her bucket back at the house, so she starts carrying the sand from a big dune to where she's building, which is a good ten yards away. I says, 'Honey, why don't you just build your little castle right next to the dune, so you don't have to carry the sand so far?' But she don't pay no mind, which was as usual. I notice that she ain't making much progress, 'cause she's squeezing the sand so tight in her hand that it's trailing behind her while she's walking, and by the time she gets to where she's going there ain't no sand left in her hand. You know what I mean, Mr. Alcover, sir?"

Billy Ray held up his fists to Virgil, squeezing them hard, sitting up straight in the rocker. The cigar dangled in his mouth, twitching back and forth as he balanced it. Virgil scribbled, then nodded.

"So I says, 'Honey, now, don't squeeze it so hard, the harder you hold it, the faster it'll slip right through. That's how sand is.' But she ain't listening. 'You're grabbing too tight, Honey. Here, use this here towel to carry the sand. It'll be easier.' She acts like she's stone deaf. I figure I better just shut up before they haul me away for talking to myself.

"She keeps at it for a long time, going back and forth with a fierce will, but she ain't getting nowhere, just trailing sand where there already is sand. Then she sits down on her little striped towel, real quiet. After a bit she looks at me and says, 'So how about that curve ball you think you know so much about?'

Billy Ray smiled and rocked faster. "Honey never did listen to me much. I tried to talk her into playing ball for Ralph's Diner, like Mama used to, but she'd have none of that. Said she wanted the real game.

"Once, she was maybe twelve, we was playing at home, and we was losing. Honey hated losing. It wasn't a good year, third bad year in a row, and Diz was feeling some heat about it, if you know what I mean.

"Anyway, Honey, she's sitting on the bench, chewing on a big wad of gum like they used to make, yelling at the ump. Then she walks over to Diz and says, 'Diz, when will I be old enough?' I'm not sure what she means, but Diz just pats her on the head.

"'When? How old do I have to be to play?' Now I understand. All the guys in the dugout start to laugh. I say, 'Honey, you've got some growing to do yet, don't you think?' But Diz, he holds up his hand for us all to hush. Then he smiles at her and roughs up her hair a bit. 'We'll talk it over later, at home.'

"She keeps at it. She stands real close to him and speaks clear. 'You always say that. Always say we'll talk about it when I'm older. Well I'm older. I want to know. When will I be old enough? How much longer I have to wait?'

"Diz starts scratching at the back of his neck. Honey's just standing there, real still, waiting. Then Hector Hurlbut, a back up catcher, says, 'You know you just a girl, Honey! Take a look out on the field. Don't matter how old you are. Maybe you could be a Bloomer Girl!' He's not saying it mean, really. He just thinks she's kidding.

"Some of the guys laugh and Diz tells them to shut up. But Honey is looking out over the field, her eyes moving slowly. Then she says, 'Tell him that's not so. Tell him when I'll be old enough, that if you're good it don't matter. Tell him it's not like this everywhere. It's not, right?'

"'We'll talk it over later Honey,' says Diz. 'You sit down with Billy Ray and watch the game now.'

"Honey does what Diz tells her. Now she was a child who liked to kick and scream to get her way, and I wait for the tantrum, but it doesn't come. She looks older to me. She's quiet the rest of the night.

Seems almost sleepy. I try to talk to her a few times but she doesn't answer. Keeps looking at Diz and the field like she never saw them before."

Billy Ray just rocked and shook his head.

"One thing I'll always remember about Honey. She did not know how to carry sand."

X.

Virgil is on the porch and Billy Ray isn't and Virgil wonders why and it seems like dusk, the evening is almost there, but in one corner a slice of sun lingers like the last piece of pie and then Virgil sees her, sees her playing solitaire. He can't remember seeing the woman before but there she is. She doesn't look up, not once, he can't see her face and when she finishes a column of cards she slaps the last one hard and the little wicker table shakes and now Virgil hears her speaking to someone.

"You ain't buying any of this, are you?"

"How's that?"

"Said you ain't buying any of this story, I hope."

"Billy Ray's story?" Virgil says.

"Nice story. But ain't a lick of it true."

Virgil says, "You mean he made it all up?"

She doesn't answer, he can't hear her and maybe it's just that he's tired from the mountain air and the long drives up or maybe the woman isn't speaking to him, maybe to someone else, where is Billy Ray and then Virgil hears her again.

"I heard this a million times. Keeps changing. Expanding. It's like the first fish you ever caught. Gets 3 pounds bigger every time you tell it."

"Did you know Honey Durant? Do you have some information about her?"

"Makes a real pretty story, don't it? Real pretty."

"Are you saying she never existed? Don't tell me that."

But he can't feel his mouth moving and then the piece of sun and the cards and the woman are gone but underneath her chair, like the button off of a coat, a mouse sits and watches and Virgil thinks the mouse is there to make sure that Virgil had heard, and the mouse is looking at him very hard, her familiar, thinks Virgil, I've heard of such things. The mouse just sits and its whiskers are like glistening steel swords and now it drops away and the porch is dark. Virgil blinks and reaches for his briefcase.

XII.

Pearl Harpham's House
1960

Pearl Harpham's blue and white china was famous in the county.

As the oldest in her family, Pearl had inherited it from her mama who got it from her Aunt Josephine who brought it over from Bavaria. There wasn't a scratch on any of it. Lighter than air it was, like the colors of the June sky and pale clouds, each piece hand painted with little blue birds dancing around the edges. In the center of each piece stood a woman and child in wooden shoes and Dutch bonnets, each offering a tulip to the other. When the day was fine, Pearl would hold a plate next to the dining room window, where the sun made a warm, white halo around the china. The painted blue birds would glow like Christmas lights as Pearl turned the plate this way and that.

Pearl never once complained that she'd had no choice in the matter of the china. Ever since she was a little girl, she'd known that it would be hers someday. This she accepted willingly and graciously. She understood that the choice had been someone else's and that her duty was to accept it, care for it, and pass it on. It was a constant in her life, a symbol of all that was good and continuing, and she cared for it with the tenderness of a new mother, always placing each piece in the same place on the shelf, as though it had never left the cabinet. She never allowed anyone else to touch it.

Pearl had hoped to pass the china on to her oldest daughter Georgina, killed in a car crash when she was seventeen years old. She had been out driving with her boyfriend, whom Pearl had forbid her to see. The police said the two crashed head on into an old oak that stood just at the edge of town. Pearl remembered walking past that oak as a child, watching it change from green to bright red each year, gathering its leaves to make place mats for her mother. Georgina was the type to break all the rules a lot of the time and Pearl knew this was her undoing. Maybe you could get away with it once in a while, Pearl reasoned, but when you live your whole life outside the rules, you are just inviting heartache and trouble with an engraved invitation.

Pearl remembered that she had tried to impress this on her surviving children after Georgina died, but they didn't get it, she thought. She was not the type of mother to overly dote on her children, something that irritated her to no end in others. Pearl could not understand how other women said they lived for their children. She could never feel that way. She loved them. Wished them well. But after all, they'd grown up and left her, none of them were really *like* her in any significant way, and they didn't really appreciate all the things she tried to teach them. How could you live for people who didn't appreciate you? But whenever one of Pearl's friends would say something like "What would I do without my children? They're all I have," Pearl would smile and nod and pat her friend gently on the hand, but she wouldn't say anything. She knew her friend just wouldn't understand.

Pearl had expected, and looked forward to, some rivalry between her surviving daughters over which one would inherit the china. But instead they each seemed determined to choose their own patterns. Pearl bore this well, seeing it as a sign of the less disciplined times in which her daughters lived, and clinging snugly to the belief that sooner or later one of them would realize her error and recognize the value of the inheritance. In any case, she secured promises from each of them that the china would stay in the family and would go only to a daughter, not to a son (there was only one boy in the family anyway) and definitely not to the wife of a son, and that the set would never be broken up. In the meantime she allowed each of them their foolishness and held her tongue when they made their choices.

Her second daughter, Georgella, had chosen a plain gold plate with a thin silver boundary that Pearl felt was the ugliest thing she had ever seen, much less eaten off. "What's the use of having freedom of choice when you go and make a bad one?" thought Pearl as she smiled broadly at Georgella during dinner, asking her to please pass the mashed potatoes.

Honey, too, seemed unimpressed with Pearl's inherited china. At Thanksgiving and Christmas and Easter, when the china was set loose from its walnut cage and dressed up with fine, delicate linens and antique silver, the invited guests and Diz too would appropriately "ooh" and "aah" over the glorious blues of the blue birds and the tiny handles on the soup bowls, and everyone would tell Pearl again and again what fine shape the china was in and how she'd cared for it so loyally, and how lucky the next owner of such a treasure was going to be. Pearl would half smile and throw her hands at them, saying, "Oh, go on now," and her eyes would sparkle. But Honey would stay quiet. It didn't seem to matter to her what she ate off of, as long as she ate, and Pearl caught her more than once rolling her eyes when others had complimented the china.

Honey's idea of significant inheritance, Pearl reflected, was dragging home pieces of other people's garbage from the Bryson City Dump, located about a mile from Pearl's house. It was just on the other side of the ballpark, at the bottom of a grassy hill. Folks took all sorts of things there, things they had once thought they'd wanted, things they'd thought they couldn't live without, but things that once gotten had become boring or broken and useless, or not living up to their billing had become a sad disappointment. And so the thing would be brought to the top of the slope where it would be tossed or given a gentle shove, and it would topple over itself and land dead at the bottom. People would stand at the top and watch their former prize until it was still; then they'd slap their hands together, shake their heads and go home.

Once in a while Honey would bring something home, a piece of something, a souvenir from someone else's life, like a miniature birdcage, or the cracked face of a grandfather's clock, its half-moon rising forever above the missing nine. She'd even found a lady's corset, still stiff, most of the laces gone. Pearl thought it was silly how Honey'd bring all that junk into the house, and the dirt drove her crazy; but Diz, he let her, and Honey kept most of the things that had been handed down to her in a little cardboard box in her closet and rarely looked at them.

The one thing Honey kept out of the box was a doll that she'd found. It was made of porcelain and was cracked and fragile as a dried oak leaf, and it had one eye and one arm and just a bit of fluff where the hair had been. It sat upright and naked on Honey's bed, on top of the quilt that Pearl's grandmother had made for her when she'd married. Pearl hated to see that ugly old doll on the quilt; it seemed to crowd the space somehow. She always meant to remove it whenever she was cleaning or straightening in Honey's room, but she never did. When she would strip the sheets to make the bed, she'd hold the doll by its feet and move it carefully onto the night table and put it back in the same manner. No matter where Pearl went in the room, the doll seemed to be watching her with that one eye, daring her to come close, and Pearl let her be.

It was a rainy evening, and Pearl had just finished drying the dishes and had hung up her yellow apron on a worn metal hook in the pantry. "All done," she said, wiping her hands on a red gingham dish towel. She glanced out the window. "Looks like the rain stopped. Now let's get the evening paper and see what folks are up to around here. Come on, Robert E Junior." He eagerly followed.

She made her way to the front porch to look for the paper. Just as she opened the front door, the paper boy flew by on his bike and hurled the paper onto the wet lawn.

"Hey, Stanley Carter! How many times do I have to tell you that I want my paper put on the porch! Now it's just soaked. And don't roll it up, neither! Last night I had to iron it so I could read Lil' Abner." She retrieved the paper from the lawn and picked it up, shaking it in Stanley Carter's general direction, but he was long gone.

Mumbling to herself, Pearl went inside and put the paper in the still warm oven to dry it.

Diz came in the back door covered head to toe with wet sand. "Lord, Diz! Looks like you brought the whole ball yard home with you. Better get those filthy clothes off and get them right in the wash basin. Where's Honey at?" Pearl got the broom and started to sweep up the sand. "She was supposed to be home at least an hour ago for chores, but she never showed up, as usual."

"Maybe she went over to Billy Ray's."

"Uh huh. Well maybe it ain't none of my business," said Pearl. She fixed her eyes on the broom head as she swept. "But she's getting older now, Diz. Time for her to be thinking about growing up to be a lady and forget all this nonsense about being a ballplayer. Billy Ray and his mama are filling her head with a lot of hooey, ask me. Cherokee wands and magic. Nonsense. Besides, I need her here. I need help, I mean."

Diz just stood there, scratching at the back of his neck.

"Thing is, Diz, she don't listen to me. You got to be the one to tell her. She's so like you. Not like me at all. All bats and balls and the game. You two talk about that stuff all the time and I got nothing to say about it." She kept on sweeping.

"Game don't make people the same," said Diz. "Besides, all this time I thought it was you she took after."

"Me?"

"She's so like you, Pearl, anyone would think you're her mother."

Pearl felt a sudden rush of excitement, felt her face flush red; she put down the broom and pushed her palms against her cheeks to cool them. "No, not like me. Do you really think so? Does Honey think so? No. How is she like *me?*"

Diz lowered his eyes. "She's strong, Pearl, like you. I'll talk to her again about helping you more around the house."

Pearl repeated the words to herself over and over. *So like you anyone would think you're her true mother.* Diz hadn't said the word *true* but Pearl felt it conjured the real meaning. *Her true mother.*

XII.

"Season ended and another one started and it was the next June, I recall, when Pearl's nephew, name of Acton Lowell Lockwood, came to town for a spell. Acton was the child of Pearl's sister. I remember his name because every chance she got Pearl would say it. 'He's my youngest sister's youngest boy. Acton Lowell Lockwood. The family lives in Richmond, you know. Old money. Acton is a very *special* boy. A bit older than Honey, fifteen and a half, and very mature for his age. This could be just the spark that Honey needs. Yes, Acton will introduce her to the young person's life. This will do the trick.' She fussed so much you'd of thought the President himself was coming to stay at her house.

"Diz told me that Pearl even had some fine handkerchiefs made up special with Acton's initials on them. *ALL.* Only the *A* sat on top of the two *L*'s. Looked like a little pyramid. She gave the handkerchiefs out to some of the folks in town as a means of introducing her nephew to "society," as she called it. Only she never called him her nephew. She always said 'my sister's boy.' Once when she was going on about him I says 'Ain't he your nephew, Pearl?' She hands me one of them hankies and says, 'He's my sister's youngest boy.'

"Pearl'd been squawking for weeks about how Acton was coming and how he and Honey were sort of like cousins and how they'd have fine times. I'm over there at dinner one night and Pearl says to Honey, 'You and Acton will have to go on down to the new theater' or 'I'm sure Acton will enjoy an afternoon canoe on Little Lake Calhoun with you, Honey.' But Honey never says a word back to her. She just sits there and scrapes her fork against her plate until Pearl tells her to stop, and Diz keeps his head down.

"Well, there was some dance coming up and Pearl gets it into her head that Acton should escort Honey to it. I ask Diz how he ever got Honey to say she'd let Acton take her. Diz says he had to promise Honey something real big to get her to go. I ask him what it was. He don't say nothing. I say 'Don't seem like something Honey would do. Must've been something big.'

"'She's been sassing Pearl a lot lately,' says Diz. 'I told her just this one time, do it for Pearl. We owe Pearl.'

"'She ain't never minded Pearl before,' says I. 'Why would she now?' Diz don't say nothing. 'You had to promise her something big, you say?' Then I laugh. 'What did you do, promise her she could play, for real?'

"He smiles. But he don't say nothing.

"So anyway, by the time Acton comes to town everyone is good and worked up. I mean Pearl has at least fifteen, twenty of her friends and relatives meeting him at the train station with her, including me and Diz. All the ladies are holding one of them hankies and waving it in his face when he steps off the train. Pearl looks like she's about to faint away from the excitement.

"Pearl presents Acton to Honey and he gives Honey a big bouquet of yellow roses, a bit wilted from the long train ride. Honey takes them. Acton leans down and whispers something to her and then he turns and greets all the relatives. Honey's standing there with her face covered in roses, her eyes peeking above the yellow. She watches Acton make the rounds. Diz is there too. He stays back, behind Honey, his arms folded across his chest.

"Now Pearl's been telling everyone that Acton looks like Rudolph Valentino, but when I see him, I think he looks more like someone's nephew. Just a plain kid. His hair is all slicked back like somebody'd hosed it down with lard. He shakes my hand real hard, pumping it up and down and smiling wide. All the ladies think he's just the cutest thing. 'So respectful. So well mannered,' they whisper.

"Over at Pearl's, that first night Acton arrived, Pearl has Acton and Honey sitting side by side on the velvet sofa and Pearl keeps pushing their shoulders together and Honey keeps pushing her back. But Acton don't seem to mind. He's smiling and smiling. He takes Honey's hand and holds it real delicate. He whispers to her. She laughs a bit. He brings her some punch. In front of everyone I hear him tell Pearl that she should have told him Honey was so pretty, he would have come down sooner.

"The party's breaking up. Diz says goodnight and goes on up to bed. I don't see Honey anywhere. Pearl is in the kitchen, getting her china all dried and stacked, jabbering with her friends. I go in the kitchen to say goodnight and Acton comes in and tells Pearl he ain't that tired yet and he's going out for a little walk.

"'Take Honey with you,' says Pearl.

"'I think she went to bed already,' says Acton. 'She seems awfully tired and I don't want to disturb her.'

"'Ain't that polite!' 'What a nice young gentleman!' say the ladies, but Pearl looks disappointed. 'Yes, I suppose there will be plenty of time for you and Honey to get acquainted,' she says, smiling. 'You are so considerate, Acton. I'm so pleased you've come for a visit.'

"I say my goodnights and when I go outside I see Acton walking down the street with someone, a girl who was at the party. Daughter of one of Pearl's friends, I think. I can hear the girl giggling. Then I see Honey sitting on the porch swing in the dark.

"'Thought you went up to bed,' I say.

"'Think I will,' she says, and goes inside.

"So Pearl spends every day working on the dress for Honey to wear to the dance. One day I go over there and Pearl's on the floor with her mouth full of pins. She looks like a little porcupine. Honey's propped up on a wooden stool looking like she's wearing a straight jacket. There's pins all over the place. Robert E steps on one and Diz and me have to take him out back and pour whiskey on his paw and pull it out. Robert E limps for a while and keeps licking at his foot. He got to sitting in front of Pearl's liquor cabinet after that, as I recall.

"Couple days later Honey asks me to take her fishing. When I go to pick her up, Honey's still in her room getting dressed, and Pearl says it's impolite to go without Acton, that if we're bound on going, then we should take him along. I say fine. Pearl calls to Acton and he comes downstairs. She says Billy Ray has something to ask him. So I ask him if he wants to come fishing with me and Honey.

"He looks like he's thinking about it, then he says 'I'd only slow you two down. Not much of an outdoorsman myself.'

"'Why it's just for fun, Acton!' says Pearl. 'Honey never does such boyish things, it's just a way of getting fresh air, you know, just a way to clear the head.'

"'I said I'd meet someone,' says Acton. 'You understand, Aunt Pearl.' Pearl raises her eyebrows but Acton comes over and kisses her on the cheek. 'Maybe I could go to a game with her.'

"'Now Acton, that wouldn't be any fun at all!' says Pearl. 'Honey and I are just girls. We don't understand anything about that silly old game.'

"Now that makes me laugh, even though Pearl shoots me a look. Honey knew the game inside and out, but truth be told, Pearl herself could have known a lot about it too, living with Diz and Honey, but she chose not to, seems to me. Kept it off her.

"So me and Honey go on down to the Nantahala River. We're sitting on a big rock that juts out over the water, but neither one of us is very good at it and we ain't catching a thing. I was surprised she even asked me to take her, since we'd only fished together once before, when she was a little bit of a thing, and I didn't catch anything that time, but Honey caught a little trout. It was all shiny blue and red and wiggled in her hand, and I told her that it would make a fine supper, that there ain't nothing better than just cooked trout that's been alive that very day, but she said 'Throw it back, I don't want it. Show me how to get it off.' After that we never went fishing again, till this day she asked me.

"So we're fishing and she's real quiet and our lines are dipped in the water and then she says 'What does it feel like?'

"'What does what feel like?'

"'Did you ever go to dances?'

"'Sure. Plenty of them.'

"'What does it feel like?'

"I smile to myself. 'It feels like you could dance and dance. It feels like everything is spread out before you like a feast. It feels nice. I went to dances with my cousin, name of Lurlene. Always fine to go with a good dancer.'

"She don't say anything else. We sit a while longer, but nothing's biting so we go on home.

"Now the funny thing is, after all that fuss, I never did see Acton with Honey that much. Only once. One night after a late game, I seen them walking away from the ballyard together. At least, I think it was him with her.

"A while later I seen Acton at a day game. He's sitting up in the stands with some other kids. Honey's in the dugout with me, and I catch her looking up at Acton, looking sideways, looking at him like she don't want to be caught looking. So I says 'That's a real pretty dress Pearl is making for you, Honey. You'll light the place up.'

"'It itches.'

"'So does my uniform. You get used to it. When's this dance, anyway?'

"'Tomorrow night, if I decide to show up.'

"'Now why wouldn't you show up? After all the trouble Pearl's been taking with that dress? I wish I was your age. I'd go myself. Seems like Acton likes you.'

"She looks at me and starts to say something, but she stops. I catch her looking up at the stands again, but Acton ain't there no more.

"Next night Diz asks me to come over to Pearl's for dinner. It's just Diz and me eating, since Pearl and Honey are upstairs getting Honey all set for the dance and Acton is getting Pearl's Chevrolet out of the garage. I can hear all kinds of thumping and running up the stairs and I hear Pearl talking in an excited voice.

"'So do you think Honey will really go?' I say.

Diz is eating some peas one at a time. He shrugs and doesn't look up.

"I go on. 'She told me she might not go. Taking an awful long time up there. Do you think she'll really do it?' Diz don't say anything.

"'You do want her to go, don't you? I mean, she's got to get out with other children sometime. Don't you want her to?'

"Diz stops eating. He's rolling one of them peas around on the plate, chasing it with his fork. He starts to answer but Honey comes down the stairs.

"She looks just beautiful. Looks like one of them china dolls in the window of a shop, all polished and still. Her hair is twisted into a little braid circling her head and Pearl is on her with the comb and spray. Diz looks like he's about to cry. He's even shaking a little.

"Honey looks so pretty and for the first time, I think she knows it. I think maybe she likes it. I never seen her like that before.

"Pearl is all busy clasping a gold locket around Honey's neck. There's a little heart dangling on it and Pearl is saying 'There's pictures of me and my sister in this locket, when we was just babies. Just babies.' Pearl seems different to me. Softer, full of sighs. She keeps fanning herself with her hand. Acting like she's going to the dance herself. She fusses over every little thing. Honey's shoes have little bows on them and Pearl is making sure they're good and even. Then she's smoothing out the light green silk of Honey's dress which falls all the way to the floor. 'That's

Sea Foam, that color,' says Pearl. 'You like it, Billy Ray? It's the latest thing.' Even Robert E is sitting straight up, watching.

"Pearl is peeking through the front shades. 'Acton went around to get the Chevrolet. I told him he could take it even though he only has his permit. After all it's a special evening and only a few block's drive. I know he'll be careful. Wait until you see the corsage he picked out! I went with him to order it.' Honey's just standing in the middle of the room, not moving. It's very quiet. Almost feels like church. We wait. But Acton never did show up that night and I never seen him again. Diz wouldn't say nothing about what happened and I didn't have the heart to ask Pearl or Honey neither.

"Down at the barber shop a while later, I heard that Acton had been found a week or so after the night of the dance in a rooming house in Savannah. He'd taken Pearl's Chevrolet, which she hardly ever used anymore, and he drove it all the way down there on his own. When the police found him he still had on the yellow rented suit and the corsage was in the Chevrolet, in its little box, on the front seat. The car was all wrecked and Pearl never did get another."

XIII.

Suddenly she is there. Pearl is asking Diz to let her throw Honey a real party, with invited girls from the neighborhood and all things properly connected with a little girl's party. Diz says there's a game that day Pearl, I promised her she could come, but Pearl argues that they've spent every birthday of Honey's at the ballpark, with just Diz and Pearl and Billy Ray and sometimes his mama too as the only guests, and Pearl cannot abide another year of listening to that old fool and his mother yabber about home runs in the sky. She wants to give Honey something real, something she can remember just let me give her a nice party, just this once. And then Pearl is putting up pink balloons and lace in the dining room and there are little hats with hearts on them all around the table and in the middle of the table is the book of fairy tales that Pearl got for her. She can't remember buying it, but there it is anyway, and on the cover is a beautiful lady riding a swan, and the lady has yellow hair and red lips, closed tight, and a prince is reaching for her hand, and she's looking down. Pearl is still hanging the pink balloons and then a child is there, she doesn't look much like Honey, she looks a little like Georgina,

Pearl's daughter. She must have lived after all, they must have made a mistake, and the child is looking at the book and asking what it is, asking who the lady is, and when she speaks it doesn't sound like Georgina, it sounds like Pearl's own voice. That's my gift to you, says Pearl, see here, the first story is Rumplestiltskin, the king tells the maiden to spin the straw into gold or he will kill her, but if she does it he'll marry her, you see, he's talking about making something out of what you got, he's talking about taking what you got and making the best of it. So she spins the straw into gold and then she gets to marry a king! But he said he was going to kill her, the child says, and Pearl can feel Robert E stirring at her feet, but she has to tell her, she says Oh, the king didn't really mean it, he was just saying that, see, the little elf helped her do it, she's right here on the cover so pretty and pink and yellow, that's how your mama looked. The child throws the book down and says No, I don't have a mama. Oh yes, everyone does, says Pearl, I know the secret but I never told, and she wants you to have a wonderful party. No, my mama is cursed, like me. Like you. And then Pearl is in the kitchen again and finds the book in the garbage and she's doing her best to wipe it clean with a worn green sponge and now she is on Aunt Ella's couch, face down, her arm dangling over the side, and she realizes that it's time to rise and shut the living room shades.

XIV.

Bryson City,
Present Day

Virgil was in the back room of the Bryson City Times-Picayune, looking through old newspapers. He'd already gone to the school board. All records before 1956 had been lost in a fire, and there was no Honey Durant listed after that. When Virgil had phoned the state capital he'd been told there was no birth certificate on file for a Honey Durant. Nothing.

He'd asked Billy Ray if he had any photos, journals, letters, anything to substantiate his story. "Let's say I do," Billy had said. "If it's proof you're after, what would it prove? I could show you any old picture of any little girl and say it was her. That don't prove a thing."

In front of Virgil was each weekly issue of the Times-Picayune from 1946-1950, which he figured from Billy Ray's accounts to be about the time of Honey's birth. He saw no birth announcements, no cute little stories about her, no photos. He did see two pictures of Diz Durant and even a short article about Billy Ray himself from the June 4, 1948 issue, in which Billy Ray discusses teaching the breaking ball to young pitchers. Virgil turned the pages of the old papers slowly, eyeing each one up and down. He'd already looked through them once and was on his second go-through when he saw the Lost and Found column from March 18, 1947. Betty Ann Harris had lost her wallet at the movie house on Saturday night after seeing a showing of *Mildred Pierce*. Anyone who might find it can just bring it right over to the drug counter where she worked. A child's bike had been stolen from his front lawn. If it was returned there would be no questions asked. Just leave it right where you took it. Someone had found an empty suitcase near the train depot outside of town. It was light tan and had a sticker on it that said *Myrtle Beach*.

Underneath the Lost and Found was another column called *News of the Strange*. Virgil hadn't noticed it the first time he went through the paper. A short note from the editor, a Mr. Moses Wilcox, said that so many odd things had been reported to the paper that month that he'd decided to run them, just for fun.

Three lizards in a blue shoe box had been found in front of the Methodist Church on Mavis Street. Each lizard had a little red scarf tied around its neck. Someone's favorite pig, a pig that had never left the farm and had always been faithful, had wandered away during a hail storm, unlikely weather for that time of year. Some locals had reported seeing strange lights in the eastern horizon each day before dawn for about a week. One farmer's wife had described the lights as "bits of lost lightning," and a girl had been born to a nameless mother at a clinic over in Cherokee. The baby, along with the mother, had disappeared in the middle of the night three days after her birth. (Anyone with information was urged to call the clinic.) A Mrs. Melba Squire reported that someone had stolen the wet laundry off her back clothes line. "I don't care about most of it," she was quoted as saying. "But please bring back the white shawl. My mother made it when I was born."

Nothing, thought Virgil.

A pretty story. But ain't a lick of it true.

His eye travelled back to the item about the baby, just for a moment. Could she have been Honey? Maybe, thought Virgil, he should go to the clinic in Cherokee and check their records. But what if it wasn't her? What if it was all a mix-up? Virgil let the questions cross his mind like threads on a loom. But no pattern formed, he only heard himself thinking *I don't want to know, I want it to be real,* and he knew that almost everything in his life that was worth remembering seemed made up, and he felt that the harder he looked the less real it would all be. So he folded the paper and put it on the pile with the rest and took them all back to the young woman at the front desk. She'd been eating a white sugar donut. A little ring of powder surrounded her mouth.

XV.

Pearl's House, 1963

One early evening, while Diz was on the road, Pearl sat on the crimson sofa pressing her newspaper flat and cursing Stanley Carter. The screen door flew open and Honey ran past Pearl into the kitchen, nearly tripping over Robert E Junior.

"You frightened me half to kingdom come!" Pearl called after her. "Where you been, child? You're late and the dishes are already done. I did hope that you were growing up some! I'm not going to spend the rest of my life being your step 'n fetch it, I hope you know!"

Pearl went into the kitchen and saw Honey with her head in the fridge, picking leftovers.

"Where you been?"

"Out."

"Out where?"

"None of your business." She took a giant bite out of a chicken leg.

Pearl folded her arms and planted her feet. "It is my business, Miss Teen-Sass. You ain't big enough to talk to me that way." She felt startled by the sound of her own voice, remembered when she'd talked that way before to a child of fourteen, and felt the presence of someone else in the room, someone who was watching her, softening her.

"You're never home," said Pearl. "Why can't you stay around here for a change? What you been doing out there, anyway?"

"Nothing." She picked up another chicken leg.

Pearl sat at the table and watched her. "I wish you'd stay. House is so quiet with Diz away."

Honey didn't say anything. She took a glass and poured herself some ginger ale, then drank it all at once. She sure is stubborn, thought Pearl. Sure is hard to talk to.

Pearl suddenly remembered how she and her Aunt Ella had sometimes played cards together. Those were fine times. Yes, she and Honey needed times like that. That was just the thing. "Say. How about we play a nice hand of hearts?"

"Yeah, right. Like I really know how to play those old lady games. See you later." Honey headed for the back door, chicken leg in hand.

Pearl stood. "You're leaving again? Where you off to now? You shouldn't be—"

"Bye." The back screen slammed.

It's the curse, thought Pearl. She remembered seeing Lurlene in the park that night, sipping pop through a striped straw. *Babies are nice.*

"She ain't your own child," Pearl said emphatically as she sat to read the paper. "She didn't come out of you. No one can blame you for it."

All this time Pearl alone had carried the burden of knowing the secret of Honey's real mother, and she found herself worrying more and more that the curse would be handed down no matter what. Why couldn't Honey act like a real girl once in a while? Especially when she knew that it would make Pearl just a little bit happy? All right, there was that sad business with Acton, but that was over and done with. It may have disappointed Honey, thought Pearl, but she seemed to have bounced back as children do, and besides, what good would it do to talk about that now? Pearl had hoped that the experience would have warmed Honey to dances and dresses, all the things Pearl had loved at Honey's age. It was too bad the way it had turned out, of course, but we all must suffer such things. Poor Acton. It wasn't really his fault, he was just confused. Just had bad influences. If only Pearl had known, she could have helped set him straight. But it was over now. Best to put it away and get on with it. Best to never mention it and let it be forgotten. We all have disappointments. They make us stronger.

Pearl remembered being made to wear a lacy white dress every Sunday when she was little. It itched like crazy around her neck (she'd rather have been wearing her soft overalls) and every time she tugged at the stiff lace collar her mother would slap her hand and say "Young ladies do not scratch at themselves," and Pearl was glad, she thought, *glad* her mother taught her that, where would she be if she hadn't?

You need someone to teach you what's right, she mused, someone to teach you how to fit in. Her Aunt Ella had been her friend, but it was her mother who taught her to put her foolishness aside and act respectably. Why wouldn't Honey let Pearl be a little of both to her? Why did she resist it so? Wasn't there *something* Pearl could give her? "You're dwelling on this far too much," Pearl said as she began to knit Diz's Christmas sweater. "She ain't your own child. If she was, then you could worry. You've done your best."

She'd done her best with Georgina, too, she reminded herself. Georgina had loved to knit. She always wanted to know how to put things together. When she was little she'd loved fancy dresses and stockings, all the things she hated when she got older. She'd had thin black hair with straight cut bangs and freckles that were like bits of milk chocolate dotted across her nose and cheeks. Pearl remembered that on Christmas Eve she'd sing Georgina to sleep and tell her that Santa wouldn't come until she was really, truly asleep, until she'd had her first dream of the night, and Pearl would think *she's all mine, all mine and no one else's,* and the memory of her seemed all yellow now, hazy and yellow and—

The clock on the mantle startled her as it chimed six-thirty. Pearl rested her knitting on her lap and rubbed her neck and allowed her eyes to travel around the room. She fixed her glance on a painting in the corner, a painting someone had given her grandmother, and Pearl remembered that her grandmother had loved it, but her mother thought it was too sentimental. And so, when Pearl's grandmother died, her mother had banished the painting to the corner. Pearl had never really looked at it before, but this evening she let her eyes rest on it as she continued rubbing her neck. She could see that there was a young girl holding a wicker basket. The girl was on a hill near a beach, walking carefully down a worn pathway that she'd walked many times before, Pearl thought, and there was some tall grass and wildflowers along the path. And she could smell the sea, it shone before her like a long piece of dark glass, and on the sea there was a small boat with a large rectangular sail puffed out wide. Pearl thought that the girl must know someone on that boat, and she's sorry he is going away, but now she'll gather some grass and flowers and shake the sand off as she lays them in her basket, and the breeze will feel a little cool against her cheek. Out of the corner of her eye, she'll see the boat sailing away. Now, thought Pearl, she'll turn her back and walk up the hill away from the shore, back to the cottage which is just around the bend, make a small fire and wake her father and try not to think of the sea. That's what she'll do. Why, that's a fine painting. Pearl lowered her eyes and lifted her knitting to her chest and began to click the needles together again.

After a while she rose and turned on the huge console radio to pass the time and keep her company. She was irritated to find that a baseball game was being broadcast from Asheville. "Henderson is down two strikes now, the count remains nothing and two" the announcer said. As she fumbled with the tuner to change the station, Pearl mumbled out loud, "I will never understand that game. What the hell does that mean, anyway, nothing and two? If you got nothing, well, you got nothing. And if you got two, then you got two. Can't have it both ways, seems to me." She found her country music station and, feeling comforted, sat back down with her knitting.

She hears the squeak of the porch swing and it seems dark. Pearl blinks and she can't quite see but she thinks it's Honey on the swing, thinks Honey is holding something close, she almost cradles it, and Pearl tries to push aside the shades but they won't move and Honey sits and rocks and holds the thing and Pearl thinks she hears Honey talking to it and she sees how careful Honey is with it, whatever it is, maybe it's not Honey, I thought she was older now, she's not careful with anything but it looks like her. Now Pearl is in the kitchen watching through the window and Honey is on her knees under the maple out back and Pearl sees her chipping away at the earth with a little twig, she should get a shovel, Pearl thinks, and the dirt sputters and then Pearl sees Honey lay the thing into the ground and cover it with some earth and pat the top of it and Pearl is saying *You can't hang on, things come and go from this life all the time, ain't nothing you can do, you got to get on with it* and she feels her mouth moving but no sound comes and Honey seems not to hear. Pearl sees that no one can hear. She lets herself stand there with no voice, watching.

XVI.

Fontana Lake Home

The afternoon sun was a warm glow. The brunch had started late to give church goers a chance to participate, and Virgil had eaten too much. He and Billy Ray sat belching on the porch near some red and purple tulips. The gardens were full of grandchildren, tugging at their grandparent's coats and running between the rows of tulips. In the garden's birdbath, some young robins splashed noisily, as though they, too, wanted in on the festivities. Some children ran by, waving their arms high in the air, and chased the birds away.

"I wish they wouldn't do that," said Billy Ray. "Them birds don't like to be chased." He scratched his neck.

"See, those same birds are here every day, sir. I'm used to them and they're used to me. The day I don't see them I'll know one of us is dead. How about a little walk?"

The two of them stepped off the porch and began to stroll around the gardens. "I dreamed I'm a woman and I'm holding a small child," said Billy Ray, "but the child wants to get free. I keep pointing to the sky and saying, 'Look there, look up and see yourself,' but the child ain't listening, it keeps trying to get free." He smiled. "Don't even have no kids. Now what do you think of that?"

Virgil shook his head a little and shrugged. *Oh no, you're not going to get me into talking about dreams.*

Virgil knew he'd stayed too long already with this interview, but after all, Billy Ray liked to ramble and there wasn't much Virgil could do about that, was there? Besides, Billy really hadn't told him the ending yet, and he liked to make sure his articles had a solid ending. That's what his readers wanted. He still hadn't figured out how he was going to write an article that was based on so much hearsay, but he'd worry about that later, he assured himself. For now he'd just stay and finish. *He must be near the end by now. Then I can get out of here and get on with it.*

He didn't like to think about it but the story was tugging at him, pulling him to a place where he wasn't sure he wanted to go, making him think about things he hadn't thought of in years. Like the time when he was ten and he'd been fighting with his older sister and he stole her watch, the one their father had given her, and Virgil buried it under two feet of snow. He denied it of course, but his tracks led them right to it. As his father stood in the knee-deep snow, holding up the watch and chain in Virgil's face, looking at him like he was waiting for an answer, Virgil had said *Well it was your daddy's watch! Why should she get it and not me?*

Maybe his father had told him that other things would be his, or that she was older, or that he was acting like a baby as usual. Virgil couldn't remember exactly. He remembered that he'd had to take her chores for a whole month and pay for the watch to be cleaned and say he was sorry. But it bothered him now to have to think about it, something that seemed unsettled, something that happened so long ago.

They walked a bit longer and as they approached the front porch, Virgil felt surprised to see Billy Ray's rocker empty. It looked as though something had been ripped away from it; when Billy Ray sat back down in it, Virgil felt relieved. Time to hear the ending now.

"Whatever happened to Honey?"

Billy Ray took out a new cigar. It resisted being lit and Billy struggled for a minute to convince it.

"Want one, sir?"

"No thanks. What happened to her? What is the ending?"

Billy Ray was already into a steady rhythm, rocking and smoking. "I'll tell you the rest of what I know. That's all I can do."

"Fine." Virgil waited with pen in hand.

"After the thing with Acton, Honey practiced a lot, but something about her changed. She still came to all the games, sitting on the bench watching, quiet. Any crumbs she could get from the game she ate like a starved orphan, like eating was serious business. I remember trying to get her to play a little pickle with me, for fun, you know. She'd say, 'Can't do it, Billy Ray. Got to work on my fielding today. Having trouble with hard grounders. Can you hit some to me?'"

Virgil knew he should be writing this down, but he was just listening, watching Billy Ray.

"Diz thought about retiring a couple times but someone always talked him out of it. Once they even asked him to be a scout for one of the big clubs, but he turned it down. Said he didn't want to travel any more than he already did. But I always wondered if that was the real reason.

"Honey was about fifteen, sixteen, and I was with her at the batting cage one day. Old Herman the Horse Hornsby comes swaggering in, bragging about the home run he hit the night before. He was the big slugger on the team, all bat and no brains, and not much older than Honey.

"'Yep. I guess I showed little Lyle Malone where to put a fat one! Did you see his jaw drop when I hit it? I gave that ball a sweet ride, I did.' Herman was not known for his humble nature, sir. 'Did you see it, Honey? Quite a poke.'

"I can tell he likes her, if you know what I mean. He's always trying to impress her.

"'I've seen longer homers,' says Honey. She wipes some tar on her bat. 'It was a gift if you ask me. Anybody could've hit that pitch.'

"All the guys start laughing, including me. We think she's just teasing him, and he deserves it.

"'What the hell you talking about? I hit that pitch a slap mile. And who says you can do better, miss girlie?'

"'I say so, Horse. You want to go up against me? Just say the word and I'll meet you at the plate.'

"'I been waiting to hear you say those words for a long time, girl.' Horse looks her up and down, whistling. 'I'd *love* to go against you. Anytime.' The fellows all laugh, the Horse loudest of all.

"Honey keeps polishing her bat. 'You're a jack-ass, Horse, and everybody knows it. Jake Barker, right over there, said so last night. Said his own baby sister could out hit you.'

"Horse starts towards poor Jake, whose mouth hangs open as he backs away. 'Now look here, Horse, I never said—'

"'I say you're scared,' Honey interrupts. 'Scared I'll beat you. I'm saying I'll out hit you, right here and now. I'm saying you're the biggest piece of chicken-shit ever if you don't do it.'

"Some of the guys start yelling at Horse, telling him to go for it. He puffs his chest out real wide. 'No problem! I'll see you at the plate in five minutes!'

"'First one to hit ten out wins.' says Honey, like she's been practicing that line for a while. Lots of jaws hit the floor when she says that. First time she ever went up against one of them that way. But I knew what she was doing. She'd waited for this day a long time, waited like a hungry hawk, circling, scheming.

"Everybody follows Herman out to the field. I appoint myself pitcher for the contest. It's pretty cloudy out. Looks like it might rain, so I tell the Horse to hurry up and get ready and he tells me to shut my face. Now the Horse was strong, but he was a free swinger. Struck out a lot. First pitch I throw him, he just about screws himself into the ground swinging at it. He misses.

"Now most of the guys are rooting for Horse, some for Honey. She comes up to the plate and stands in. Takes a few practice swings, digs her feet in, looks at me and nods, her eyes fixed like an old barn owl.

"I throw her a hard one. The guys are all cheering, messing around. But the sound of the ball as it hits her stick shuts them all up. That ball leaves the yard like a rocket to outer space. Now everyone gets real quiet, and then they all start yelling, 'Come on Horse! You can do it!'

"Horse looks a little pale. He yells, 'Hey, Billy Ray, you trying to pull a fast one? What kind of shit you throwing? That ain't the same pitch I got from you! I should've known you'd be on her side. Hey Rocks,' he says, pointing a fat finger at him, 'get in there and pitch. And don't hold back.'

"Rocks Hamlin threw hard, sir. Harder then anybody on the team. Couldn't hit the corners, though. Everything was right down the middle. Horse knew he could hit him.

"So Rocks throws his first pitch to Honey, who's still up on account of she's leading, 1-0. Honey swings and fouls it straight back. Had a good cut at it, though. The guys all cheer, and now Horse is back up.

"'Ain't so easy with a real pitcher, is it?' says Horse, leaning on his bat. 'Let me show you how it's done.'

"Horse hits the next five pitches out of the park, then misses with a long fly ball. Everybody's cheering mighty loud for old Horse, even though nobody really likes him that much. Then I see Gil Turner, the general manager and Diz's boss, come out of his office. He sits down in the stands as Honey comes back up to the plate.

"She digs in her feet like a filly before a race. She sets the bat up on her shoulder, swings a time or two, then nods at Rocks. I seen that look on her face before, on a beach.

"Rock throws a straight heater that Honey gets hold of and sends out over the right field fence, special delivery. I see Gil Turner stand up. The boys get quiet again as she takes him out four more times, then misses. There ain't no sound at all save for the crack of those balls heading for the sky. Even I was surprised at her power. They'd all seen her hit from time to time, but only in practice, when the ball is just lobbed. Never seen her hit for real. All those years were with her.

She'd been watching for a long time, listening, learning, and nobody ever thought anything of it.

"Honey leaves the plate since it's Horse's turn now. I see Gil Turner start to walk towards us. Horse doesn't go to the plate, he just stands there leaning on his bat, grinning.

"'What's so funny?' says Honey. 'Come on, it's your turn.'

"Horse puts his bat on his shoulder. 'So you can hit a little,' he says. 'So what? Tell me what good it'll do you.'

"Honey shifts her feet some as it starts to drizzle. 'Somebody'll notice me one of these days,' she says. 'Teams can always use a good hitter.'

"'Sure, sure they can. What do you think, fellahs? Those offers should be pouring in anytime now. All these years Daddy Diz let you play. All for nothing.'

"'Shut your filthy mouth about Diz,' she whispers.

"Horse can tell he's getting to her. 'What you gonna do when Daddy Diz ain't around? Nobody else'll let you anywhere near the field!'

"'I said shut up about Diz!'

"'You're nothing! You got no rights here! And Diz knows it, too!'

"'I'm telling you for the last time to leave him out of this! This is about me and you!'

"'Me and you? I like that idea just fine, girl. Been waiting for you to come around to the right way of thinking. We know why you like the feel of hard wood in your hands, don't we boys?'

"Nobody is laughing now except for the Horse. Honey starts walking towards him as the rain comes harder. I get between them and say 'Settle down now, Horse, you're bigger than she is,' but Honey tells me to shut up and the Horse gives me a hard shove.

"'Back off, ball boy. This is between me and the girl.' He faces her square on. 'Why do you think Diz stayed here all these years? Because of you! He could've gotten out. You think they'd let you anywhere near the field in the Bigs? Think they'd let you ride them fancy jets? Diz stayed here because of you and everyone knows it. That curse you got has rubbed off on him!'

"In the thundering rain Honey charges the Horse and jumps on him, beating him on the head and kicking him in the sides, while he laughs. I'm trying to pull her off him and then Gil Turner is there yelling at everybody to break it up. Horse throws Honey off and she lands on her side. Gil is already gone and everybody else starts to leave, but the Horse is still laughing. Honey's all covered with wet sand and her face is starting to swell up under one eye. Horse picks up his bat and walks away. I help Honey up but she shakes me off. She's breathing hard and says, 'Where's Diz at? Did he see it? Did he see me hit? Where'd Gil go?'

"I tell her that Diz is inside, I think, and Gil went back to his office. So she goes in to find Diz and I follow.

"As we get inside we can hear Gil yelling at Diz. Honey slows her stride as she listens and the two of us stand still as hunted deer outside Gil's office.

"'Here it is. I know she's your kid, but it's gone too far this time. It's bad enough that she's in the dugout and rides the busses. I'll tell you, Diz. The guys have been complaining for a while now, ever since I've been working here, and I don't blame them. It was one thing when she was younger. But she's grown now. And she's pretty, too. It distracts the players.

"'Now I admit, I'm impressed. If things were different—but things aren't different. You've got to get control of this thing.'

"Honey is real still, her lips pressed together tight. She don't even blink.

"'Look, Diz, you've been with us a long time,' says Gil. 'You've been a good manager. A great manager. You've stuck with us when you could have moved on. But we're having another bad year here. Worst in a while. Expansion is starting to take its toll. I'd hate to see folks start to lose their jobs. And you know that someone will have to pay for it. The big club is breathing down my neck. They want us to produce. The last thing I need for them to hear is that a sixteen year old girl can out hit my biggest slugger.'

"I look at Honey and she's smiling. 'I can play, he knows I can play.'

"'You know the rules of the game, Diz. Made your own bed on this one. You let her play all those years and now she thinks something will come of it. Thinks some team is going to pick her up, for Chrissake! I guess you can let her think what you want to and it's none of my business. But it is my business when it affects this team.'

"Diz nods, holding onto the back of his neck. He doesn't say anything to Gil, which surprises me. I wait for Honey to go in and rip Gil's head off. But she barely moves, a leaf froze in ice.

"'Maybe I should have had this talk with you a while ago. I see that now,' Gil says. 'But I thought it would take care of itself as she got older, I thought she wouldn't be around so much. But it's got to stop now. Game's been tampered with enough as it is, you know that. You know what I mean.'

"Diz still ain't talking and I'm thinking, 'Come on Diz, make your move. She's watching you.' I look at Honey again and I see her eye twitch a little. She looks at me and smiles, a strange kind of smile, then turns and walks away.

"It was quiet in the office for a minute or two, and as I was looking sideways at Diz I notice for the first time that he looks older, and it surprises me.

"Then Diz speaks, softly. 'What am I supposed to tell her? That she ain't good enough? She knows that ain't true. What was I supposed to tell her all those years?'

"Gil is getting riled now, seems like. 'I don't care what you tell her. It stops now. That's all I care about. Not on this team. Take care of it.'

"I wait for Diz to come out, and when he does, I act like I don't know nothing about it, and he don't say nothing. 'Cause like I told you before, if Diz wants you to know something, he tells you. Better write that down.

"The rain has stopped, and we go off to batting practice as usual. But Honey, she don't come back. First practice she ever missed, except when she had the chicken pox."

XVII.

Pearl Harpham's House
August, 1963

She'd always made a habit of trying not to wonder about things, especially things she couldn't do anything about. But this particular day, the very day that Honey challenged Horse on the field, as Pearl stood drying her blue and white china, wondering crept into her mind.

Pearl had gotten the china out for the Bryson City Ladies Bridge Club, a group she despised, but they did give her fine compliments about her china. They also questioned her, with raised eyebrows, about Honey.

"Has she started seeing any young men, Pearl?" "I don't recall seeing her at church last week. Is she ill?" Now Pearl knew that *they* knew that Honey had hardly been to church in her life, just at Christmas and Easter. Pearl herself went only sporadically. But if you want to show off your china, thought Pearl, you have to put up with some stupid questions.

It was Diz and Honey that Pearl was wondering about at first. She remembered what Diz had said to her, that Honey was so like her that anyone would have thought Pearl was her mother, and Pearl tried to believe it. But she could see it wasn't so. She herself had borne five children, some of whom resembled her strongly in features, but all of whom were so different from herself that Pearl wondered how they'd grown inside her. Honey was a child who'd been left in a basket in a dugout, left for Diz to raise whether she was his or not, a child who looked nothing like him and came from who knows where, and yet, was so like him.

It was the game that held them together, Pearl thought, the game that she didn't get at all. No, maybe not the game itself; like Diz said, the game don't make people alike. It was something else, something that Diz and Honey understood, like nothing and two going together. Pearl saw how it was between them, and their familiarity puzzled her. Honey wasn't his own child. But it was as though they recognized each other from the very beginning. She'd seen it that first night when Diz brought Honey home, saw how he held her like he knew who she was, something found that was the safest and best part of himself. Something else hung between them too, though, something Pearl couldn't quite grasp; an odd kind of sadness, or maybe an old secret.

It was at times such as these that Pearl would remember her own secret, the secret of Lurlene. She'd never told anyone. It comforted and warmed her, made her feel a part of something whole; she pressed it close and it became a kind of companion, a consolation in times of confusion. *I know this, only me.*

Pearl didn't really see her own children all that much, but she tried not to wonder why that was. And when she did wonder, she'd just get busy doing something else, something she could touch, like making sure her china was arranged just so or seeing that the fringe around Aunt Ella's sofa was not tangled or dusty, and soon her wondering would pass.

When Georgina died, Pearl wondered more than she ever had. She wondered if Georgina had been in love with the boy who died with her, if she'd had a favorite time of year or a favorite dress and she wondered mostly why it was that she'd noticed so little about her daughter all those years, except that she was so different from herself.

Before the funeral, Pearl wondered about all those things. Then she took out her sewing basket and in two nights made a silk dress, blue, with a white lace collar that she crocheted herself, and buried her daughter in it. Then she put the sewing basket and her wondering aside.

There was just so much Honey could expect, thought Pearl as she dipped a china bowl in the warm suds. Who does she think she is, anyway? It ain't like she's the first child to not get her way on everything. After all, it ain't the end of the world. She can still like the game without playing it. She can go to games and watch, some girls do that, Pearl supposed. Pearl had made a good life for herself and done without a lot of things. Some things you got to learn to live without, and once you get used to it, it ain't that hard, ain't that bad, really, it just becomes your life and you can do just fine, doing without. No, she ain't my own child, she thought, but if she'd let me I could show her this one thing, just this one thing. Honey had a chance to escape Georgina's fate. Maybe if we spend more time together, thought Pearl, maybe then—

"That you, Honey? Where you been?" Pearl walked to the back pantry entrance and saw Honey, dripping wet, covered with sand. "You look like you been dragged through the mud! And your eye! It's all swolled up. What happened?"

Honey just stared at her.

"I'm talking to you, girl."

Honey wiped her nose. "Nothing. Nothing happened to me."

"Don't look like nothing, You been fighting again. Are you bothering some boy? Sixteen and still fighting." She clicked her tongue loudly. "You get those filthy cleats off. Don't drag your mess through this house. I've just now cleaned. This is what comes of your wish to play that game. Tangled hair and swolled up eyes. Some young lady you are!"

Honey bent down and began untying her cleats. Pearl sighed. "Practice still going on? Where's your daddy?"

Honey didn't look up and spoke quietly. "I don't know where my daddy is."

"All right. Just get cleaned up. If I had a nickel for every time I've swept sand out of that pantry—" Pearl stood for a moment, wiping her palms on her apron. Then she bit her lip a bit and turned to Honey.

"Say, how about this? Since Diz is working late, how about you and me go on down to that new movie house out on the highway? I hear they got five different kinds of popcorn and three shows to choose from. I haven't been to the pictures in ages."

Honey stopped untying her cleats and stood. Her mouth hung open slightly as she stared at Pearl.

"Honey, you hear? I said how about a movie?" As Honey stood staring at her quizzically, Pearl felt a sudden rush of embarrassment. "I--I know we ain't spent much time together lately, so I thought--"

"Not tonight."

"Why not?" Pearl walked over to the counter and continued washing her china. "Carlene Swanson told me that she took bus number five out there easy as pie. Good place to meet some nice children your own age." The sponge squeaked against the wet bowl, the only sound in the room. "I just thought—"

"You never asked me before. Why now?"

Pearl wiped her hands on the dish towel but didn't look up. She felt her face get hot. "I remember going to the picture with my daughters on a Saturday afternoon. We'd get dressed up and—"

"I'm not your daughter, Pearl."

Pearl felt that odd uneasiness again, as though she were disappearing in her own kitchen. *Babies are nice. She'll get used to me.* "I just meant that if we could spend more time together—"

"No."

Pearl continued to wash as she felt something pushing up from inside, and then she heard Honey walking through the kitchen with her shoes still on.

"Get those cleats off my floor!" Robert E Junior flinched and left the room.

Honey spoke sternly, her voice focused. "Stop it. You can't tell me what to do! You ain't my mother!"

"Thank goodness for that!" said Pearl, but what she wanted to say was *I could have been if you'd ever let me near,* that's what ached in her, and she wanted to run, to escape this conversation, but instead she picked up a wet plate and began drying it hard, turning away from Honey. She spoke almost to herself.

"I've told myself all these years that you ain't my own child. No one can blame me. I've turned my back on the whispers and given a child no one knew a home. Never asked for nothing of my own. Never asked to be thanked for it. I've kept the secret and—" She cut herself off, hoping Honey wasn't listening.

"What are you mumbling about? What secret?"

Pearl began to feel invisible, felt herself shrinking; and as Honey stood waiting Pearl put the dish down and turned to her, calmly as she could.

"Nothing. Just get them filthy things off your feet. Do it now."

"No. Tell me what you're talking about. Is it about Diz? Something about Diz?"

"Always Diz! He's always the one you think of, ain't he!"

"Is he all right?" Honey took off her wet cap. "What secret? Is it about me?"

Pearl slid her hands hard into her apron pocket. "I've been good to you, haven't I? Taken a child nobody wanted and nobody knew and tried to make you a nice home—"

"It was Diz who done that! You never wanted me. Don't you think I know that? It's in every look, every word you say to me! I know you hate the game—"

"It ain't ever been about that."

"Then what? Why do you hate me? I never asked you for *nothing*! Not a thing. I got everything I needed from Diz. He's the one who wanted me. He's the one who loved me."

That's right, you never asked me for a thing.

Pearl's voice was low and flat and she pointed a long finger at Honey. "Diz never wanted you. I had to talk him into keeping you. Why would anyone leave a baby with him? Your own mama left town because she hated you! It was *me* that you were meant for! Me! That's the secret!"

Pearl knew it was a lie and didn't care but when she saw the look in Honey's eyes she wanted to snatch the words back into her mouth, push them back down where they came from, put it all back together, but it was too late. She saw herself in Honey's face, she could see that Honey's hatred of her was complete now, and Pearl lowered her eyes and tried to speak and was barely aware of Honey moving past her. She did not see when Honey picked up a china bowl, freshly dried and still warm. Honey didn't throw it hard, she just sort of let it go. Smashed blue china scattered like stones on a pavement. Honey kept her eyes on the floor and then walked out the back door. It was just that quick.

The sound of the china hitting the floor seemed to awaken Pearl slowly; for a few moments she stood slumped and still as she surveyed the blue and white chipped sea. It was the lie that did it, she thought. Years of care was in ruins before her and she knelt by it and knew that no rule can save you. The china was crippled and her daughter was dead. In the shattered glass around her she saw it at last. She could see that the curse troubled everyone, not just those who live outside the lines but everyone, and kneeling quietly Pearl felt the sticky glass ghost of a babyfood jar brush against her cheek and heard the sound of a smashing car and saw the china, the game, her daughter, her self, saw that all of them were in pieces, none of them whole, and she suddenly felt that it had always been so.

And then, a kind of pained contentment came over her. Something like a smile unfolded inside. All those years she had imagined only her grief should the china ever be damaged, she'd never imagined the relief. And in the same instant Pearl saw what the game was to Honey, saw the broken-ness of it, even felt the game stir inside. *Her own child.*

She knelt a while, trembling, waiting for the feelings to pass; and then, rising, she swept the dead bluebirds into her copper dust pan and tenderly laid them to rest.

XVIII.

Virgil hadn't slept well at the Cool Waters Motel, conveniently located on Route 19 in Cherokee. It wasn't a bad place, really, a little close to the road, but clean. Virgil was tired and fretful as he sat and ate his over-easy eggs and sausage in the Cool Waters Diner.

Virgil's life had been one long parade of them. There was no family, no wife sitting in a bright yellow kitchen waiting for his call, no son to play catch with, or daughter either. There was just him and his over-easy eggs, just him and whatever was in front of him. During the off-season he had this little one room apartment up in Richmond, but he was only there a few months out of the year. He didn't really know anyone in the building. There was one woman, a brunette who lived on the same floor as him, and they'd nod to each other once in a while when they were picking up their mail or taking out their garbage, but Virgil had never even asked her name. What would be the point? He'd just be off in a few weeks and not come back for seven months and she'd forget him, she'd tire of waiting.

When Virgil first heard of the girl pitcher, the one in Watertown who may have been Honey's daughter, he shook his head. Another great assignment. A publicity stunt, no doubt, a politically correct move on the part of baseball. But now, in a way he never expected, he looked forward to seeing her as she walked onto the field, to watch the faces in the crowd when she threw her first pitch, to witness her first out. This surprised him, and he thought about Billy Ray's voice and could hear him asking *Why should I tell you this story?* and Virgil felt he almost had an answer.

There was no hard evidence for any of it. No journals or letters or photos. In fact, there was no record that such a person ever existed at all, but he found himself not caring about that any more. It was the connection that bothered him. He wasn't used to it and he didn't like it. It made him nervous, suspicious. He was used to forgetting and moving on. He traveled light and though he recognized his emptiness he felt at peace with it, or thought so. In a strange way it had become his companion. But now, as he drove back up the mountain for his last interview, there was this restless curiosity that wouldn't let him alone.

Billy Ray was already half way through his mid-day cigar. "I trust you slept well, sir, at the Cool Waters."

"Not very."

Billy Ray straightened his tie and smoothed his white cotton pants. "So what do you want to ask me today?"

"Tell me what happened. Tell me the rest of the story."

"Why?"

"I want to know what's real."

"I can't tell you anything about that," said Billy Ray.

"Then what has all this been about?"

"You asked for the truth."

"Is that what you've given me?"

Billy Ray said nothing. He just puffed and rocked.

"Give me a straight answer for once! How am I supposed to write an article without any evidence, without the facts?"

"Is that what you came here for?"

"Is it real? Is it the truth?"

"Those are two different things, sir."

Virgil sighed with frustration. "What are you talking about? That doesn't make any sense."

"The truth might not be real. What's real may not be true."

Virgil sat pressing his palm flat against his cheek.

"You see that white rowboat?" said Billy Ray. "Down at the bottom of the hill there, near the shore?"

Virgil nodded.

"When I close one eye, that boat seems like it's next to the oak tree. But when I open that eye and shut the other one, the boat disappears behind the oak. That's how it is from where I sit, anyway."

"So?"

"Which is it? Is the boat next to the tree, or is it behind it?"

"That's just a trick. An optical—"

"They're two different things, sir."

Virgil sat for a minute, staring out at the lake. Then he shut his notebook and put it away in his briefcase.

"I want it to be real," he said.

"Then I'll tell you the end."

Billy Ray folded his hands across his chest and shifted the cigar back and forth like a metronome.

"After the thing with Horse, Honey hardly played on the field at all. Just by herself once in a while, before the rest of the team came on the field. Then she'd sit on the bench, off in a corner, legs twitching, squeezing her mitt like sand between her fingers, her cap pulled tight around her eyes.

"It's late afternoon and I'm locking up after a day game. Diz'd already gone home. I'm the last one there and I walk out of the office and it's that time of day, sir, maybe you've noticed it, that time of day when day meets evening just for an instant, a slow blink; they sort of stand and salute each other and then, when it's over, day just lets go, just like that, because it knows that ain't the end of it.

"There's Honey on the field alone, standing at the plate with just her bat, swinging in the air. She looks like she's a ghost, floating over the diamond. She doesn't see me, I stay back.

"She's pretending to hit. She swings at a phantom pitch and watches it sail to the outfield, and she even jogs around the bases a couple of times. Seems like she can feel the line drive in her arms and the field looks like the sandy bottom of a rippled lake, like somebody just ran their finger over it this way and that. I never seen Honey like that before. But in that instant I seen how it was.

"After a bit I walk out of the shadows and she sees me and I ask her, 'Want me to throw a couple to you, for real?' She starts to nod, but then she says no, says she's done her hitting for the day. Says she'll see me tomorrow and I say the same.

"Next day is the last game of a long homestand and her itch gets itchy. She asks me to pitch a few to her before the guys come out on the field, so I do it. I know Gil don't like it, but I do it anyway. She's hitting them all over the field, just tearing it up. The balls she hits are just sitting in the outfield like unhatched eggs.

"The opposing manager that day was Captain Pete Peterson. He was in the army and everybody just calls him the Captain. Old friend of Diz's. I see him out of the corner of my eye going into his dugout, and I tell Honey it's time to quit, but she wants a couple more pitches, so I do it.

"The other team is filtering into their dugout now, and so are some of our guys, but she keeps asking me to throw to her. I see the Captain over there with his fists stuck to his sides. Then he says, 'Billy Ray Poole. Get her outa there right now. She ain't supposed to be around at all from what I hear.'

"Diz comes on to the field now, holding up his hand, 'She ain't bothering nobody. Just take it easy, Cap, don't get all worked up.' I'm surprised he says anything.

"Most of the guys from both teams are in the dugouts now, and they start paying attention to what's going on. 'She's bothering me and my boys and I'll get worked up if I want to.' The Captain's head is waving back and forth like a flag. 'Everybody in the whole league thinks you're nuts. And I always defended you. Wake up, Diz! Get her off the field. Let's play a clean game.'

"'She's got a right to be here, just like anybody else.'

"'Oh no she don't! Now get her off the field. I'm only going to ask you one more time, as your friend. Then I'm going to get mad.'

"Diz walks slowly over to the Captain, who starts coming out of his dugout. The guys are waiting to be released. Waiting to defend their leaders. Now I believe that the boys on our team are mighty fed up with having Honey around, but they'd fight for Diz quick as anything. Some of them start yelling at the Captain's guys. 'Nobody does Diz that way! Bring it here!'

"'Come on, Diz,' says the Captain. 'You look like a damn fool. You look like a stupid army mare! And for what? She's just showing off! I hear she already made a fool out of the Horse there.' Horse yells, 'Shut up, meat!'

"'You got to take control of this, Diz. I never thought that some-one like you would tarnish the game. You don't belong here no more! It's like you're spitting on the game! Now get her off or we'll make you make her.'

"Diz just stands there, shaking his head, standing his ground. Captain says, 'What's the matter with you? What's happened to you?' He says it like he really wants to know. He's face to face with Diz now and pushes him backwards.

"Both dugouts empty and start to head for each other, howling, rolling up their sleeves, spitting. Diz is in the middle of the whole thing and just when it looks like it's about to explode Honey hits a line shot right though the middle of the mob and then holds her bat high over her head and everyone stops. Then she walks over to Diz and without saying a word, hands him her bat. He tries to give it back to her but she won't take it. She just stands there and they look at each other for what seems like a long while. Then Honey, she walks off the field kind of slow, savoring the sand under her spikes, and disappears into the tunnel.

"I don't see her for the rest of the game, till the eighth inning or so. Then I spy her up in the stands, where I ain't never seen her before. She looks kind of strange sitting up there. And she sits there for the rest of the game."

Billy Ray stopped rocking.

"After that, I believe, Honey never played no more. Didn't see her much. Missed her, I did." He began rocking again and then he spoke quietly, more to himself than to Virgil.

"Now Mama always said that the baseball gods were fair, but unpredictable. But that day, I didn't hardly believe in them anymore."

...and the sun is beginning to dip a little, as though it is melting into the lake, scattering bits of itself across the flat water, and Virgil is heavy and sleepy and then he feels the glare on his eyes, like a flashlight in a mirror at night, but he doesn't look away and he doesn't reach for his sunglasses either, for he thinks he sees, he does see, almost over the water, or maybe it is just some gulls, he thinks it's Honey, grown, with a child. He sees all the years from then to then laid in a row and it seems long and he feels them pass as one turns the pages and then he thinks he sees Honey leaning over, tall and dark and handing something to a little girl. It's a mitt.

He wonders where is Diz but sees that Diz isn't there and now he can hear Honey talking and he leans in a little and hears her tell the child that it was her daddy's mitt when he was little, and Virgil can see that the leather is spongy and soft and that the stitching is loose here and there and it smells of June and fresh grass and he wonders if Billy Ray can see them too, or is Billy telling it to him but his voice is gone and now Honey is showing the girl how to slip her hand inside where it is cool and dark and carefully she shows her where to place each finger and tells her how it should feel when it's on just right. Now she is showing her how to spit on it when it gets too dried out and where to rub the oil on it just so, not too much, she says, just enough to keep it supple and strong, so the ball will just get sucked right in, like sipping chocolate milk through a straw. And now that she's shown all that, now that she's told her all she can, Honey takes the mitt away and shows her daughter where to hang it up, near the back door on a worn brass hook next to her own, where it will always be when she wants it, where it will always be waiting.

Isn't That Just Like You?
by Eric Anderson

Isn't That Just Like You?

"They looked like children," she told me. And that thought frightened her, because she always felt that only children are capable of everything."

—Gabriel Garcia Marquez
Chronicle of a Death Foretold

I.

Rona's grandmother Merrilee had a black tooth, right in front, and she liked to tell long stories about where it came from, and what it meant, and how Rona was the only one who could see it, and that was because Rona was magic, or at least someday she would be. Even when she was sick, even right before she died, Merrilee still believed this, and if Rona's parents wouldn't have been happy about those stories, it didn't matter. Rona didn't want to be like them. What she wanted, more than anything, was to be like Merrilee.

Merrilee had been born in West Virginia, the youngest child in a long line of mountain witches, women who spent their whole lives in the hills, curing people of whatever. Standing in her kitchen at the stove, Merrilee would tell Rona about the doctoring she had done, and the cures she had learned, and the magic she had seen. She was always stirring something, the pots on the burners bubbling like gossips. "I could do little things, like make sure no one saw my tooth. No one wants a girl with a black tooth. But you saw it, Rona. I couldn't stop you."

Rona was twelve and she collected first names; she hated the idea that she had to call anyone Mister or Mrs. just because her parents insisted on it. She wrote real names down in her diary like they were codes she cracked. She knew the truth about her teachers and the mailman and all her mother's friends, even her father's drinking buddies, most of whom wanted to be called by their first names anyway. In Rona's head, her parents were Agnes and David, Agnes and David, Agnes and David. The hardest name to get had been her grandfather's, and even then it turned out disappointing; Garland, like the decoration. It made Rona think of Christmas trees before the ornaments went up. Everyone, even Merrilee, called him by his last name, Tate.

To Rona, it seemed like the truth was always disappointing.

All she remembered of her grandfather was walking into the hospital room right before he died. Her parents brought her all the way from California, though she only knew that now, in retrospect. She was four at the time, but that was the kind of thing her parents did, take a baby to the hospital. David especially never put any thought into consequences, like how for the rest of her life she would have these strange memories of long, plastic sheets hanging over a bed, a light glowing inside, the whole thing like some terrible bird's egg about to hatch. Rona hadn't been able to see her grandfather behind the plastic, only the dark mound of his chest, quivering and collapsing, this terrible breathing sound, like someone trying to suck the whole world through a straw.

At Merrilee's funeral, Rona knelt beside the coffin, pretending to pray. She was curious about that tooth, and she thought that maybe the undertaker had pulled it out. Undertakers did things like that, prying off gold fillings and wedding bands, unlatching retirement watches. That's what Rona would have done, if she were an undertaker. Think what they were called; the under takers. The ones who take you under.

In the casket, Merrilee might have been taking a nap in a fancy bed, lips tight together, as if troubling over some dream. She was a big woman and her body pressed against the velvet sides like bread rising in a pan. Rona tried to peek into the closed half of the casket; in the darkness down there she knew that parts of her legs were missing because Merrilee had diabetes and wouldn't take care of herself. Rona couldn't see past the shadows and frill, though, she looked back to Merrilee's face; with her lips pursed like that, she seemed to be trying to keep some secret, trying not to tell Rona something.

Rona leaned a little closer, hoping to glimpse the black tooth past the thin line where the lips touched. Over her shoulder, people stood in little half-circles, all of them facing away from the casket, having quiet conversations. This was her first ever funeral; Agnes and David had the good sense not to take her to Tate's, at least. Still, Rona felt like she had been to a thousand funerals because in the books she read, people were always dying or in love with someone who died. Rona knew, just knew, that no one would turn around in the next five seconds. Even if anyone saw her, it would only look like she was reaching towards Merrilee's face. Her hand hovered over her grandmother's mouth for a moment; she had to will it downwards. Her fingers jumped back as if Merrilee's lips had kissed them.

Taking a breath, Rona tried again. The lips, too stiff, only as warm as the air-conditioned room, wouldn't separate. She pressed harder, nervously waiting for the kissing sensation, and leaned in. There was an almost clear crust of glue just barely visible between Merrilee's lips.

Rona turned back towards all the mourners. I knew it, she wanted to seethe. Why else would they glue her lips together if they hadn't stolen the tooth? An undertaker would know about talismans. Rona looked around at her grandmother's friends and the relatives up from West Virginia, Agnes and David and her bald-headed little brother Wyatt. The anger went out of her in a sigh that made her chest feel small and empty;

she couldn't tell them about the tooth. They'd give her that strange girl look and go back to pretending no one in the room was dead.

But later, after everyone had said, "Poor dear," and, "Sorry about your loss," and, "She's in a better place," Rona fixed the undertaker with her most evil glare, and when he saw the way Rona was looking at him, he flinched. His hand went up to his chest, as if he'd hung the tooth on a necklace and wore it even now, under his white, white shirt.

After the funeral, all the relatives came to Merrilee's old farmhouse. The house was a pale blue color and the old women rolled out of it like waves, crested with trays of food. Rona sat with her parents and Wyatt at a picnic table on the back porch and watched everyone moving about the yard, withdrawing their names from her memory one by one. Some of them she had only seen in the framed pictures that sat on every flat surface in Merrilee's house, or hung on the walls like keyholes through which distant people could peek into what Merrilee called her Up North life. The relatives stood close to each other and told quiet jokes, laughing in a hushed way, so that no sounds came out even though their whole bodies shook.

Wyatt sat at the table and glared out into the yard. Three years ago, he had leukemia. He was eleven now and the doctors said the cancer was gone, probably forever, but there was something different about him. He mostly sat and stared like he was watching some boring TV show where he already knew what would happen next.

"You know what I heard the doctors tell Mom and Dad?" he said to Rona, right after he first came home. He would go to the hospital and Rona wouldn't see him for weeks, which was hard because they used to get along and he was the only person she liked to play with. She remembered he offered to let her feel his head, but she had been afraid to touch him, almost like he was contagious. He asked again and again, almost excited, running his own hands over his scalp. Two years later, there was no sign of the hair growing back. Wyatt said, "The doctors told them I was going to die. They said it right in front of me, like I was too dumb to understand them or something."

"Everyone's going to die."

"Not tomorrow, they're not."

That was the way Wyatt's mind worked, and Rona watched his dark eyes flick back and forth around the yard, two flies on everything clean. One of Merrilee's sisters, Evanelle, as un-magic a woman as Rona had ever seen, brought a tray with four pieces of cherry pie and set them down, one by one.

"No sign of Head," she said, her voice going up at the end, like a question, or maybe an accusation. Head was David's half-brother, whom Rona had never met. David just shrugged and picked up a fork. Evanelle looked younger than Merrilee even though she was a decade older. No matter what the doctors said, Merrilee wouldn't listen.

"Well, it's my life," she said all the time, especially to Agnes, who would bite down on her cheeks to keep from saying what she wanted to say, her face pinched between invisible fingers. Agnes worked in a nursing home and Merrilee didn't like nurses either. She was the kind of grandmother, Rona thought, the words like a little eulogy, who would cut a piece of cake then leave the piece and eat the rest.

Everyone picked at Evanelle's pie in silence, except for Wyatt, who used a fork to smash his slice into pulp. Once the last of the relatives left, Rona's father went through the house, shutting off all the lights. The kitchen smelled like cake before the frosting. On the back porch with the whole house dark, David locked the door. Ordinarily, Rona wouldn't have said anything, but Agnes and Wyatt were already in the car and she was alone with David, and in a moment of weakness she told him about the glue on Merrilee's lips. Of course, he knew why.

"It's to help the mouth stay closed," he said, and told her how he had a job in a mortuary when he was going to med school, before he decided he was better suited to the teaching life. Not that he was actually teaching now, or had ever taught anywhere that Rona knew of. He'd always had a lot of jobs, even in California before Tate died and they moved back to Ohio.

David told her the people in the funeral home had made fun of him, saying anyone could operate on a body that's already dead. "They had a list on the wall, all about the strange things dead bodies do. The first one was Breathing Sounds."

Rona's house was less than a mile from Merrilee's farmhouse, which sat on three acres of land, surrounded by smaller houses like the one Rona and her family lived in. At one time, Rona's grandfather owned all the land in the subdivision, but he sold it all off, bit by bit. He was always making bad deals, and Merrilee said he only pretended to be a farmer so no one would ask why he wasn't at work. When the fields got too ragged, he tried dairy farming, but he let the cows dry up and he took such bad care of the poor animals no one would even buy them for slaughter. They all died of old age on the farm, sway-backed and gap-toothed.

Rona knew all this because she was the kind of child who liked to sit and listen to grown-ups talk. They always shooed her away at first, but she was quiet enough that no one noticed when she came back. Relatives would come up from West Virginia to talk to Merrilee, and sometimes they brought her things from the mountains; ugly roots that looked like fists with extra knuckles, or burlap bags of splotchy mushrooms, or jumbles of bright berries and stalks that reminded Rona of discarded game pieces. Sometimes Merrilee would cook for them, adding the powdery ingredients she stored down in the cool basement. Merrilee never used recipes; she kept everything in her head.

"Rona, put a pinch of this in," she'd say. "Just a baby pinch; your fingers are the perfect size." The relatives would sit in the kitchen while Merrilee started to cook the regular food, using her visitors as an excuse to make all the things she wasn't supposed to eat. She thought the whole world should be covered in gravy. Rona would pretend to be busy helping, not saying anything, letting everyone forget she was there.

They would all eat and afterwards David would make a bonfire behind the house, out by what was left of the old orchard. Everyone sat around drinking, even Merrilee, who always made sure that her guests went home with a Mason jar full of whatever they came for. The more the adults drank, the more Rona learned, especially when Merrilee and David sat together on the porch. Then Rona would hear how her grandfather was the kind of fool who never spent one penny when he could act like a big deal by spending two. If Agnes was there, she might tell David how he never should have let Merrilee buy the house in the subdivision for them, and how if he'd tried to teach when they were in California he could have gotten tenure and they would've had health insurance when Wyatt got sick. And on those rare nights when Agnes and Merrilee drank together, Merrilee would swear she didn't want the money back, not for that, not for a sick child.

David, drunk with his friends, once stood up on a chair and swore he wouldn't give the doctors a penny, not a penny, even though they saved his son's life. It wasn't honorable, having the power to save a child and then charging the parents to do it. "Shut up," Agnes told him, her voice so quiet it just sounded like more flames in the fire. That's what David did, then, and so did everyone else. Finally, when one of her father's friends eased back into talking about baseball and how the season went wrong, David just sat and listened. It was a summer night and warm, but the mosquitoes weren't bad yet. He stayed out all night, sleeping in a lawn chair, and Rona stayed with him. In the morning Merrilee's rooster, a mean old bird which she only kept because it was too stubborn to die, began to scratch around the weathered coop. When David woke, Rona was watching him. He rubbed his eyes and said, "What are you doing out here? Go to bed."

Rona thought about the Breathing Sounds as they drove down the gravel drive that twisted along the back of Merrilee's farm, towards their house in the subdivision. When David saw that Wyatt had left his bedroom light on again, he said, "You know, it's no big deal for me to calculate how much it costs to run that lamp of yours all night and subtract it out of your lawn-mowing money."

This was her father; two minutes ago he'd been joking about his mortuary job, and now he was angry. His eyes welled up as he spoke. Wyatt got out of the car without saying anything, and Rona followed him. Her mother and father stayed behind, their heads close together in the front seat.

Money was the only threat that mattered to Wyatt, but nothing could stop him from keeping the light on all the time. At the dinner table after he came home from the hospital, he'd told them how dark his hospital room was at night.

Agnes said, "Really? It has to bright enough for the nurses to work."

Wyatt looked hurt, and David tried to smooth things over by saying something about hospitals being like hotels, only the concierge keeps showing up to poke you with a needle. He always said the weirdest things without even wondering what anyone else would think, and Wyatt didn't think anything was funny, which might explain why they weren't getting along. Rona and Agnes had their own problems, too, now that Rona was twelve. Rona thought it was because of the way her breasts had just shown up, all at once, at the end of fifth grade. She couldn't figure out the new way Agnes looked at her; sometimes it looked like a kind of pity, which made Rona either uncomfortable or angry, or it was a kind of blame, like Rona had somehow grown them on purpose.

Rona loved and mostly hated her breasts. She liked to catch the boys in her class looking at her, but she couldn't stand how it made her feel. She would sit with her shoulders curved forward, like they were wings she could use to cover herself. At the same time she would imagine what would happen if she arched her back, just the tiniest bit. Boys would fling themselves from the monkey bars, forget to raise their hands to catch the kickball before it smashed their faces.

Wouldn't that be a kind of magic?

Without a word, Wyatt and Rona went to their rooms. In Rona's room, there were a few posters of some cartoon animals she no longer cared about, mostly there to cover the cracks in the walls, and some bookshelves filled with mostly picture books that she knew by heart even though she hadn't looked at them in years. There were a few young adult books Agnes had given her to read, things like *Go Ask Alice* and *Are You There God? It's Me, Margaret.* But behind those books Rona had hidden some other books, books that Agnes would think she wasn't old enough to read.

Rona sat on her bed and looked around. It looked like a little girl's room. She thought about the funeral and figured she ought to be more upset. She thought about Merrilee and how many days they had spent together while Wyatt was sick. For weeks at a time they lived together, and sometimes she slept right in Merrilee's bed and all night her grandmother would talk about the mountains and magic and how lonely she was for that world when she came to Ohio.

"I was just a girl, then," she said, and her voice was so clear in Rona's head, Merrilee could've been sitting right next to her. I should be crying, Rona thought. So she stayed still and thought about her grandmother's tooth until finally she did.

Rona wasn't sure, but she thought that Agnes had left David and that if Merrilee hadn't died just then, Agnes might not have come back.

Agnes always left lists of chores for Wyatt and Rona. Wyatt's side of the list usually concerned the yard work, things like mowing the grass or weeding the little garden behind the garage, or even painting the back fence, which Agnes had inadvertently put on the list twice that summer. Wyatt said it was proof that she didn't care if he really did anything, that he only got jobs to do because Rona was getting them, too, and their parents were hung up on fairness.

"Maybe it's because you did a lousy job the first time," Rona said.

"She's losing it," Wyatt said. "She's got mow the yard on there again.

I just mowed the yard yesterday. We might as well have Dad giving us stuff to do."

Rona's side of the list was all about housework, dusting and sweeping and washing dishes. Sometimes, like some immigrant, she would have to walk down to the little strip of stores on the corner and buy milk or bread and then carry them all the way home. The only good thing was that Rona would keep the change from the grocery money and go to Burton's Book Shop, next to the convenience store. The old man who worked there, Burton himself, didn't care what kind of books Rona bought.

"Where's my change?" Agnes would ask, when Rona got home, and she would say "I gave it to Dad," or, "Downstairs with the laundry."

The lists were always long and painfully specific; dust under the beds, it would say. Take down your grandmother's china, wash, carefully towel dry. Two loaves of white bread from the back of the shelf.

Rona suspected that Wyatt was right, that Agnes was only trying to keep them both busy. The house's usual state was one of wild disarray, unless they were expecting company, or unless Agnes couldn't sleep; then she would wake Rona up in the middle of the night. "Come on, I need your help waxing the kitchen floor," she would say. Or, "Let's clean the silverware." Rona would sit at the dining room table, half-asleep, the strong smell of the polish occasionally pinching her awake.

Then, impossibly, Rona and Wyatt finished their lists, and two days went by with no replacement chores. David was busy doing a jigsaw puzzle. He didn't do puzzles like ordinary people. Everything seemed normal enough at first; he would turn the pieces right side up, then study the picture on the front of the box for awhile. Then he would put the box somewhere he couldn't see it and stare at the pieces until, finally, he would pick up two and click them together. He would go on that way for hours, never touching a piece until he was sure where it went. His hands looked like a pair of slow, patient birds, tilting their heads to listen to the ground.

The only time he stopped was to answer the phone whenever someone called for news on Merrilee, who was in the hospital at the time. David's voice was soft as he talked into the phone, his head bobbing up and down as he answered questions about operations and procedures and the chances. "Things look better," he said. At supper time, he would go to Merrilee's room for the end of visiting hours. Wyatt and

Rona weren't allowed to come; Merrilee had already lost one leg up to the knee, and her other foot was in danger. Rona hadn't seen her in a month.

David would come home from the hospital with some fast food, and in the mornings Rona made everyone toaster waffles for breakfast. She made peanut butter sandwiches for lunch. David didn't shave or change his clothes for the first two days of the puzzle. As more of the picture came together, he began to work faster.

On the third day of the puzzle, Rona began to look for clues about Agnes. She asked Wyatt if he'd heard their parents arguing, not believing for an instant that she could have missed it. Her parents' arguments were both terrible and oddly entertaining; Rona saw them as a great opportunity to learn things that no one would normally tell her. Agnes was a yeller and screamer, and Rona wished that David would yell back, just so she could get his side of the story. They argued mostly about David being out of work.

"My mother's sick," he said. They were arguing on the back porch and Rona watched from around the corner of the house; Agnes tapped the check book like a baton in her palm. David held a beer in his lap, little beads of perspiration dripping down the sides, onto his leg. He said, "She might need me."

"For what, exactly?" Agnes said. "A beer run?"

As discreetly as she could, Rona checked the calendar on the refrigerator where her mother wrote her work schedule at the nursing home. Briefly, she considered calling to ask if she was there, but she finally decided against it. It seemed too easy; if Agnes had really left them, Rona didn't want her to know she was missed. But by the evening of the third day, Rona stopped in the dining room to talk to her father, still at work on the puzzle; a country scene, autumn trees around the edges, red outbuildings, a white house, some indistinct animals, either cows or horses. There was a well beside the house. David was working from the outside in. He picked up a piece. He set it down perfectly.

"We're out of toaster waffles," Rona said. David looked up and stared at Rona as if he didn't recognize her. He nodded once, then went back to the puzzle.

"And peanut butter," she said. David didn't look up again.

In the morning when she came downstairs, the puzzle was done and David was cooking breakfast. Already at the table, Wyatt stared at his plate of black bacon and pancakes that were runny in the middle. The eggs were almost scrambled, almost fried. Lunch was even worse; undercooked bacon and burnt pancakes. When it was time for supper, her father said, "Come on, let's go out."

The three of them climbed into the cab of David's pick-up. Rona had never seen her father so frenzied; it was like he had nowhere to put all of the energy he had devoted to the puzzle. Driving too fast, he ran his fingers savagely through his hair, which was short-cropped but somehow still managed to look as though he had fallen asleep in the middle of a headstand. He tugged on the scruff of his beard, as if trying to make it longer. David drove away from town, out into the country along a twisting, two lane road, tailgating the cars that came up in front of them, finally swerving around, waving off the angry honks and dirty looks. At a dip in the road where a set of railroad tracks cut across at an angle, David hit the rails going so fast that the truck bounced into the air, and everything in the cab jumbled all over the place, including Rona and Wyatt.

"McDonald's?" David asked, to no one in particular. Wyatt and Rona quietly slid their seat belts on. "McDonald's it is."

Along the way, they passed Frank's Roadside Bar. David drummed his fingers along the wheel and then he groaned like he did whenever Agnes forced him to make a decision. He slowed down enough to make a U-turn and went back.

As he parked in front of the bar, he said, "I have to meet somebody for a minute."

Rona and Wyatt both nodded. Rona asked, "Where's Mom?"

"Be right back."

While he was inside, Rona fidgeted with the handle that rolled for rolling up the window. She locked and unlocked the door. Wyatt kept looking over at her and huffing through his nose. It was getting dark. Finally, Wyatt said, "Do you think Mom's gone?"

It wasn't like him to sound worried, but he did. Rona said, "She'll be back. Probably some kind of emergency. Anyway, Dad's got it covered."

"Oh," Wyatt said. "Yeah. Everything's fine."

By midnight, they were both starving. Rona found half a package of sunflower seeds in the glove box, and she poured the contents out onto the seat between them. They took turns picking a seed, chewing it up, spitting the little shreds of shell on the floor of the cab. Their fingernails were blue and red from the neon lights in the bar window. Draft Beer, it said, and then, On Tap!

"Maybe we should go find him," Wyatt said. Rona listened to the muffled sounds of some too-loud music coming through the walls. She could see burly men and thin women as sharp as shadows going back and forth in front of the window. Wyatt asked again, a little louder, and Rona shook her head.

David came out at two. He was wobbly, stopping to lean his head against the hood of the truck. After a minute, the bartender came out and stared towards the cab. Rona put her hand on Wyatt's shoulder, guiding him lower into his seat.

"You okay, Dave?" the bartender called.

David just waved his hand in the air. He threw up beside the truck, and when it was over, he said, "Better now."

He slid into the cab and looked at Rona and Wyatt, huddled together on the floor. He said, "What are you doing down there? Let's grab something to eat."

The pickup made slow arcs across the centerline, almost like it wanted to be on the wrong side of the road. As they pulled up towards the dip in the road and the tracks, the crossing lights came on. David eased to a stop, but when the gates came down the truck was on the wrong side.

"Dad?" Rona said. She looked over and he was asleep, his head tilted back on the seat. Down the tracks, a single headlight came towards them. The whistle howled, splitting the darkness.

"Dad?" she said. The truck crept slowly forward, the engine idling just fast enough to ease them up the incline that led to the tracks, and then the cab flashed with light and the train was on them, rumbling and shaking. Wyatt put his hands on the dashboard and pushed himself backwards. Rona put her hands on David's shoulder, shaking him, but then she was afraid he might wake up and stomp on the gas. The train was right in front of the hood, rushing past, the blasts of wind between cars rocking the truck back and forth, pulling them closer. Rona's throat tightened as the shaking grew worse, jerking side to side, and then the last car roared by. Rona heard the springs creaking as the truck rocked to a stop.

David sat up and looked around, blinking at the dark fields as if they were pressing against his eyes. He fumbled with the gear shift, glancing sideways at Rona and Wyatt as if they had been trying to do something behind his back, and then he eased the pickup towards home.

It was almost four in the morning when they pulled into the driveway. Agnes still wasn't back. The phone rang as they walked into the house. David answered, leaning against the counter and nodding as if the person on the other end of the line could see him. He left without saying a word, getting into the truck and driving up to the hospital, and it was only later that Rona learned that Merrilee had died.

II.

After the funeral was over and all the relatives went home, Rona's mother gave her some cardboard boxes and told her to start packing her things because they were moving into Merrilee's house. The news didn't surprise Rona at all; she'd been listening in the other room when her parents made the decision.

"We could have that big bedroom upstairs," Agnes said. "We could put the kids all the way at the other end of the house."

"Sounds kind of creepy." David's voice was quiet and guilty, but also a little rushed, almost excited. "Being in the house with all her things."

"All that old wallpaper," Agnes said, "with those flowers the size of basketballs. We'll have to re-do everything."

They were quiet. In her head, Rona could see the sharp light in her mother's eyes, David wringing his hands, working them against each other.

Rona had a talent for being in the right place to eavesdrop on interesting conversations. She was sure it had something to do with her magic. Once she was hiding under the back porch at her grandmother's house when she saw Merrilee come up the driveway, carrying one of the chickens from the coop. There weren't many of them left. At the top step, Merrilee took the plump bird by the neck and held it tight as she flicked her wrist. The body twitched at the end of her arm like someone shaking out their fingers. Agnes came out onto the porch. She said, "I suppose that bird's on your diet."

"It's for Rona and Wyatt," Merrilee said.

"And for you."

"Not everything's about what you like," Merrilee said, her voice dripping with kindness. Rona could feel her mother coiling up, trying not to let the conversation escalate into an argument. Merrilee said, "One little serving. I have to eat something."

"It doesn't matter how little it is if it's bad for you. You know that."

At the dinner table later, Agnes sat eating a salad, stabbing the dark green lettuce with her fork. When she came to a crouton, she crunched it loudly between her teeth. Merrilee slurped the thick, creamy gravy off her spoon. She said, "You and David should move in. Then you all could cook for me."

"You be careful what you wish for," Agnes said, and not long after that the doctors took off Merrilee's heel. She'd clipped her toenail too close and when it ended up ingrown, her whole leg got infected. David had a big hospital bed brought in and they set Merrilee up in the living room, propped up on pillows so she could spend her time watching soap operas and talk shows. What was left of her foot looked terrible, all bruised and swollen like it had been stuffed with something rotten. Rona pretended to watch TV while she listened to Merrilee and David talk.

Merrilee was staring down her leg at her toes. She said, "Five little tombstones on an old green hill."

David smiled. This was the way they sometimes talked, some kind of language that was half poetry and half lunacy. "Didn't your mom have diabetes, too?"

"It's like watching death crawl up my body. It'll be toes, then foot, then all the way up."

"Well, that's sure to screw up how the covers lay on the bed."

They both laughed. Merrilee said, "If I was little enough, I could run the record player without plugging it in. I could stand with my stump on the spindle and kind of hop things along."

They laughed some more. David said, "You know what record you could play?" He crooned for her, smiling, "All of me. Why not take all of me?" which made Agnes get up and leave the room. She had been a nurse so long that she couldn't stand people who wouldn't help take care of themselves, especially ones who spent most of their time making things worse. Rona once asked her mother why things seemed to be going so wrong for the family, health-wise, and Agnes said it was bad genes.

"And all the moonshine and incest," Agnes added, snorting at her own cruel joke, probably because she didn't think Rona knew what incest was, but Merrilee had given her half an explanation one night as they lay in her bedroom. They were under a quilt and Rona could smell the liniment Merrilee rubbed into her swollen feet. She told Rona a ghost story about a girl killed by her father because he couldn't stand how he felt for her. The way Merrilee said love, Rona knew something was wrong.

"Down the well she went," Merrilee whispered, "an old well up on top a hill. There was a farm there where no one lived anymore and that's where he took her, and after she fought him he was so ashamed, he lifted the cover off the well and said, 'Look down here.' But every night after that, he heard her calling and calling, sure that she was still alive. And he threw himself down to save her, and if you go there today and put a bucket down that well, who knows what you might pull up." Then Merrilee rolled over and faced the darkness and said, "Now go to sleep."

Agnes could make all the jokes she wanted, but Rona thought there were a lot of things her mother didn't know, and that was because she was always too busy going to work, or having a meeting with one of the nursing home's committees, or gossiping with her sewing circle, which Rona knew was really a drinking club because she liked to hover outside the room and listen to her mother's friends talk about their husbands. There was the sound of ice clinking in glasses, and whenever Agnes said something about David, her voice dropped too low to hear, rising only at the end to be lost in the slur of laughter.

Filling the boxes was easy because there wasn't much Rona wanted to take. The only things she really cared about were the books she'd hidden on her shelf. The best thing to do would be take a few at a time, hiding them in with her clothes and her notebooks and whatever toys she was pretending still interested her. Agnes had given her two boxes, and Rona put a couple of books in each of them, pausing over each cover, the bare-chested men, the half-dressed women heaving out of whatever remained of their clothes. Rona carried the boxes out to the car, where Wyatt and Agnes were waiting, and after they dropped off the boxes, Agnes drove them back home. As they pulled in the driveway, she looked at her watch and said, "It's the swing night, so I'll probably take two shifts." She turned towards Rona. "Make your brother lunch and the two of you can walk some boxes back down to Grandma's house and I'll see you later."

Then she rushed them out of the car and backed down the driveway, giving them her I mean business look before she pulled away. As soon as she was out of sight, Wyatt started down the sidewalk, away from the house.

"Where are you going?"

"She's nuts. I'm not walking any boxes anywhere."

Rona watched him walk away, his head pale as a basketball that's been left in the sun too long. At first, she thought she wouldn't pack any boxes either, but then she thought it might be a pretty good time to get as many of the books as she could out of the house and into her new room. And it would be nice to have Merrilee's to herself, to plan how things should be and the best way to make everything happen the way she wanted, before her father had time to fill the whole house up with his garbage, his piles of books and papers and those charts he liked to make that seemed to be about nothing at all.

David was writing a book called *The Dangers of Understanding Evil.* Rona liked to go through his various files and folders and notebooks when he was safely away somewhere, out in the backyard by the fire pit, or playing football with his friends. He'd been working on the book for years, all the way back to California. There were stacks and stacks of typed pages, and photographs tacked up to the walls of his den; skulls in a pile, a naked girl walking down the road, bodies stacked together like cords of wood. Rona liked the ones of bombed cities the best, although liked probably wasn't the best word for how they made her feel. She would lean closer and closer to the photographs, until it felt like she was inside of them, the walls around her flattened into rubble, the horizon stretching farther and farther away.

Whenever she asked David what the book was about, the answer was different. The last time, he had said, "Whenever you study something, no matter how good your intentions, you have to accept it a little. Say somebody does something really wrong . . ."

"Like what?" Rona asked. They were sitting in the drive-thru lane at McDonald's, Wyatt and Agnes back home. Rona liked to be alone with her father; often she would imagine there was only the two of them, no Agnes and no Wyatt.

"I don't know, somebody murders somebody." Disappointed, Rona sat back in her seat and twisted her lips doubtfully. Her father said, "Okay, somebody comes into the house one night and kills me and Wyatt and your mom."

Rona sat forward, re-interested. She had to wait while David yelled their order into the crackle of the speaker phone. She was so anxious she wasn't even offended when he ordered her a happy meal.

"So you're so upset by all this, you go away to college and you learn all about psychology and you go interview the guy who killed us. If there's any justice, he's on death row. He tells you how he was abused as a child and how he used to torture animals and how it wasn't personal or anything. He could have killed anybody along the way, but he just happened to come across our house first."

The girl at the cashier window smiled at David, the way that women always did, and pressed the change into the palm of his hand. David didn't seem to notice. He was quiet until after the food came and they were on their way back home, and then he said, "So you might not agree, but maybe you sympathize a little. You think about how awful it must have been, being abused and torturing animals. Maybe it really wasn't personal. But your family's still dead."

"But maybe because now I know so much about psychology, I can help the next guy who wants to kill a whole family in their sleep. Were you sleeping?"

David nodded. "Sound asleep. But understanding why somebody did something doesn't make what they did any less wrong."

To which Rona said nothing, though she had to wonder what the alternative was; you couldn't go around not knowing things. Once, she asked if he was ever going to finish the book.

"The problem is," David said, "they keep changing what's evil."

David was good at saying They. Rona could always tell just the kind of people he meant.

She over-packed the box with books and it started to tear while she was walking to Merrilee's. Even though it wasn't that hot and the walk was only a little over a half-mile or so, it seemed like twenty miles because the Jeffers boys, who had moved in across the street at the beginning of summer, came out and walked down the sidewalk on the opposite side of the street. There were two of them, one a year younger than the other. Looking at just their faces, it was hard to tell who was who; they both had sharp noses and close-set eyes, but their bodies were completely opposite. Rona figured the fat one was probably eating the skinny one's food. They had a hungry way of talking, too, circling around and biting the ends of each other's sentences. They kept pace with Rona, walking just behind her, so that she had to turn over her shoulder if she wanted to see them. They were debating what might be in the box.

"Probably a shitload of money," the skinny one said.

"I bet her grandma willed it to her." The fat one, his voice deeper.

"Yeah, willed it to her. She can buy herself a bra."

"Yeah, that bra she almost needs."

The way they snickered sounded like two dogs gobbling from the same dish. Rona quietly gave them the finger; not so they'd notice, just pulling her other fingers back so only the middle one wrapped around the corner of the box. She wanted some of Merrilee's magic, then; think of the things she could do to them! At the very least, she could keep the box from falling apart and give them something to really laugh about.

When she got to her grandmother's gravel drive, the boys turned and went back to their own house. Rona told herself to think up something nasty for them, something she could write down in her diary. Someday when the magic finally came, she would go back through her notes, remembering name after name, spell after spell.

She kicked through the little fine stones, passing the dilapidated chicken coop, where she could hear the demented old rooster inside, scratching at the walls.

◈ ◈ ◈

Inside, Wyatt was sitting at the kitchen table. Rona said, "What are you doing here?"

"There were some kids down at the park." Wyatt always thought that everyone was staring at him. When he first came back to school after the leukemia, most of the boys in his class had shaved their heads, but that just made him feel more self-conscious, especially when their hair grew back and his didn't. He was always getting in fights, then saying it was all because someone made fun of him, though this was only sometimes true. It was impossible to say what would set Wyatt off next; all it took was the wrong kind of look, a little misinterpretation. Once, it was because the kid in the desk next to Wyatt's wanted to borrow a pencil.

"Here," Wyatt snapped, throwing his whole supply box across the room, and when the teacher came over, Wyatt said, "He called me bald!" Which would cause all kinds of trouble for whomever Wyatt framed, until the teachers caught on, and then they sent Wyatt to the principal, who would write a note and send it home for Agnes and David to sign.

While Agnes and David were busy yelling at Wyatt, Rona would sneak into the other room and read the letters, how Wyatt should go to a psychologist, how he had failed to adjust, how his behavior affected the classroom environment. David hated psychologists almost as much as he hated doctors.

"Trust me, I know all about them," he'd say, and Agnes would just look at him like she knew she couldn't win. The letters got to be such a big deal that Wyatt came to Rona and asked her to forge Agnes' signature, which was something Rona could do pretty well. It was easy because Agnes had such neat handwriting. Rona agreed to do it, hoping maybe to make things between them better, or at least to have something she could use against Wyatt someday, if only to get him to leave her alone.

Once summer vacation started, everyone hoped Wyatt would calm down. During the last week of school, Rona walked past the teacher's lounge and heard one of the old biddy teachers, Mrs. Murch, whose first name was Eunice, talking to Principal Harrocks. His name was Roger. Eunice Murch said, "There's always been a dark streak in that family."

Eunice was about a hundred and fifty years old and she used to teach in one-room school houses and all of her opinions were based on mean little rumors she often started herself. A million years ago she'd had both David and Agnes in her class, and then Rona, too, a long, miserable school year that slowly filled Rona's diary with the cruelest spells she could imagine.

Rona just barely managed to get the box of books down on the counter when Wyatt said, "You want to play Death Squad with me?"

The last thing Rona wanted to do was play Death Squad. Wyatt made up the game when he was in the hospital, and it was the only thing he liked to do except to think of ways to make money. Ever since he came home, he had been trying to get rich. He'd heard David talking about how much everything cost and Wyatt thought if it was such a problem, keeping him alive, then he'd just pay them back and be done with it.

He sold Rona's whole Barbie collection to the prissy girl who lived next door to them, whose name was Stephanie, and all he got for them was ten dollars. Wyatt told Rona he was her agent, then he gave her nine dollars and kept one for himself.

All the money he made, he wadded up and crammed into a big jar he kept under his bed. The jar had a screw top lid with holes punched in the top because it was where Rona and Wyatt used to stick the lightning bugs they caught towards the end of every summer. There would be so many of them the jar would glow a greenish yellow that looked like a cartoon monster's eyes.

Stephanie spent a whole week having the most elaborate Barbie social event ever, a big ball with fancy dresses and lawn furniture and tiaras, and the whole thing happened in all its glamorous detail right on the other side of the chain link fence. Rona, who had outgrown Barbie seemingly overnight, still couldn't keep herself from watching her ex-dolls go about their new, sophisticated lives.

"So do you want to play?" Wyatt asked again.

"We're supposed to be packing," Rona said.

"If you don't play Death Squad with me." Wyatt said, using a voice so flat and sure of itself he sounded like a grown man, "I'll tell Mom and Dad how you broke my arm."

Which was true. Before the leukemia, Rona had broken Wyatt's arm, accidentally. At the time, Merrilee's hens were still alive, and Rona and Wyatt would gather up the chicks and take them down to the creek that ran through a low gully beside the farm, and past that a big woods and a park where hardly anyone ever went. From down by the creek, nothing of the subdivision could be seen. Even the noise of the main road disappeared, shuttered out by the leaves and the brush between the trees.

One by one, they would dip the chicks into the water, just like they had seen some preacher doing on television, and Rona and Wyatt would take turns saying, "I baptize you in the name of the father, son, and common sense."

Around her head, Rona wore a cloth napkin she had borrowed from Merrilee's linen drawer. It was embroidered with fantail doves, red-edged with gold stitched into the tips of their wings. Rona wrapped her head with the napkin, and Wyatt had a white handkerchief tied around his neck and knotted in the back so he'd look like a priest. But in the middle of the game, for no reason either of them could later explain, he swiped Rona's napkin and ran around the little wash-out. She dropped her handful of chicks and chased after him. They were both laughing, the chicks like little balls of soggy fluff scattering around their feet, but Wyatt was too fast for Rona to catch. He skipped rock to rock across the creek.

On the opposite bank, there was a huge oak tree with some boards nailed to one side, running up like a ladder, and Wyatt climbed up. Not only was he fast, but he was agile, too, and he went most of the way just by using his hands, holding the napkin in his mouth. Rona plodded up; she went slow because she hated the way the old boards creaked when she put her weight on them. The first big branch was about fifteen feet up, and it shot out from the trunk at right angles. Wyatt went scooting out, sitting down with his legs dangling over the sides. Rona followed.

"Give it back," she said. Wyatt laughed, scooting away. Once she got close enough, he balled up the napkin and dropped it. It puffed out as it fell and landed on the surface of the creek. They both watched it float, the water carrying it away.

Looking over his shoulder at her, Wyatt smiled at first, proud of his strategy, that Rona would have to hurry back down the tree and chase after the napkin, but then she saw that he looked wary, too, like she might keep him trapped at the end of the branch. He glanced down at the ground, gauging his chances. All at once, Rona couldn't stand how he looked, there on the branch, so sure he would still escape. She reached out and pushed him, hard between the shoulders.

It wasn't a long way down, but Wyatt twisted, falling sideways. There was a loud crack. At first, Rona thought the branch had snapped beneath her, but then Wyatt tried to roll over and his arm seemed loose, somehow, slow to follow his body.

By the time she got down, Wyatt was howling. He looked like he was made of white wax that had been melted down over and over again. Rona scurried up the embankment, and she saw Agnes already coming from the house, her apron flapping like one wing trying to fly. Merrilee stood on the porch, watching.

At the hospital, the doctors wondered why it was taking Wyatt so long to stop bleeding where the bone splintered through, and not long after that they had their answer.

As soon as he had the chance, with the plaster still fresh on his arm, Wyatt swore he would never tell, and he had meant it the way only a little boy could mean something. Rona wasn't even sure he still remembered what really happened; it couldn't seem like much, compared to leukemia. Still, there were times when Rona thought about how she felt, that moment when she thrust her hand forward and felt it slam against Wyatt's back, between his shoulder blades.

And she also knew that Wyatt wasn't the same little boy; that promise came before Wyatt laid awake all night in a dark hospital room, which was nothing like a hotel, filled with doctors who were not concierges. It was a promise made by a boy who had heard what the doctors said when they thought he wasn't listening.

"Fine," Rona said. "Let's play."

It was immensely complicated, playing Death Squad, a game invented by someone with nothing to do but think of rules and how to break them. Wyatt took the name from a book about mercenaries which Rona had bought for him at the bookstore and then smuggled in to him at the hospital.

Wyatt made the Death Squad soldiers by holding his fingers in different, sometimes painful looking positions. Each position made a new type of soldier. There was the Sitting Assassin and Standing Man, Running Freak and Flying Freak, Shooter and Ax. There were variations all the time, and special powers, and revised rules. Most of the time, Wyatt played the game by himself, sitting cross-legged on the floor with his fists flashing against each other, but sometimes Rona let him talk her into playing. She had only won once, and that was because Wyatt had started to cry when she made up Death Breath, who could kill any of the other soldiers just by breathing on them.

"That's what Grandpa Tate sounded like when he died," Rona said, and Wyatt was so shaken that he couldn't come up with anything to counter Rona's sudden flashes of inspiration, Bullet-Proof Soldier, and then Bomb-Proof and Fire-Proof. By the next game Wyatt was back to form, fully armed with Proof-Proof Soldier. He was too good at making up rules, a flawless logic always at work, a pattern Rona could not recognize.

In Merrilee's kitchen, he was defeating her again when he suddenly stood up. "You aren't even trying." Rona watched him stomp onto the back porch, where he threw himself into the swing and sullenly made his hands continue their battle. Rona stayed in the kitchen, wondering if he would really say anything about what had happened to his arm by the creek, what could have possibly made him decide to use that information against her all this time later, what would happen if he did actually tell. The summer was almost over, but it wasn't over yet, and if he was bored enough, there was no telling how many ways he could find to make her life miserable.

Rona gathered up her box of books and took them upstairs to Merrilee's old room, the one with giant flowers on the wallpaper, even though she knew that was the one that Agnes wanted. It was the biggest and it had windows on three sides. Without Merrilee's things, all of the rooms in the house seemed eerie and empty. Every time Rona turned, she looked for chairs that weren't there, tables that were missing, pictures of old people that used to hang on the walls. There was a fireplace in the living room and on the mantel Agnes had already put out some of their own family pictures. There was one of Merrilee; she stood on the back porch, looking down, but she must have been saying something because her smile was blurred, just slightly, and her tooth looked like a smudge on the film, some dust on the lens.

What if the tooth was still in the house? If Merrilee had prepared some spell, some way of leaving her magic for Rona to find?

For the rest of the afternoon, Rona went about the house opening and closing all the empty drawers and closets, feeling morbid and anxious and optimistic but finding no clues about the tooth. The idea started to seem ridiculous until she opened the door to the basement and looked down the steps, remembering the boxes where Agnes and David had stuffed Merrilee's things, hauling them down, some of them while Merrilee was still in the hospital.

The basement was Rona's least favorite place because of all the doors; one for the swaying wooden steps going down through the middle of the house, and one for the outside entrance and the sandstone steps which filled with water when it rained. There was a door for the workshop where her grandfather's old tools hung rusting and one for the room lined with shelves of dusty canned vegetables, the food inside the glass canning jars pale and puffy; the contents made Rona think of fingers, eyes, baby hearts. There was a door to the coal chute and a bulky gray furnace that looked like an octopus, its tendrils reaching up into the house, its dry search never ending.

There were other doors Rona was too afraid to open, because Merrilee claimed to have brought a hooly-hoo with her up from the mountains when she first came to Ohio. "I brought him up in a jar, and you should have heard him howl when I let him out. I had to bring your great-grandmother up just so there'd be enough magic to make him stay. Hooly-hoos like mountains and woods, they don't care anything for old stone cellars. But I thought I might need someone to guard the place, so that's why I brought him."

"What's a hooly-hoo," Rona had asked her mother, the first chance she got.

"Something your grandmother made up." So that was how Rona knew Merrilee was telling the truth; Agnes didn't want her to know anything. David, at least, would tell her if he knew, because he didn't care what Rona and Wyatt learned or what they read or what they watched on television. He thought children were basically indestructible, if they had half a chance to figure things out on their own. Of course, he only thought this when Agnes wasn't around.

One side of the basement stayed pretty dry, but the other side was always damp and Rona was careful not to touch any of the black, cobwebby stuff that clung to the walls. Her parents had stacked the boxes along the dry wall. There was one window in the whole basement, late afternoon light golden on the beat-up cardboard. The boxes glowed like the sun was shining just for them, the world having spun into place for this one ray of light. Those boxes seemed like the perfect hiding place, but as she walked toward them, Rona felt a rush of cold air coming out from under one of the doors. Without really thinking about it, Rona reached to push the door open and saw her own hand reaching towards the rickety handle.

Inside, the room was all shadows, but there was an old light switch on the wall. Rona twisted a little knob to turn it on. The light flicked once, and then shone down on a low, rectangular pool of water with a circle at one end. It looked like a huge, rippling keyhole laid flat on the floor. As she watched, a few bubbles rose to the surface. Rona could see her breath, and then there was something beyond the chill, and the hair on her arms rose, as though her skin wanted to unpeel itself from her body.

She shut off the light and slammed the door, forgetting the boxes and running upstairs.

Rona told herself that she was too old to be scared of a puddle of water, no matter how creepy it seemed. She knew it didn't have any-thing to do with the hooly-hoo because eventually Merrilee had told her everything there was to know about them; how they were miners that died in a cave-in, or a baby that shouldn't have been born, or a girl who killed herself over the love of someone who didn't love her in return. At night, a hooly-hoo howled and sounded just like the wind coming through the holes in the house and the loose frames of the doors. But Merrilee had never said anything about the keyhole of water in the basement.

Rona was thinking about all this as her mother yelled at her. Agnes had found the books in the bottom of the box, and there was no way Rona was getting the biggest room in the house for herself, no matter what she imagined her grandmother would have wanted, and there was only one person who was in charge, and that person damn sure wasn't a twelve-year-old girl who spent her time reading books she wasn't sup-posed to be reading.

"Maybe you think you understand what's happening in those stories, but you don't," Agnes said, which Rona thought only showed how little her mother really knew about her.

"They're historical," Rona said, picking up the books as Agnes took them out of the box and threw them down on the floor, so that they bounced up and flapped open like wounded birds. When she was mad, Agnes' legs went stiff and her shoulders swung back and forth. Rona thought she looked like a rotating sign, an advertisement for Anger.

"I see where the bindings are broke," Agnes snapped, throwing another book.

"I buy them second hand. I use my own money!"

"You use the change from the grocery store. You think I don't know that?"

Rona was sitting on her bed, and she stacked the books behind herself.

"*Tropic of Cancer?*" Agnes said. "*Justine?* Rona, I don't think so!"

Then Agnes held the book in her hands, staring at it as though she might start to cry. Rona felt an immediate twinge of regret, because she hadn't actually read *Justine* yet; she had only bought it because of the way the girl on the front looked, her clothes dangling dangerously, everything miraculously held in place by one shoulder strap.

Agnes had never laid a hand on her, but Rona thought this might be the time. A long, shuddering sigh came from her mother as she looked back and forth between the books still in the box and the books Rona tried to hide behind herself. She drew the long breath back in. "Look. I know there are things you're curious about, but I read *Tropic of Cancer* in college. You can't possibly understand anything but the worst parts of that book."

"It's historical!"

"You aren't old enough."

"Daddy says if I'm old enough to ask a question then I'm old enough to hear the answer."

Agnes stared at her. She took the copy of *Justine* and went off to find David.

Rona took the remaining books and put them back in the box, happy that she had won, at least temporarily. Her mother was gone and she wouldn't have to hide her books anymore. She carried the box down the hall to the room that was going to be hers, the room that had been assigned to her, and sat it by the door, and that was where the books stayed for weeks and weeks, completely forgotten.

"Give your mother a break about the books, all right?" David said, the next day. They were out in the yard behind Merrilee's house, late in the afternoon. David had the hood up on the pickup. He looked at the engine while he talked to Rona.

"Okay," she said. "What's that thing in the basement with all the water in it?"

"A spring. That's where they were supposed to keep the milk, but your grandfather never really used it." Then he went on for awhile about how her great-grandfather had found the spring with a divining rod and they had built the house on top of it. The long rectangular side was where the milk cans would go, and the round side let the water up. Then he talked about how the old barn looked before it fell, and how the place was never farmed like it should have been.

Merrilee used to talk about the farm the same way, wistfully, but only when she was busy with something else at the same time, as if those memories would only come to the surface when their owner was distracted by some other little task; hanging the laundry, rolling out dough, or teaching Rona string games like Cat's Cradle or Baby Diamonds. She could make the most amazing string animals, too. Sea snakes, and fish, and lizards. "Look, Rona, there's an owl in the house," Merrilee said to her once, and then pulling the string tight between her fingers showed Rona the owl, which had his wings outstretched. Merrilee wiggled her fingers and the wings flapped, and then the owl rose into the air and flapped around the room three times before perching again on Merrilee's open palms. Rona felt herself staring, but Merrilee only smiled at her and set about looping the strings again, as if nothing unusual had happened at all.

Whatever David was trying to do with the engine wasn't going well. He had a crescent wrench, but couldn't seem to get a hold of what he wanted. The wrench came loose and he cracked his fingers; the wrench went flying across the yard. He gripped his fingers, cursing, then saw Rona staring at him.

Immediately embarrassed, he shook his fingers and grinned. "Sorry about that," he said. "I guess you've seen enough angry people for a couple of days." Rona nodded, and he said, "I've got to go pick something up." He took the prop bar out of the hood and let it close quietly, pushing down on the latch with his uninjured hand.

"Can I come with you?"

"Not this time," he said, then climbed into the truck. "Stay out of your mother's way."

Which was not something Rona needed to be told. She walked around the farm, past the chicken coop, through the old orchard with its twisted up apple trees. One of the trees had been struck by lightning and all that was left was a stump and the wood David had cut up with the chain saw then left lay. There were always ants climbing in and out of the stump, and Rona liked to watch them, walking around in their straight little lines, going places that probably seemed like the end of the world to an ant.

Once, she had dabbed nail polish on the back of one of the ants, just so she could try to keep track of how many trips in and out of the stump it would make. When the ant didn't turn back up, she dabbed another, and another, until the nail polish bottle was empty, and then she thought of the ants down in their tunnels, glowing red, the dirt walls lit as if by lanterns.

Rona walked over to where the barn used to be and tiptoed down the two sides of the foundation that were left, and then past the foundations down to the creek. Merrilee always said the only thing that kept her sane up here in all the Ohio flatness was that creek and the way it cut a little path beside the farm.

"I used to stand out there in all that field and I'd never seen anything so flat in all my life. I'm a hill girl, Rona, I need land with curves on it. I'd get scared, looking at that house in the nightfall with its pale little lights and the nearest neighbors a mile away and nothing beside me but Tate and he was laughing at me. 'Told you you'd hate it up here with nowhere to go hide,' he'd say."

Whenever Merrilee talked about Tate, it sounded like her voice was echoing around in a tin can. "When he was off pretending to be a farmer, I'd come down to the creek and throw stones. Sometimes the water ran so still I could sit and look at my tooth and wish it wasn't there."

As Rona got back to the house, a pick-up that looked even worse than David's pulled into the driveway. On the back of it, someone had built a big wooden box, weather-beaten now, rusty nails poked out of it and only some of them hammered sideways. The driver honked twice as he rolled past, and a huge hand popped out of the driver-side window and gave Rona a wave. The hand was so thick and fat it looked like the fingers wouldn't be able to bend. Rona ran in the house and told her mother someone was there, and they went to the back of the house to see who it was.

"Oh, no," her mother said. "It's Head."

Out of the truck came a huge man, as wide as he was tall, wearing jeans that were torn in both knees. He stretched and turned and no sooner was he out of the cab then a gang of kids came out after him. They moved so fast and in so many directions that Rona lost track of them. She thought there might be six of them. Some went towards the old out-buildings, some the creek, others the orchard, as if they had lived on the place their whole lives. The littlest of the bunch wore bib overalls and stood beside Head.

"Say there, Agnes." The man came across the yard. "I guess this is a surprise."

Before her mother could speak, Rona's father came pulling into the driveway. David's face dropped as he spotted the big man and drove past.

The two men met in the yard and shook hands and then stared at each other. Head said, "Sorry I missed the funeral."

"That's okay."

"Had a job I couldn't leave and all."

Agnes muttered something too low to hear. Head came up on the porch and looked down at Rona. She saw at once how the man had come by his name; he had no neck whatsoever, and his head was so fat it didn't look like he had any ears. He was bald completely on top, and the hair on the side of his head was shaved to stubble. He leaned over her, held out his hand and said, "Rona, I haven't seen you since you were a baby."

His hand reminded Rona of the time she had got her own hand stuck in the knot hole of a tree. She thought for a moment he might never let go, but then Wyatt came through the door. Head looked at him and said, "Boy, we got the same haircut."

Wyatt turned and went right back in the house. Rona moved to the side and watched as the adults continued their awkward conversation. Merrilee had never said much about Head; he was Tate's son from a previous marriage, and Tate and Head had fought all the time and by the time David was five, Head had left home. He was only fifteen at the time. Though her house was filled with pictures of relatives, there was only one picture of Head, as a little boy, standing on the back of a tractor which had one of its wheels missing.

Head kept saying how long the trip from West Virginia had been, how tired and beat they all were. Agnes told him how they just finished moving in and how they hadn't even been to the grocery store yet. Finally, David asked if anyone was hungry, and how about if he ran down to the store and got a couple buckets of chicken.

"Better make it three," Head said, and he bellowed once, something so loud that Rona couldn't understand it, and then all the kids showed up, right away, as if they had been hiding around the edges of the house the whole time.

As they ate, Head licked the chicken grease off the stubby, jointless appendages that passed for his fingers. His kids did the same. There turned out to be eight of them, seven boys and one girl, and the boys all ate with their mouths open. The whole kitchen sounded like something wet being run through a grinder. Rona and Wyatt sat pushing their food around their plates. Occasionally, Rona would pick up a piece, move it towards her mouth, then set it back down.

"I'm surprised you all moved in here," Head said. He ate so fast he was sweating. "I always thought this place was haunted."

"We like it," her father said. "It's a good chance for us."

"Mmm-hmm." Head turned a drumstick long ways in his mouth and pulled the meat off with his teeth, gristle and all. Around the mouthful, he said, "What's happening with your old place?"

"We're going to rent it," David said.

"We've rented it, already," Agnes said. This was not entirely news for Rona; she had heard her mother telling Stephanie's mother about it, who said she thought that was a really nice idea, even though it sounded like she had to swallow hard to say it. Rona knew this because she just happened to pick up the phone in the middle of her mother's conversation, and she listened for awhile because, she thought, they might be done talking soon. No time in the rest of their conversation, though, had her mother said anything about the place being rented already.

"Don't say," said Head. He picked apart a chicken breast. Head's girl sat so straight it looked like someone was pulling a string through her back. She smiled at Rona, keeping her teeth hidden behind her lips. Head pulled off a long piece of skin and said, "I've got a job lined up, up here. Looking to make a fresh start and all."

The adults talked about jobs and David explained how he was

between careers right now, but they were getting by. There were always prospects. Head nodded solemnly. He said, "You know, your mother told me one time I could have this place after she died. That was before you all came back from California."

David nodded. Rona watched his jaw clench. He said, "Well, like you said. Before."

Head studied David for a moment then turned to Wyatt and said, "Hey, boy, you still doing that choir stuff?"

"He's not in choir anymore," Agnes said. Wyatt had been in a chorister group before the leukemia, and everyone thought he had a beautiful voice, though Rona wasn't sure how Head would know this. Agnes said, "Not since he was sick."

Head blushed. Rona looked at all Head's rough kids in their dirty clothes and said, "Do any of your boys do that choir stuff?"

Everyone stopped eating and looked at her. Head looked at her from under his eyebrows, then turned to her father. "Say, didn't your mother buy that house in the subdivision? The one that's up for rent?"

"Rented already," Agnes said, correcting him. David nodded. Head picked at the little crispy pieces stuck to the side of the chicken buckets. He said he thought they might stay a little while. David said he didn't think there was enough room and Head said not to worry, he'd brought some tents for the boys and maybe the girls could stay together. Next, Head asked what they'd done with all Merrilee's things, and when he wouldn't stop asking, David suggested they go downstairs and he would show him where all Merrilee's things— where all his mother's things— were.

"And all," David said.

"That's a fine idea," Head said.

The two men went downstairs and then there was the sound of raised voices and one loud bang that seemed to shake all the walls. Rona and Wyatt stared at Head's kids across the table.

The sound of voices came through the floor, almost laughing, and then Head and David climbing the stairs, back into the kitchen, smiling. They walked right outside and Agnes went to the window to watch and Rona hurried over so she could see as well. Together, the men began putting up the tents. As soon as they were done, they started a fire and they sat around drinking and laughing, something which just a few weeks before had seemed a sure impossibility to Rona. All night, she sat on the edge of the fire and listened, and the next day the two men packed up the tents and Head and his family moved into Rona's old house.

III.

Rona and Wyatt spent the last weeks of the summer trying to avoid Head's kids. As if they weren't bad enough, there was Head himself, hulking around the farm like a huge, lazy bear. Rona did her best to fit the pieces of his history together. She could have just asked her mother for the details, but getting information from Agnes was like trying to pull a nail out of a board without a hammer.

"Which one was his mother?" Rona asked one night, casually, after Head and the kids had left. They spent all day at Merrilee's, apparently just so they could snoop around and break things.

"Noreen," Agnes said, grudgingly. The next day, David said, "You know his mother died in childbirth, don't you?" He was talking with Agnes as they washed the dishes, watching Head through the window by the sink. Head's family had just wolfed down lunch and then hurried outside without bothering to help clean up. "Look at the size of that head!"

"And it's all brain, too," Agnes said. David watched his half-brother and his half-nephews and his half-niece. They seemed to be having some kind of wrestling match. Head kept picking up the boys and throwing them in the air. They cartwheeled around and sometimes he didn't bother to catch them. Agnes said, "Moonshine and incest."

Rona believed Head was her grandfather's son, though, because she'd found a picture of her grandfather down in the old boxes and the two of them looked exactly alike, except her grandfather had a skinny body to go with his big head. She also found out that Head's name was Harold. There was a bible down there that looked like it hadn't been opened more than once or twice, and there was a family tree on the inside. In one of the branches she found her own name, then her parents, then Merrilee. Beside Merrilee's name someone had very faintly written Garland Tate, as if maybe they were hoping to erase it somewhere down the line.

The eight cousins were Fulton, Aubrey, Dewey, Guy, Hugh, Clay, Hack and Irene. During the day, they had the run of the farm, but it seemed to Rona they were mostly concerned with sticking ice down the back of her shorts, particularly Hack, the oldest of the boys and the same age as Rona. He had red hair and pale skin that seemed too angry to tan, and teeth so crooked they could almost be fangs, and shoulders that curved forward so he looked like half a question mark.

The cousins were like a dog pack; one would stand in front of her, mumbling some question Rona could barely understand because of that accent they all had, and while she was trying to figure out what they were saying, another one would run up behind her with the ice. Whenever it was Hack, he tried to put his hand down her shorts, too. It got to be that Rona couldn't see one of them without looking over her shoulder to see where the others were at.

They constantly asked Wyatt what it was like to have leukemia and then told him how lucky he was to miss all that school. Rona and Wyatt both felt like they were always in danger, and the presence of the cousins brought them briefly back together, so that nothing bad was said between them, except for when they were down by the creek one day, watching the cousins skinny dip. Rona and Wyatt hid behind the giant oak tree with the boards running up the side, and Wyatt said, "Look how high up that branch is."

Rona pretended not to hear him, and glanced at the cousins, all of them naked and laughing. When Hack rose out of the water, Rona saw the shadow on his body, a little line of pubic hair. She felt herself blush. Quietly as she could, she crept back towards the house, scared to death that she would fall down or that the leaves would crunch under her feet and they would all find out she had been watching.

At the house, Rona arrived just as the mailman pulled up in his little white truck. His name was Burke Van Meter. He was the mailman from their old house, and Rona liked him because he was young, with long hair like a rock star. He also smiled at her whenever she went out to meet him. Merrilee's mailbox was by the road, instead of by the front door. Burke saw her coming down the driveway and waited for her to get to the truck. "Rona," he said. The smile. "And how's the new digs?"

"Hello, Mr. Van Meter," she said. Her father didn't like him because he said all mailmen should look like someone you can trust, which was ridiculous, because there were about a million pictures of her father in California with his hair down to his waist.

"Is there a letter from my boyfriend today?"

"Your boyfriend?" Burke raised his eyebrows. "Aren't you a little young for boyfriends?"

"We met in West Virginia. He writes me all the time. Love letters."

Burke whistled low, and it was hard to tell behind his sunglasses, but Rona thought maybe he glanced from her face downwards. "Well, don't get tied down too soon," he said. Below his sunglasses, the smile. He handed Rona the mail and drove off.

There was an abandoned power pole between the house and the old barn. The sun was still hot, but it was coming down in the sky and the pole cast a long, straight shadow across the yard and Rona and Wyatt took turns running down the path it made, even though Rona knew she was too old to play like that. Still, she loved the way it felt, her arms out on either side, the shade cool on her neck, hands hot in the sun, her heart pounding from running, and how her face felt, and the horizon vibrating like it was her footsteps that made it quiver.

When David came home, all the cousins reappeared, swarming around his pickup. He got along great with all these new nieces and nephews and they liked him too, maybe because he was so different from Head. There was something with him in the front of the cab that made all the cousins clap their hands against their thighs and peal with laughter.

In the passenger seat, there was a black dog, with eyes so dark they might not have had pupils. It didn't share in the cooing excitement of the cousins; sizing up its new situation, it had that flat, almost human gaze some dogs have. As soon as David opened the door it slipped out of the truck, and it let the cousins pet its back and rub its ears. There was no tail-wagging, only a stillness, as if it only tolerated this abundance of love.

It's not even a puppy, Rona thought. It was full-grown and medium-sized, with tight muscles running along its sides that made it look something like a clenched fist. Rona was thinking of how mad Agnes was going to be, but then the cousins all started to squeal again; there was a lamb hanging its head over the bed of the truck.

Obviously, David had lost his mind. Rona and Wyatt didn't like animals anyway, but their mother really hated them. Moving closer to her father, Rona wanted to ask if he had any idea the kind of trouble he was causing everyone, but he was too busy accepting congratulations from all the cousins and going on and on about how much grass a sheep can eat in a week and what they would do with the wool and how the dog was supposed to be a great sheep dog.

"And it's the perfect relationship," he said. "One boss and one worker. That way it's more like a partnership." Irene swept the lamb up in her arms and held it like a baby, swaying with its weight as it began to bleat. Despite herself, Rona smiled. The boys packed themselves around Irene and Rona noticed for the first time how different they all looked, like all eight of them could have come from different mothers.

Head wandered over, appearing from behind the chicken coop and Rona thought of the way he had devoured the chicken on the day they arrived, and she had a sudden urge to warn the rooster.

Leaning down around his own gut, Head tried to pet the dog but it took a couple of slow steps forward. He watched it pace away and said, "You picked out that dog's name, yet?"

"It's already got one," David said. "Stella, like the movie." Head just stared at him. David said, "You know, with Brando. Stella!" The cousins stepped away from him as he yelled and he laughed.

"You ought to let your boy pick a new one." Head turned toward Wyatt. "Boy, what you want to name that dog?"

Wyatt kicked at the little stones in the driveway and didn't answer. Head leaned back and looked down his belly at Wyatt, and then over at Rona. She crossed her arms in front of her chest. The dog was squatting over by the chicken coop to pee.

"Stella!" Head yelled, so loud that the poor dog flinched and trotted away. Head laughed and went walking down the lane, all eight kids bouncing around behind him like fleas, yelling Stella! Stella! The lamb stood off by itself, looking confused, and Stella lowered her head, wolfishly, and watched them go.

Agnes was so mad, she started slamming things around in the kitchen. Rona and Wyatt listened outside the door as David bore it all, never saying a word or fighting back, just like he always did whenever they argued, unless it was one of those quiet arguments no one was supposed to hear. Agnes wanted to know where the money came from and who was supposed to take care of them and how in the hell were they supposed to feed two animals when they were already feeding Head and his eight kids and it was only a matter of time until Kitty showed up and Agnes was the only one in the whole world with a job, and David said it was a fair trade and the kids could help and did she know how much grass a sheep could eat in a week.

After a stiff and silent dinner, Rona went in to watch the little bit of TV they were allowed to see when their mother was home. Agnes let them watch nature programs or game shows, assuming the game shows were the kind with people who knew a bunch of things that didn't really matter. Rona longed impossibly for music videos. As she came into the living room, however, Rona saw the empty space where the TV usually sat, and she ran to the kitchen and told Agnes, who just looked at David.

"Baaaa," he said. Then he said, "Woof! Woof!"

So that, thought Rona, was her father's idea of a fair trade. She couldn't believe he would do such a thing, and not even the fact that he showed up a week later with another TV made her feel any better. She felt used and the new TV was smaller than the old one and it was all like her grandmother said; you couldn't trust anyone, so it helped to have some magic on your side.

"One time my grandmother poisoned a man," Merrilee told Rona, on one of those sleepovers late at night, Wyatt home from the hospital but still not well. "Some black man, came sniffing around my mother. He was West Virginia black, which meant you could only tell by what his last name was. He kept saying he was sick and needed something for his stomach, and nothing my grandmother gave him seemed to work. Every day, standing by the lane, smiling at Momma on the porch. So she gave him something for his stomach, all right. Now, that's not a good thing to do," Merrilee said, stepping out of the story the way she sometimes did, capturing Rona's attention, bringing her back to the real world, but also making her long for that other place, half-imagined but somehow more real than the real world. "But," she said, "the truth is what it is."

Rona spent the last weekend of summer vacation going through the boxes looking for more clues about Head or wistfully for Merrilee's tooth or anything else mysterious, and in one of her grandmother's old cookbooks she found a letter that Merrilee had written but never sent. The only way Rona could have been more excited was if Burke Van Meter, his hair pulled back in a pony tail and his mirrored sunglasses low on his nose, had delivered it himself.

The pages were yellow and there were little rips along all the old creases, as though the letter had been folded and unfolded a hundred times.

Dear Momma,

How are things back home, I miss everyone and wish I was there. Ohio is so flat I don't think I'll ever get used to it, but there aren't many trees and you can see all the stars at night, just like when we'd go up to the top of that old bald hill and Pop would make up names for the stars.

The creek is high because of all the rain and I wonder alot if you all ever get the same weather. There's no one up here that can say what the weather means like you, though I try to do my best, but your son-in-law don't care to hear it, anyway. All he worries about is when he should go into town, it's a nice town but not for me, though I do like going down to look in the shop windows. I've been having some problems with Harold, but you know how his father is and they're just like each other, that's why they can't get along for anything. The baby's fine, though he does tend to cry alot.

I've been thinking alot about that night Harold was born and you took me down to help with the hot water and all and that was the first birth I ever saw, except for that calf of Pop's, ha! But Noreen was screaming so much I thought I never wanted to see another one and that's what I thought about the whole time I was pregnant. I kept telling myself, don't let this baby kill you before it even comes. Thank the Lord he looks like Pop and not his father, I remember how   terrible Garland looked that night. He was over in the corner watching everything happen and of course you didn't see because you were trying to save Noreen and you'd already handed me that baby all covered in blood. I handed it to Garland and he gave me this awful smile, it was the worst thing I ever saw.

Then I think about how you yelled Noreen's dead, my daughter's dead. You didn't see, but Garland just handed me back that baby and sat down with his hands over his eyes and they were all bloody and his face had that blood all over it like some awful mask. I guess I don't know why I'm telling you all this, don't let Pop read this, just tell him I'm writing him his own letter to read. You know how he loved Noreen, I never thought before about the way I was so scared of Garland that night and how I fell in love all at the same time. He was so sad, Momma, and I was only ten, what else could I do?

There, I wrote this all down but I don't think I'll send it, you don't want to hear this stuff anymore anyway. I will sign it, though, your daughter,

Love, Merrilee

Everything was unfolding in Rona's head but, like the letter, seemed on the verge of crumbling apart. She got up and found the Bible with the family tree in it, running her finger along the branch with Merrilee's name on it. There it was, the first name on the line; Noreen. And beside her name, in the same faint letters, someone had once again written Gar-

land Tate. Merrilee had married her dead sister's husband. She had been
there when her sister died and Head was born and there was blood
everywhere.

Blood. Merrilee standing at the sink, right after she killed the chicken
for Rona and Wyatt. She was cleaning the bird and there was blood on
her hands. Merrilee stopped working and stood staring down at her
hands and the dead bird, its guts splayed on the cutting board, then she
turned to Rona and Wyatt and she said in a voice that was sharper than
the knife in her hand, "You two stay out of that basement."

She pointed her finger at both of them, one and then the other.
After a moment, she smiled at them as if her own warning didn't
really mean much and as she went back to working on the chicken, she
said, "I just sent your father down to put out some mouse traps and I
don't want to have to worry about your sweet toes."

Rona slipped the letter back into the old cookbook and closed
the box. Merrilee had hundreds of cookbooks, and Rona imagined letters full of family secrets in all of them, and recipes for magic and poison
and the summoning of things like a witch's mark. She'd even settle for
one of her own teeth turning that ugly black, provided she could learn to
hide the tooth from boys like Merrilee had. It would be all right as long
as only other witches could see it. Still, she was careful as she thought
about her teeth; she knew enough about magic to be careful about things
like stray thoughts.

From behind her, Rona cold feel the draft coming out of the
room with the cold spring. The door tapped against the frame, and there
was another noise there, something like a small animal would make, a
rustling, a crackling. Rona opened the door to the dark room and clicked
on the light. There stood Merrilee, though she disappeared so quickly that
the image was gone from Rona's mind before she realized what she had
seen. There had been something in the water, she thought, and she was
breathing hard, and her skin felt tight and clammy between her shoulder
blades.

How far down did the deep end go? In her mind it seemed like
it might go down forever, a current pulling on her legs, and no way
back to the surface. She kicked off one sandal, sat down, and stuck her
foot in the water. Nothing there, but she scooted forward and reached
with her toes, and when the cold water was almost touching the hem of
her shorts she could feel something hard. It must have been the shelf
where they kept the milk cans. At the other end, there was a semicircle

and there she felt only the water and its brutal iciness, seeping into her joints, so quickly that her foot was numb when she pulled it out of the water.

As Rona put her sandal back on, the world seemed very small all at once, like she could draw a detailed map of it on the back of a place mat. She could draw the farm and the creek and the curve in the road that led to her old house. There would be room for the school and the book store. She could even draw the lamb trembling in the grass and the dog, its dark eyes ever-watchful. She could put herself in the map, a little dot somewhere in the picture, something that might not even get noticed. And off the edges, there would be the West Virginia mountains she had never seen and even the upstate New York mountains where her mother's people came from, having no magic that Rona knew of, and beyond that everything that was interesting in the world.

Whenever possible, Rona trailed after Head. She did this the way she imagined people who made documentaries about animals would, peeking from behind the chicken coop, or through the railings of the porch, or from the window of her room. He seemed like some kind of omnivore, something which wasn't usually but might sometimes be dangerous. Most of his time was spent hanging around the farm, and he kept a silver flask on the inside of his bib overalls, which he drank from whenever the cousins caught up with him, but not until after he had listened to whatever they had to say, nodding or shaking his head or pointing sternly back towards home.

The flask was filled with moonshine that Head brought up from West Virginia; Head had told this to David one night as they sat drinking by one of David's bonfires. They passed the flask back and forth, both of them making terrible faces each time they sipped. Once the flask was empty, Head went stumbling down the lane, right past Rona, who was watching from the orchard. He came back with a whole bottle of the stuff.

"I got this right after Kitty left," Head said. "It's the best they had."

"I'd hate to taste the worst," David said. David had a way of asking questions when he wanted to be serious, lowering his head, speaking directly to the ground and then looking up for the answer. "You think she'll come back?"

"That wall-eyed hussy?" Head said, his voice strained. He made a motion that seemed to make his head sink into his body. "She'll shack up with somebody. She has her ways, bad eye and all."

Rona tried to imagine the woman they were talking about, if she was Head's wife or girlfriend or some woman he picked up in a bar, one eye pointing away from her face. Like he knew what she was thinking, Head said, "I loved that eye, you know. You all can laugh, but when she looked at me, I liked to think she was seeing a second me there. Me, but better." He raised the flask and made a toast. "To the thought that counts."

Head also carried a long knife inside a leather sheath which he wore on his belt, and he kept a sharpening stone in his pocket. He worked the blade back and forth as he sat by the fire. The blade dragged along the stone and Rona's skin tightened the way it did whenever Agnes took her to the dentist to have her teeth scraped clean.

Head spent a whole afternoon in the orchard, throwing his knife at the ants' stump. Maybe half the time, he hit his target. What would the ants think, the blade splitting their hard-worked tunnels, slicing the larvae, cutting soldiers in two, coming closer and closer to the queen? Head certainly didn't seem bothered by his limited success; Rona watched him until finally Wyatt found her and made a big show of it, probably because he wanted Head to know she'd been spying on him, just the way he had been trailing after Rona, spying on her.

Wyatt still seemed scared of Head, and he would hide in the house when Head was around. If Agnes was at work, he would watch the church channels on television. He liked the ones with the yelling preachers that kept wiping their heads with white handkerchiefs, especially if someone was hollering about Hell. The Baptists broadcasted the same sermon about eighteen times a day and when it wasn't a sermon, they showed strange cartoons about the end of the world or sometimes a movie that someone probably made in their own backyard. Wyatt also liked the Catholic channel, which sometimes had real monks on it. They only showed a mass twice a day, but Wyatt somehow managed to memorize whole parts of the ceremony, and he picked up other things, too..

"Confession is awesome," he told Rona. "The priest turns into God and everything's forgiven."

"Everything?"

"Everything. Even if you murder someone, they forgive you."

"Then you could go right out and murder somebody else."

"You have to be really sorry."

"I could be sorry."

"And you have to do this penance thing."

"Okay," Rona said. At least David and Agnes didn't make them go to church. They went to a Catholic church every Christmas, but that wasn't so bad because there was usually a choir and Christmas songs and the priest always seemed nice, if a little shy, or maybe nervous, or even tipsy. Rona especially liked the parts where he sang by himself, and she liked the stuff about the body and bread, the blood and wine, and everyone walking up the aisle with their hands cupped together like they were carrying birds with broken wings. That wasn't enough for Wyatt; he wanted fire and brimstone.

One time Head showed up at the end of the driveway in his pickup truck and walked down to the creek. He was carrying some metal contraptions over his shoulder and they clanged against each other as they bounced against his broad back. On her belly, Rona watched from the top of the bank while Head worked. They were traps, and Rona saw Head put them along the edge of the creek, six of them altogether, and then he came over and sat not too far from where she was watching. He was close enough that Rona was afraid to move. He picked up a dead branch and stripped off all the bark with his knife, whittling it down smaller and smaller. The two of them sat there like that for what seemed like hours, until there was a pile of shavings at Head's feet and Rona had to pee so bad she thought she might wet herself. Finally, there was a terrible springing noise, and a squealing at the closest trap. Something small and brown whipped around, frantic, trying to flop itself loose. Head strolled over and looked down. There was the flash of his knife and the small thing stopped.

Rona wasn't even sure what it was when Head lifted it by the hind legs. She backed away from the top of the bank. Head cocked his head like maybe he heard her, but then he knelt down and jabbed his knife into the ground, cleaning off the blood.

The first week of school went pretty well, except for the way Wyatt walked so slow every morning. He was a heavy weight around Rona's ankle. She could practically hear him scraping like an iron ball along the sidewalk. She dragged him past their old house, surprised to see that it hadn't yet been run into the ground by Head and the cousins even though they hadn't been living there more than a month. The yard actually looked better, except for Head's pickup, its homemade cap spiked and with nails. Rona knew the cousins were all hiding out inside so they wouldn't have to go to school, which was fine with her. Sooner or later someone would find out they were her relations, and it was already bad enough, having Wyatt around.

As if they had been great friends, Stephanie would wait on her porch for Rona and Wyatt to come past, and then she would float down her driveway like a cloud full of happy coincidence. She usually wore something with Barbie on it, shirts so covered in faces it looked like Barbie's smile was eating her alive. The Jeffers were always waiting, too, grinning like they smelled something good to eat.

"How do you like your grandmother's house, Rona?" Stephanie would ask, or some other annoying question, but even then Rona felt an unexpected pang of loneliness for her old house and this girl she didn't like much. Before Rona could prove she could be just as prissy as Stephanie, the fat Jeffers said, "I bet she likes being rich."

"Being rich, yeah," the skinny one said, then he reached over Rona's shoulder and grabbed at her chest, digging his fingers in. Rona squirmed away, but the boy squeezed harder, then took off running. The other Jeffers followed, knocking Wyatt down as he went past. He yelled sorry in that way which meant he wasn't sorry at all, and Wyatt got up, glaring at Rona like she was the one who ran him over.

Wyatt made her late everyday that week, and finally her teacher, Mr. Edson, who was a new teacher at the school and whose real name Rona was still in the process of acquiring, had no choice but to punish her. He made her write one hundred times, I will endeavor to be more punctual, Mr. Edson. It was an insult, each time she had to write Mr. Edson on the end of that sentence, as if he had guessed how much first names meant to her and enjoyed that she had to spell out her failure over and over again.

Mr. Edson had a paddle and he made a big show of waving it around that first week, telling everyone and all the boys in particular how he liked to use it. He had dark hair with two gray streaks just over top his ears, and the one time Rona went to his desk to try to act sweet and maybe get a look at something with his name on it, he just stared at her like he knew what she was up to and sent her back to her seat.

Rona was glad this would be her last year in elementary school and she could move on to the junior high, where there'd be some real books to read and not these goofy little kid stories about learning to survive in the wild, or being a circus performer, or overcoming the odds, her least favorite of all. She hated those kinds of stories, where someone learns something they should have known in the first place. The Christmas before, Agnes gave Rona a diary with a little lock on the front. For the first two months, Rona wrote down all the things she did, which at the time was mostly wait around to see if Wyatt was going to live or die. When she went back and read what she'd written so far, she hated everything. Who wanted to remember what they ate for dinner or the boring things in school or how she could hear Agnes crying herself to sleep over Wyatt? The only things that were the least bit interesting were Wyatt's narrow escapes and the stories Merrilee told; Rona always wrote as much of those as she could remember, but it was more fun to just make things up. Rona invented whole days for herself.

Dear Diary, she would write. When I woke up this morning I found the whole house empty. I looked everywhere, but everyone was gone. I went to the hospital and all the doctors and nurses wore black. Everyone's sick, they said. Even you. I clapped my hands like Merrilee would and BAM! they all stopped moving. I got away.

Dear Diary, I discovered today that I have the power to move things with my mind. I can turn people inside out. Enclosed you will find a picture of my brother Wyatt, reversed.

Dear Diary, when I move my hands a certain way, people love me more.

Dear Diary, I can heal people, even the dead. I can make Merrilee better.

The world was better that way, Rona thought; for one thing, the days had definite beginnings and definite endings and nothing lingered, nothing seemed like it might last forever. Eventually, it seemed natural to just leave herself out of the diary altogether. Mostly, though, Rona made up little one page stories, and the characters didn't do anything like the boring characters in school books. Sometimes they even did really bad things, but Rona always made sure they got what they deserved by the end of the page.

On the first day of the second week of school, Principal Roger Harrocks came to Mr. Edson's room and asked Rona to step into the hall. Mr. Edson came with her and the first thing she thought of was that paddle and the second was that maybe Mr. Edson had seen her going through the top drawer of his desk when she thought he wasn't looking. Roger Harrocks knitted his eyebrows together and said, "Rona, would you come with me down to your brother's room?"

Rona nodded and followed the prinipal as he waddled away, rolling along like a lopsided ball, Mr. Edson keeping pace with his crisp, military walk. As they went down the hall, the nurse came towards them, leading along a hunched-over boy who was crying and holding his hands tight to his belly. The light through the bright doors behind them made everyone look like they were tangled in their own silhouettes. It was the skinny Jeffers boy, the one that grabbed Rona on the way to school. There was blood on his hands, and little drops of blood on the linoleum as they came closer to Wyatt's room.

Inside, Wyatt had a hold of both sides of Eunice Murch's desk. Eunice stood between Wyatt and the class, the kids were pressed against the far wall, a row of desks turned upside down, a bookshelf emptied; how's that for a dark streak, Rona thought. There were a couple other teachers in the room, too, and even the janitor, holding his broom out defensively. He was trying to talk Wyatt into letting go of the desk. Rona stepped towards Wyatt and stopped, not having any idea what they expected her to do. It wasn't like he was going to listen to anything she said. Roger Harrocks leaned down and whispered in her ear, "Can you get him to calm down?"

Rona looked at the man as if he'd just asked her to levitate across the room. She shook her head. Mr. Edson said, "Son, you can come with me or I can drag you out."

Wyatt flung his head from side to side like there was a bee in his ear, his mouth clenched, an animal noise straining out of his throat. Mr. Edson took two quick steps, put his arm around Wyatt's waist, and tugged. Wyatt didn't let go, and the teacher was caught off balance. He regained his footing and pulled harder. The desk screeched against the linoleum tiles. It was halfway across the room before Wyatt couldn't hold on anymore, and then he came loose, wailing as if his fingers had been torn off. Mr. Edson carried him, thrashing and struggling, down the hall, Roger Harrocks bumbled after him, saying, "Take him to the office, Rudy! Take him to the office!"

So that was how Rona learned Mr. Edson's first name.

The other kids stayed away from Rona, whispering to each other whenever she went past. Eunice Murch had probably told them all her theories about the Tate family, and now the whole school was waiting for Rona to go berserk, too. She had no luck finding out what set Wyatt off; all she knew was the other kids started chanting, Why, it's Wyatt. . . . Why, it's Wyatt in that evil sing-song melody the children of cavemen probably used on each other, and that Wyatt had responded by diving out of his desk and sinking his teeth into the Jeffers boy. Wyatt ended up suspended for a week and grounded indefinitely, though the grounding didn't really mean much since Agnes was always at work and nothing seemed capable of yanking David's attentions away from jigsaw puzzles and the travails of the sheep and Stella and his late night work on The Dangers of Understanding Evil. Sometimes in the afternoon, he would go out job hunting, or so he said. He would get in the pickup and drive off, and watching him go Rona would think about Frank's Roadside Bar, Draft Beer On Tap, and the night of the train going past the bumper.

The suspension made Wyatt a hero to the cousins. Head had finally made them go to school, and the fact that Wyatt was home alone all day seemed to make him glow in their eyes, as if his ability to escape was something like magic. In turn, each of the cousins, except for Irene, took on the role of classroom terror, tormenting their classmates whenever they could. Dewey tried to re-enact Wyatt's tantrum but tripped over an overturned desk and had to get four stitches in his lip for his trouble.

Rona was getting along better with Rudy (short for Rudolph) Edson, now that she knew his first name. She had two of her cousins in class, Irene and Hack, and one afternoon on their way home Hack strutted over to Rona, smirking like he'd just finished eating her lunch, and said, "Wyatt said to ask you how to baptize a chicken."

"I'll baptize you next," Rona said, and Hack just stood there with what was supposed to be a grin on his face.

"Why would anyone baptize a chicken anyway? I got to know why you'd do something dumb as that." Rona started to walk away and Hack said, "You got to do my math homework for me."

"I got to?" Rona said. "Maybe I should do your English homework, too."

"Wyatt said you got to or else he'll tell Uncle Dave what you did to his arm."

Rona turned and said, "What about his arm?"

Hack gave her the grin again. His teeth looked like someone had twisted them around with a pair of pliers.

"What about his arm?" Rona asked again, and when Hack's face faltered just a little, she figured Wyatt hadn't told him anything, and when Irene came over to see what was happening, he retreated.

Irene liked walking home with Rona; Rona wasn't sure she felt the same, because Irene seemed like a bright, talented girl, and Rona didn't like anyone with real talent. She couldn't stand being jealous, but she also couldn't stand hearing other people praised and Rudy always complimented her by saying what a fine addition she was to the class and Betsy Menke, the Art teacher, put Irene's collage project on the Art room's bulletin board, and even Rona's room at the old house seemed better since Irene moved into it. Judging from the kind of things she said on the phone, Agnes seemed to believe Head's family would treat the house the way locusts treat crops. Our investment, Agnes called it. How would they ever rent it again, she asked, as if of the air, not that they were really renting it now, since it wasn't like Head had given them a dollar or even paid the utilities.

Even Rona wanted to see the house collapse, the ground open up, a volcano erupt. But it was impossible not to notice the way the place looked healthier, while Merrilee's house looked worse, the grass long because David refused to believe the sheep wouldn't eventually start to eat it, and all the flowered wallpaper stripped out of the upstairs rooms but not yet, and possibly never, replaced. If only Head would leave, gather the cousins and drive in his pickup back to West by God, which is what he always called West Virginia, even if he meant it sarcastically.

"You all got everything up here," he said one night by the fire, drunk with David, Agnes sitting nearby, so still that not even the light from the flames could make it look like she was moving. "You got it all, but it still ain't West by God."

"This place looks more like West by God everyday," Agnes said, directing her words at Head but then turning to David, and in her face expression Rona could see all the things she longed to have done.

Rona suspected that most of the changes to the old house had been accomplished by Irene, who was so nice that Rona felt she couldn't be trusted. On the way home, though, Rona liked to stay for awhile on the front porch. For one thing, the cousins usually scurried ahead to Merrilee's, where they could raid Agnes' refrigerator. For another, that was the time of day when Burke Van Meter delivered the mail.

"Why, Rona," Burke said, "what are you doing back here?"

"Just visiting, Mr. Van Meter," Rona said, tempted to reveal that she knew his first name just to impress Irene, who sat beside Rona on the bottom step, fluttering her eyes at Burke and blushing. Burke gave her the smile. He said, "I don't believe we've been introduced."

Reluctantly, Rona made the introductions. In a way that would let Burke know exactly what she meant, she said, "Her father rents the house from us." Rona expected more of a reaction, but Burke only nodded and handed Irene a packet of junk mail and walked back down the walk.

"Have a nice day," he said, his voice smooth and low, "ladies."

Irene sighed and watched him walk, her eyelids still fluttering and Rona immediately envied the thickness of her lashes and even the color of her eyes. Irene was always, always sweet and the only time Rona liked her was when she would ask questions about Merrilee. Casually, Rona would mention some small bit of magic she had seen Merrilee perform—the string owl, or how she could make the sugar double itself in the glass bowl she kept on the counter, though Rona never mentioned the hooly-hoo or Merrilee's tooth—and Irene never acted like she was crazy, or that she had only imagined seeing such things. They traded stories about the family history, and that was how Rona learned that only two of the kids who came to Ohio with Head were really his: Irene and the youngest, Aubrey. All the rest belonged to Kitty. Rona asked if anyone in West Virginia ever said anything about Agnes or David.

"Only that your father went crazy while he was in California and your mother hates everyone and Wyatt almost died. Nothing about you, though," Irene said, brightly, as if this were a good thing.

Irene was also the kind of girl smart enough to listen when she wasn't supposed to be listening. But she did some silly things, too; she made her own posters of rock stars, drawing their pictures out of magazines and then painting them with watercolors and hanging them on the walls of Rona's old room, sometimes writing out song lyrics on the paintings with a calligraphy pen she showed to Rona as if it were a family heirloom. She even made up her own lyrics and put those on the paintings.

"Just imaginary verses," Irene said, shyly.

"Sing one," Rona said, but Irene just shook her head and looked down at one of the paintings that wasn't finished yet. It sat on a small brown desk that used to be Rona's, and she covered the painting with a notebook. There were also pictures of dogs and angels and dragons.

The dog pictures were really good, and when Rona said so, Irene said thanks, but so quietly Rona wasn't sure she'd said anything at all.

"Do you draw?" Irene asked, after a long moment.

"Sure," Rona said, but she lied. She thought drawing was kind of stupid, at least her own drawings, and that people who drew were wasting a lot of their time. Wyatt had liked to draw. He had drawn really good dragons and monsters and battle scenes.

Hanging above the desk, there was a picture of a dog smiling out at nothing, with little lines to show its tail wagging. What a stupid picture, Rona thought, angry at it for no good reason, and also mad at herself for being angry, and for not being able to draw.

Head's big voice called Irene out of the room. While she was gone, Rona looked closer at the picture of the dog. There was a house in the background that looked a little bit like Merrilee's house. Carefully, with just the tip of her finger, Rona reached under the edge of the paper and lifted. She heard it rip around the tack, and then she did the same thing on the other side, and then she popped to her feet to go home. She could hear the poster, flapping in the breeze against the wall as she left.

The leaves were changing colors and some of them had even started to fall, so Rona didn't see much of Wyatt during the day. He was too busy making money by raking leaves with the cousins, though Wyatt did very little raking himself. Just like he had with Rona's Barbies, Wyatt acted as an agent. He would pull his knit hat down low and go from door to door, looking for customers, bargaining and bill collecting. Then, as soon as it was dark enough, he and the cousins would sneak back out and kick the leaves out of their piles along the curbs.

When they weren't raking, the cousins were busy learning how to play Death Squad. Wyatt didn't want to play anymore, but he seemed to like being the official judge for all the battles. The rules became increasingly complex, and only Wyatt knew for sure what was right and what was wrong, though to Rona it seemed the rules of the game changed with Wyatt's moods. She tried to point this out one day as she watched the boys argue over what should happen next, but they all turned to stare at her with such a calm dislike that she stopped breathing for just a second and then Wyatt snarled at her to go the hell away. Back in school, Wyatt was as unmanageable as ever, though he somehow kept himself from getting suspended again. Mrs. Murch walled off a section of the room with some big cabinets, hoping to keep Wyatt separated from the other kids, but she made the mistake of turning the doors and drawers towards Wyatt and he spent the whole day hurling things over the top of the cabinets.

"Your stupid brother hit my sister in the head with a book," one of the boys in Rona's class said. "I'm going to kick his ass."

"Sounds good," Rona said. Even though Wyatt was only in the fifth grade and the boy outweighed him by twenty pounds, it was Wyatt who won the fight. The boy came back to Rona's class a week later, both his eyes still black.

At night, after the cousins went home, Wyatt was too tired to pick on Rona, as though exhausted from being so problematic all the time. That's what David called him; problematic, as if by labeling him this way he had solved the whole problem and could then go about starting whatever project he was going to leave unfinished next; he had torn the plaster out of the downstairs bathroom, but now that the demolition was done he'd lost interest. As for Agnes, her time was almost completely occupied with the town's annual Apple Festival, which was sponsored by the nursing home where she worked. She was on the booth selection committee. The chore lists stuck to the refrigerator grew longer and longer, and always with more to do on Rona's side than Wyatt's.

Wyatt used his extra time to dominate the television. He wouldn't stop watching the religious channels no matter how much Rona begged for just five minutes of music videos. Disgusted, she spent most of her time in her room, writing diary entries about bald-headed little boys who got all the fire and brimstone they could stand.

Everyday, Rona went out to wait for the mail. Burke always stopped to talk for a minute or two, and she imagined he was flirting with her, even though he only ever told her about things that happened on his route. "I had a dog chase me this morning. Can you believe that? Like in a cartoon." The smile. Or he might say, "That lady on Fairwood opened up her door and was stark naked. Again. I'm thinking she's doing it on purpose." Or, "That pervert on Jamestown? Got more things in brown wrappers today. How about that?" The smile, the smile, the smile. "Say, you've got a letter here."

"I do?"

"Yes ma'am." He held up the envelope and looked at the return address.

"Maybe it's from my boyfriend." Rona said, though she already knew where the letter came from; she had mailed it to herself, stealing a stamp from her mother's desk. She'd written herself a very romantic letter, with some racy parts and everything, and she decorated the outside of the envelope just like she figured a real boyfriend would do, although she wasn't sure whether or not to put little hearts over all the i's. In the end, she did, and she colored them red with a marker, because she thought maybe that was what Irene would do, and it felt a little bit like putting a spell on the letter, like one of the hexes Merrilee talked about, the ones that used to hang under the eaves of the house.

Burke looked at the letter for a moment, then handed it over. He didn't have his sunglasses on, and there was a gleam in his eye that Rona knew was probably jealousy.

"It's from Sebastian," she said, so pleased with herself that for a moment she'd forgotten what name she'd put on the envelope. On the inside, of course, she'd signed the letter, Your Darling Burke.

"Rona, don't you go running off on me, now," he said. "Make sure this guy makes you an honorable woman." Rona blushed as she went back to the house, and she tried to put a little sway in her hips, but she felt so awkward doing it that she was afraid to look over her shoulder as she heard the mail truck pulling away.

In the house, Rona folded the letter and put it in her pocket. Later, she would slip it into the shoe box she kept tucked under her bed, but for now there were so many cousins in the house she didn't want to risk one of them following her up to her room. They were always milling around, the way mice run along the corners of the room, and they ate as much of the food in the house as they could safely get away with. Rona had a suspicion that Wyatt was leading them up to her room because sometimes she found her things in different places. When she told Agnes, Wyatt denied everything, though even Agnes looked like she had her doubts.

After Wyatt finished lining up the next day's jobs for the cousins, he would sit on the back porch, watching the dog and the sheep stare at each other. Sometimes when the sheep turned its back, Stella would sneak up and nip at its back legs, then Wyatt would grin just a little bit, as if he had predicted the exact moment such a thing would happen, as if he had made it happen himself and was waiting to make it happen again.

It wasn't until they threatened to expel Wyatt from school that he finally began to settle down. At lunch, a substitute teacher had made some kind of comment about Wyatt's hair, something well meant which came out wrong and all the kids started to laugh. Wyatt climbed onto the table and kicking the lunch trays around, and the cousins jumped onto their tables, too, and that afternoon Roger Harrocks came to the house, bringing with him a list of new classes Wyatt would have to take and special assignments to keep him busy. He would have to bring home a behavior report every week and have it signed. There were consequences, he said. There were only so many chances.

Everyone except for Rona sat at the dining room table, talking in calm, measured tones. Rona went to the basement and listened through the heating vent that ran directly into the room. Their voices had a flat, metallic tone, as if they all belonged to robots. They talked about discipline and how Wyatt should go talk to a doctor and that was the only time anyone started to raise their voice. David said there weren't going to be any more doctors for Wyatt, and if that was what they wanted they might as well go ahead and expel him.

"Maybe I can do better," Wyatt said. He said it so quietly that Rona was amazed she could hear him, but at the same time it sounded as though Wyatt's voice was in her head, that his words had been born in her thoughts. For a moment, she could see through Wyatt's eyes; the bare walls of the dining room, Agnes and David, all sadness but also a kind of relief, and Rona knew that they weren't seeing the real Wyatt. They were seeing Wyatt before he was sick, and Roger Harrocks was seeing him, too, also relieved, as if someone had blown across his life and dusted it off. Rona could feel, then, what Wyatt was feeling; his own relief, entirely different than anyone else's at the table. He was glad because he knew he had fooled them. They believed him, and they would go on believing him. He didn't even have to pretend, really, that he was trying harder. They believed for no other reason than that's what they wanted to do.

In closing, Roger Harrocks went on to say all the things a principal was supposed to say; how they had to approach this like a team and how none of them could afford to have any more violence in the school. While Agnes and David walked him out to his car, Rona came into the dining room and said, "Some bad kid you turned out to be."

"Like I care about school," he said. "I just don't want to get stuck here all day."

For the rest of the night, Rona felt like a balloon someone had inflated then let go. In bed, she tried to dream about Merrilee's tooth but instead lay awake, thinking about what Merrilee had said when she found out Wyatt was sick. "Momma had the touch," she said. "If she were alive, she'd lay a hand on him. Then he'd be better."

She told this to Rona one of those nights when Wyatt was in the hospital, Agnes and David sleeping on the vinyl furniture in one of the parents' waiting rooms, and Rona in Merrilee's big, soft bed. Merrilee stroked Rona's hair, as if her fingers could make it softer, could make it long and flowing like the manes of women in television commercials. Merrilee could braid one-handed; Rona could feel the braids fall against her cheek, and then one soft finger sliding through, undoing the weave.

"That boy needs a different kind of love," Merrilee said. "But who's going to give it to him?" Her eyes were black and wet as she looked at Rona, like she could see the answer right in front of her, hovering between them. The wind against the window made that sound; hooly-hoo, hooly-hoo.

There was no dream of the black tooth, but just before dawn a familiar weight settled on one side of Rona's bed, and then rose and was gone. Rona opened her eyes, the smell of Merrilee's liniment everywhere in the room.

Eunice Murch was under strict orders to keep the kids from teasing Wyatt. Everyone was afraid of him anyway, and he made sure things stayed that way by substituting strangeness for violence. He rocked back and forth and chewed on his fingers and scratched at his head like he couldn't stand his own skin. He yelled things out for no reason. If the whole class laughed, he laughed louder. He refused to answer questions. If there was a fight, Wyatt made sure it happened at recess, in the little strip of trees beside the jungle gym, where none of the teachers could see from their windows. No one wanted to fight him anyway.

Except for the Jeffers boys, who came down to the farmhouse one Friday after school and lurked around the end of the gravel drive, waiting for Wyatt to show. There was still a line of little half-moon scabs on the skinny one's hand. Wyatt and Rona and the cousins watched from the porch as the Jeffers puffed themselves up like a couple of overblown actors in an action movie. The fat Jeffers was the meaner of the two, and he stood staring up at the porch. He started calling up for Wyatt to come down.

Rona told him not to go, but Wyatt jumped down the porch steps and walked down the driveway. He picked up a couple of rocks along the way, and the cousins followed him, but at a neutral distance. Rona went too, still trying to talk him out of it, until finally he told her to shut up. As they got closer, Rona watched the Jeffers, circling around each other, their heads tilted back like they were sniffing for weakness.

"Look," the skinny one said, "he brought his sister to protect him."

"Watch out she doesn't hit you with her tits," the fat one said, and never saw the flat rock spinning towards him, whistling through the air, smashing him between the eyes. The skinny one watched his brother fall to his knees and might have stood there staring forever if Wyatt hadn't slammed into him, climbing up the side of his body like he was scaling a fence. He held the other rock in his hand, and the blows he landed had a heavy, wet sound to them. The cousins descended on the fat one, kicking him and throwing punches down from over top their heads. Rona turned to run back to the house, but David was already on the way, and as he got closer the cousins scattered, the Jeffers scrambling back home, stumbling over each other. Only Wyatt stood there, leaning forward, panting.

IV.

"One time, I almost pushed that mean old bastard out the hayloft. I came that close," Head said, pressing his thumb and index finger together, "to doing it. The winch was bound up and he had his back to me, cursing the whole time how I screwed up. Nobody would've thought twice. Just like that. That close."

Head thought Wyatt did the right thing when he went after the Jeffers boys, and even David got this excited light in his eyes whenever he talked about the fight. After all, the Jeffers were bullies, weren't they? Head and David re-lived the whole scene every night by the fire for a week, and they talked in drunken, song-like tones about the bullies of their pasts. The stories all followed the same pattern. There was this kid in the fifth grade, David would say, and we fought at lunch, and there was the time Tate told me I couldn't go to California because he needed me here. I said, For what?

There was the Barrett boy at the farm next door, Head would say, and we fought in the barn, and that time the old man came after me with the belt and he was so drunk I knocked him on his ass and the next morning he acted like nothing happened.

There was that woman when I adjuncted in California that tried to get me fired. Never hit her, but I wanted to.

Well, it's a good thing you quit first.

And the time Tate was so mad about the way I mowed the lawn, he came home and decked me, right in the front yard.

I fought Junior Phipps on the bus. And there was that time in the hay loft.

"That close," Head said again, mostly to himself. He stared at his finger and thumb like he could hold the memory there and mash it.

"Do either of you two realize," Agnes said, a little on the drunk side herself, "what it means to hit someone with a rock? What kind of damage that could do?"

Once David was truly drunk, he admitted how he really felt; he was glad Wyatt could take care of himself, because it looked like there was nothing but trouble ahead of him, and probably worse all the time. "He's just like Daddy," David would say, and Head wouldn't say anything, not yes or no, just sitting there, running his knife back and forth across the sharpening stone.

As punishment, Wyatt didn't get to go to the Apple Festival, which made Rona wish she'd thrown some punches herself. Agnes wouldn't stop talking about the booths that were going to be there ("Some of which I had to fight for," she said, pride illuminating her voice. "Fight for, Rona!"), and also about the parade. The cousins were as wound-up as Rona had ever seen them because they had never been to a parade before. From the way they acted, Rona thought that maybe they had never even seen one on TV.

The festival was the same as always; between the smell of boiling grease and the crowds half-stepping along the jammed sidewalks of the town square, Rona was sure she would have to scream or pass out to stay sane. There was a band, and all the musicians wore cowboy hats and yodeled into some squealing microphones that balled her ears up like little fists. By the water fountain, someone propped a big plywood apple with a green worm sticking out of it, and Agnes made Rona stand behind the apple so a photographer could take a picture that made it look like her head was on the worm's body and even though she refused to smile, Agnes showed the Polaroid to every half-acquaintance that walked by, and she knew almost the whole town. During the parade, Agnes went to pass out flyers beside the Festival organizer's booth. Rona didn't know what was more embarrassing; her mother standing in the booth like someone running for mayor, or the cousins howling and squealing and begging Head for more to eat.

David had stayed up all night drinking with Head by a fire in the backyard, spending most of the time trying to explain the dangers of understanding evil.

"The problem is, they keep changing what's evil," he said, just like he had told Rona in the truck at McDonalds, his voice the same, the way he moved his hands, as if the whole conversation had been rehearsed. Rona felt like a guinea pig, like someone her father practiced his speeches on until it was time to talk to somebody more important.

"C'mon," Head said. He was sharpening his knife.

"I'm serious. The definitions keep moving around."

"Listen," Head said. "You know real evil, don't you? Don't you know what real evil is?" The two men flicked their eyes at each other across the fire. "Evil never changes. The definition or whatever might change, but wrong is always wrong."

There was a quiet, then, only the sound of the wood burning. Head said, "It was wrong, how the old man was. Whatever else you want to call it."

David eased back in his chair, holding his beer on his chest. It looked like a stake driven there. "You know what your problem is," he said. "That accent. That's why people up here hate southerners. We just can't believe that someone who sounds like that might actually be intelligent."

"Y'all's been brainwurshed by them there movin' pictures," Head said, thickening his voice with the same care that Merrilee had used when she stood at her stove. Head went back to his knife. He dragged it ten times across the stone in one direction, then changed directions, then repeated the same process but going one less time after each group. Nine times, eight times; when he got to one, he started over again at ten.

Head and David ended up so drunk that no one remembered to tell Rona to go to bed. She sat and listened as David swore up and down that he could get the farm working again, and he was going to find a way to buy back all the land his father pissed away, and then he was going to tear all the houses down and be a farmer; there was some honor in that at least. He only wished he'd understood that when he was younger instead of running away, and Head said, "It's not an easy life, farming. There's nothing you control. It's all weather this and weather that. Although some crops always pay off, if you didn't care about the law."

"Then I'll be a sheep herder." David stood up on his lawn chair.

Teetering back and forth, he said, "Or an arsonist. I'll just burn all those goddamn houses down." He cupped his hands around his mouth and yelled towards the subdivision, "Get off my land!"

This last bit came out half-laugh and half-howl. The lawn chair gave out and he landed on the ground in a heap. He was deadly still for a moment, and then he started to snore. Head stood over him, looking down, his overalls stretched tight as a sausage that was about to burst out of its casing. Rona couldn't figure out the expression on his face; she thought at first that maybe he was going to drag her father over onto the fire and watch him burn, but there was something tender there, too. Head leaned down, hoisted her father's body over his shoulder like a sack of potatoes, and carried him up to the porch, flopping him into the bench swing, then he gave it a little push, the way he'd start a baby's cradle, and he walked back to the fire.

He poured some more of the moonshine into his glass and looked at Rona. "What you think? You want some of this?"

Rona considered for a moment; she'd sneaked beers before, and one time she stole an almost empty bottle of Jim Beam from the cupboard where her parents kept the liquor, but this seemed different. She reached out and took the glass. She held it under her nose and made the mistake of inhaling; it felt like someone had flicked a lighter inside her nostrils. Holding her breath, she took a big swallow.

It's possible that something could taste worse, but Rona didn't want to know what it was. She tried to keep her face straight. Head watched her and started to laugh and then she couldn't hold out anymore. She stood up and coughed and spat and handed the glass back at Head.

"You know, I knew your grandmother pretty well," he said, splashing what was left in the glass into the fire. There was a whoosh and a half dozen little flames popped up like blue tongues flicking out of the logs. He filled the glass again. "She was only a few years older than me. She was sixteen when she married Daddy."

Rona was surprised to hear herself say, "The mean old bastard?"

Head shook his head, just a little bit. For just a moment he looked like David when he was working on the jigsaw puzzle.

"Merrilee was pretty close to being my mother. Not that she tried to be. I think, anyway, she wanted us to be friends." His voice was slurred, but his hand was steady as he raised the glass. "She was quiet, like you. Wanted everybody to think there wasn't a thought in her head. But the whole time, you're both working things. Merrilee kept everything right here," he said, and tapped his forehead so loudly that Rona could hear it over the fire. He pointed at her. "I bet you think your head's almost full."

And that was when Rona had stomped back to the house. David was still drunk the next morning and had to stop twice at the Apple Festival to throw up into the garbage cans beside the sidewalk. Rona kept on walking, trying to leave behind the terrible embarrassment of the sound. To make things worse, Irene stayed right beside her the whole time, all wide-eyed like she was taking everything in so she could write more imaginary lyrics. Rona pictured her trying to come up with rhymes for lemonade, or apple fritters, or chicken divine.

At noon, it was time for the parade (rhymes with charade, Rona thought), so David led the squabbling, ecstatic pack of cousins down to the street that ran right through the middle of the downtown. Head stayed over by the courthouse in the square, talking to some long-haired, rough looking guys in blue jean jackets, so Irene was in charge of the cousins. They mostly listened to whatever she said, though some-times Hack would make her repeat herself just because he thought it was funny. He tried to act like he didn't care about the parade, but Rona could tell he was excited because he kept playing the drums on his thighs in time with the still distant sound of the high school band. The cousins crowded in front of some people and sat with their feet right in the gutter. David, who had carried the remains of his twisted-up lawn chair with him, tried to unfold the chair. After he bent it back into a useable shape, he sat down. Despite the drums coming closer, his head began to loll from side to side, and in a moment he was, snoring, his face tucked into his shoulder.

Rona thought she would die before the parade ended. She felt like it was her family on display, the whole town watching them march past. Every time a fire truck or an ambulance or a police cruiser went by, a new wave of frenzy swept over the cousins, and they howled back at the sirens and jumped up and down as if the sound lifted them off the ground. They fought and clawed at each other for the cheap candy the firemen tossed towards the curb, and it wasn't long before two of them had bloody noses and one a split lip and the littlest one was crying be-cause no one would let him have any candy. Even Irene had a scrape on her elbow; any semblance of the brief control she had maintained over her siblings was gone, and all she had left to do was shriek at them in a high, fierce voice that cut through the sirens and made the drummers in the band turn their heads.

Eventually, Irene abandoned even that pretense and while the boys rolled and sprawled in the gutters, she sat down with her chin resting on her hands and said to Rona, "This is the most beautiful thing I've ever seen." She stared at the baton twirlers as if they had walked right out of one of her rock star paintings, the drum major strutting like some kind of Russian god in his high, furry hat, beads of sweat running down the angles of his face. Even the plastic flowers stapled to the sides of the parade's cheap floats seemed worthy of praise. Irene stood up and saluted the ancient soldiers in their uniforms and said, "There's more people here than the whole county where I grew up."

Rona barely heard her. She was looking down the road at the end of the parade. Very slowly, as if proving that it could creep along slower than all the slow, creeping things that preceded it, a lone hearse came down the road. It looked like the one black beetle in a long line of lady bugs.

All the noise and celebration turned to silence as both sides of the street stopped to watch the hearse. The side windows were tinted so dark Rona couldn't see into the back, but she could see the driver. He had on his black hat and gloves, but she still recognized him as the same man she had seen at Merrilee's funeral. He had come all the way down the street with both hands on the wheel, looking dead ahead, but as he came up to where Rona stood watching, he tilted his head towards her and gave a little wave. He grinned and there was a small, square shadow in his smile, and Rona had a sudden image of Merrilee, riding around in the back of the hearse, still in her coffin, her dry pink tongue probing the spot where her tooth had been.

Rona took a step towards the hearse, wobbling as she did, but it was already past her, and the crowd came into the street behind it. The cousins stopped mauling each other long enough to help the littlest one, whose arm was stuck in a sewer grate. Irene sighed, still sitting on the curb, and everyone walked around in the middle of the road like they were trying to wake from a long, unending dream.

The day after the Apple Festival ended and all the carnies hooked up their run-down trailers, Wyatt woke up and said he didn't feel well. After breakfast, he threw up and Agnes and David practically carried him to the emergency room. They came home a few hours later; Rona had never seen people so happy about a case of the food poisoning, even Wyatt, a relaxed grin still showing through his generally green complexion. By late afternoon, he was back to his old self, silent and sullen on the couch because Agnes wouldn't let him watch TV. Since Roger Harrocks' visit to the house, Agnes had been watching Wyatt more closely; she wanted to take him to a new doctor for some other kind of tests, something to help settle him down. David hated the whole idea, of course, and he argued that Wyatt's grades were still good, in spite of everything. Rona listened from the top of the stairs as they sat in the living room late at night.

"No boy his age is that dark all the time," Agnes said.

"He's not that way when he's around his cousins."

"He just sits and stares. Or if he's not staring at something, he's attacking people."

"He's been through a lot. And what he stares at is the television. That's how it works, you know." He was teasing her. "You have to stare at it or it's not the same."

"If he needs help, and we don't get it for him, then what?"

"I've had that kind of help. It isn't help at all."

In all these conversations, Rona never once heard her parents use her name. There was never a What about Rona? How's Rona holding up? Once, her father called her Ronar. She was in the basement looking through the boxes when David banged through the back door into the kitchen and said, "Where's Ronar? Is Ronar listening?" He said something to Agnes which was too low to hear and they both laughed.

But that was the way Rona wanted it, or at least she thought that was probably the way she wanted it. One day, she came back in from recess to get her coat and with the room all to herself, she took the opportunity to look in Rudy Edson's file cabinet, finding her own file. All of her grades were listed and that was it, except for the space at the bottom of the page where the teacher could write comments about the students. By Rona's name, Rudolph Edson had written, "A quiet child of average abilities."

Is that me? Rona wondered. The room shrank a little, and the air buzzed at her ears like an insect. She could hear the class coming down the hall, and shoved the file back in the drawer and hurried over to her desk, and when Rudy came in, he looked at her as if he knew exactly what she'd been doing.

Someday, they would all catch on to her, Agnes and David and Rudy and Burke, and maybe they would try to corner her like Head that night by the fire. They would accuse her of things. But what had she done? Wasn't she only doing the kinds of things everyone does?

As it was, Rona tried to use her time alone to her best advantage. She found another letter from Merrilee, but it was too short to make much sense.

Dearest Momma,

I already sent you all one letter and it's nice and normal but I just wanted to write this down. I didn't get married just because everyone said I had to, though I know in the eyes of some people who think they know everything that's what we had to do. I know Pop felt that way, and maybe even you did too, and maybe it was wrong, but there is a kind of love in him, you have to believe that. Here when I started this I thought I could explain how he makes me feel, but I'm too stupid to make any sense. I just keep

. . . and that's how the note ended. Rona would never have guessed that Merrilee would call herself stupid. She had ideas about everything except how to take care of herself and how to cure Wyatt, once the leukemia started. Even if she didn't have her momma's touch, she should have been able to come up with something else. Or a cure for diabetes. Rona even broke down and asked Agnes.

"Those old women," Agnes said, washing dishes at the sink with her back to Rona, "killed more people than they ever cured."

"That's not true. They had mountain magic."

"They had mushrooms and moonshine and old wives' tales. They did awful things just because they were too ignorant to know better. Wyatt's fine where he is." Agnes scrubbed the dishes harder, like there were things stuck on them that might never come off. Finally, Rona asked Merrilee, more than anything to prove her mother wrong. Merrilee only smiled, sadly, her tooth like a dark little door opening to nowhere. "It's only magic, sweetheart. It can only do so much."

And that had proved true later, hadn't it? When Merrilee was sick with her own disease, the bottom of her leg gone and her thigh turning green. She wouldn't let Rona look, but Rona knew anyway because she had to know everything, and she climbed into the hospital bed that filled up the living room. Merrilee put a heavy arm around her shoulders and the two of them watched this old guy singing on the television. Merrilee was humming along, brushing Rona's cheek, her fingers warm like a fever, and Rona felt the weight of her own body sinking down as she fell asleep.

Rona kept mailing herself letters, too, though the style of the contents began to change. More and more, she wrote directly to Burke, passionately, as if she could put an aura around the words which would be irresistible to him, something he could sense through the envelope and have to open, even if it cost him his job. She wrote about sex as much as she could, wanting it to be like her romance novels, at first, but then it seemed too flowery and vague. Trying a few dirty words, she liked how they looked on the page, but she liked them cautiously. She even showed one of the letters to Irene, one that wasn't too dirty, though she left the Dear Burke off the top.

"You've got the kissing all wrong," Irene said. "It's not like that. The tongues shouldn't jab each other."

"Well, I didn't mean jabbing, really."

"It's really soft, kissing someone. Kind of weird, but you get used to it. Then it feels good."

Rona blushed. For the first time, the whole idea shifted inside her head; what it would be like to kiss somebody? The idea began to lose its abstractness as she pictured Irene and whoever putting their lips together, moving their tongues back and forth, touching each other. Tasting each other. What does another person taste like?

Now all that flowery vagueness seemed like just the kind of thing some little kid would make up. A strange feeling went up and down Rona's spine, and then she had a sudden ache for the truth and she was sure she would die if she didn't find out soon.

The next day Rona went out to meet Burke at the mailbox. Stella waited with her, having lost all interest in the sheep, barking half-heartedly at the mail truck, as if under some obligation to act like a dog for once. In his hands, Burke had the letter Rona wrote the day before.

"That's one prolific boyfriend you got," he said. "Must be true love." He looked over his sunglasses at the dog. Stella turned around in a circle and laid down with her back to the road. "Say, what's that dog's name?"

"Stella. You know, like the Brando movie."

"Well, did you know Stella's going to have puppies?"

Burke drove off and Rona went directly to David. "The mailman says Stella's going to have puppies."

"That mailman ought to stick to delivering letters," David said. He walked around in the shed that was attached to the back of the house for awhile, muttering, and he mumbled some very unflattering things about Burke and the postal service and how neither of them knew their asses from a hole in the ground. By that evening though, he was standing with his hands on his hips, looking down at Stella, who was wagging her tail as if that should explain everything. A little while later, Head came heaving himself up the drive, and knelt down by Stella, feeling her sides with his big, stiff fingers.

The two brothers stood, taking turns shaking their heads and nodding their heads and shrugging their shoulders, then David walked slowly towards the house to tell Agnes that Stella would have to sleep in the house for awhile.

The next day when Rona went out to tell Burke he was right, Wyatt was standing by the mail truck. Hack was there, too, and when Burke saw Rona coming he said, "All right then, boys," and the two of them ran off. She saw that Wyatt had something brown rolled up under his arm.

"So, I was right about the puppies," Burke said. The smile, but a different version of it, still charming, but knowingly so. It seemed unnatural. Rona wasn't sure what it was, but the idea that Wyatt had told Burke the news first made her furious.

"My father said you don't know your ass from a hole in the ground," she said, as sweetly as such a thing could be said. Burke leaned away from her, the smile gone, like a light going off. "He said you should stick to delivering the mail."

"Well," he said, "you can tell your father that's just what I'm going to do." He winked at her and drove off.

It took almost a week to find out that Burke had given Wyatt and Hack a *Playboy*. In all that time, Burke never stopped once to talk to her, even though she waited for him on the porch everyday. The mail truck did little more than slow to a roll as he came to the mailbox; he tossed in the delivery with a well-trained flick of the wrist, gave Rona a quick little wave, and then he was off to the next house. Somehow that wave was the worst part, the way it meant he saw her. She wrote about this in the letters, which had taken on a sad tone she could not remedy, no matter what she put in them.

"There are some things for sadness," Merrilee had told her, or at least Rona believed Merrilee had told her such a thing. It was hard to tell, because sometimes her grandmother's voice sounded fresh in her head, as though she were right beside her, whispering. "But none of them really work. Sometimes the cure is worse than the thing itself. No one ever wants to believe that's true, but it is."

Rona wouldn't have discovered Wyatt and Hack's secret at all, if she hadn't been down in the basement going through the old room with the shelves of things Merrilee had canned. She wasn't sure what she was looking for, but sometimes she found the best things that way. Most of the jars had little brown labels on them, carrots or peas, tomatoes or green beans, even squash. In the very back, some of the glass jars were too murky to see into, and some kind of brown gunk leaked out around the edges of the lids. In even the best looking jars, the contents looked brown and flavorless, as if waiting patiently to come out and bore some poor person's taste buds to death.

What did you expect, Rona thought. Eye of newt? Bat wings?

It was starting to seem like Agnes was right about mountain women.

She heard someone at the top of the stairs and shut off the light, pressing herself against the shelves so she couldn't be seen. Wyatt and Hack came down and turned the corner. They went into the room with the spring in it and closed the door. Listening outside, Rona heard Hack say, "Turn to the black-haired one."

"One at a time."

"Turn to the black-haired one!"

There was a rustling of pages. If she closed one eye, Rona could see them through a crack in the door. Wyatt was holding a magazine in one hand and Hack stood a little too closely beside him. They turned the pages with a studious slowness, tilting their heads occasionally as if someone in the magazine spoke to them.

"God," Hack said, then continued, "damn. God damn." He reached down and grabbed himself through his jeans.

Wyatt was turning another page as Rona stepped into the room. Neither boy noticed her at first. She cleared her throat. Wyatt whipped the magazine around behind his back and they both turned a bright red. Hack positioned himself behind Wyatt.

"What's that?"

"Nothing of yours," Wyatt said.

"Let me see." Both boys shook their heads. It had been a long time since Rona felt the power of being the oldest person in the room. "Then I'll go tell Mom."

Slowly, Wyatt brought the magazine from behind his back and handed it to her. Hack gave him a disgusted look and shook his head, and Rona glanced knowingly at the front of his pants, which only made him blush even more.

The women in the magazine stared back at Rona like people who knew more than she could ever know. Their lips were slightly open, their eyes half-closed. She saw the curves of their bodies, and their hands seemed to be moving, and their breasts were all so beautiful, Rona could feel her own dying of embarrassment, getting smaller as the naked women swelled dangerously. She started to throw the magazine into the water, but the look on Wyatt's face stopped her; instead, she held it over the spring, trying to think of something mean enough to say. Wyatt watched her, steadily, almost daring her. Dropping the magazine on the floor, she kicking it towards them and turned to leave. Hack said, "You should show us yours."

Rona turned and looked at him. Wyatt was looking at him, too, and for a moment his whole body took on that same coldness he always wore just before he fought. He picked up the magazine and carefully slid it back into the brown wrapper, as if the covering were the most important part. He turned back towards Rona and said, "Yeah, why don't you show us?"

Rona sneered at him before moving towards the door.

"They're probably ugly," Hack said. "Those little titties."

"Maybe I'll just tell Mom anyway," Rona said, and Wyatt said, "Then I guess I'll have to tell them where I got it from." The water rippled in the spring; the whole room shimmered, dull light reflecting off the surface of the water. Wyatt stared at her chest, but it was like he was looking into her instead of at her. He knew how much she liked Burke. He knew she would do it. His gaze flicked back up at her face.

She found the edge of her shirt and she pulled it up, catching her bra on the way. The cold air closed on her skin before she covered herself back up.

"Wait a minute," Hack said, walking towards her. "I want to touch them."

Rona aimed for the front of his pants and kicked, and he went squealing to his knees. She ran up the stairs, Wyatt's laughter bouncing up the steps after her.

There were so many things Rona could have done then; she thought about just going to Agnes and David and going all the way back to Wyatt's broken arm and working her way forward. She could tell them about the magazine and maybe even make things in the basement a little worse. What if the boys had been doing something to each other? She could tell Irene and Irene was so perfect she would be obligated to tell Head. Rona had seen Head mad at his kids before; once he'd caught some of the cousins poking the old rooster with a stick and whipped four of them in a row, youngest to oldest, each one a little worse than the one before. A beating like that would look pretty good on Wyatt.

There were rumors she could spread around school, true stories she could make up. She could even try to set Hack and Wyatt against each other; what if she told Hack he could touch her, but first he had to beat-up Wyatt? She relished the image of the cousins swarming over Wyatt the way they had swarmed over the fat Jeffers boy. Would it be worth it to let one of the boys touch her? What if they all wanted to?

Mostly, Rona just wanted to take it out on someone. So she waited for Burke to bring the mail, and this time she stood practically in front of the mailbox so he'd have to stop and said, "That's some magazine you gave my brother, Mr. Van Meter." He gave her a look that was half I know what you mean and half I don't know what you mean. She said, "I was wondering what my parents will say when they find out where he got it."

"Now, Rona, those boys brought that magazine to me."

Rona said. "I bet you'll probably get fired as soon as your boss finds out." She took the mail from Burke's hand, and that hand stayed stiffly towards her, as if he were still hanging onto something. At the door to the house, she turned and gave him a wave.

The next day was the first chilly day of the fall, and the breeze was cool enough for Rona's face to tighten every time the air touched her. There was a thin pair of gloves that Merrilee had made and given to Rona the Christmas before, knitting them in her hospital bed as the television played in the background. The needles seemed to zig and zag in the air by themselves. "I'll teach you how to do this someday," Merrilee said.

The gloves were orange with a black stripe around the base, and Rona had been waiting to wear them again. They were a little smaller this year, but she wore them anyways, keeping her hands curled in her pockets. When Burke stopped by the mailbox, Rona made him wave three times before she came down from the porch. She took her time. The sway came into her hips naturally this time, not like when it had felt so awkward before. He said, "All right, I gave that magazine to your brother."

Triumphantly, Rona said, "You probably did that just because you were mad at me."

"That's not true," Burke said. "I asked him if he knew about the dog being pregnant and that other boy . . . What's his name?"

"Hack," Rona said, as though the sound of it left a bad taste in her mouth.

"Yeah, Hack. He had some wrong ideas how something like that happens, and I shouldn't have but I tried to set him straight. They just kept getting more confused, so remember that pervert? The one on Jamestown?"

Rona nodded.

"Well, I figured what's the harm in just showing them? So I opened up one of the magazines, just to show them the basics, and that's when your brother asked if they could have it. Again, shouldn't have, but I did. Anyway, it's not like the pervert's going to notice one of them missing." He tried the smile but Rona didn't smile back. He said, "Why am I even bothering with this? You don't know what I'm talking about anyway."

"I know what you're talking about." Rona said.

"Rona," he said, like he was talking to a child. "You couldn't possibly know."

"I know exactly." Rona said, with the kind of indignation that let him know how much she was enjoying herself.

"Now, how would you know something like that?"

"I've already done it," Rona said, before she could stop herself. Her cheeks turned warm, but she didn't stop looking right at Burke, and with one hand she swept the hair on one side of her face behind her ear.

"You have not," he said, quietly. Then he leaned closer. "With who?"

"My boyfriend in West Virginia," she said. She couldn't remember what she said his name was. "He's older. Like you."

Burke laughed, but Rona could hear it wasn't a real laugh. He was thinking about something while he was laughing. He said, "You know, I'm only twenty-three. That's not so much older than you."

"Someday, we could meet in a bar or something, like ten years from now, and no one would even look at us funny."

There was the laugh again. He said, "Rona, every day's something new with you." She could tell that part of him wasn't there anymore; something had gone deep inside of him, or something different had come to the surface. There was a quickness to his voice. "Listen, do you ever go to that park on the other side of the woods?"

"All the time," Rona said. She couldn't remember the last time she did, though.

"I'm almost done with my route." He'd decided something. "Why don't you meet me there in about an hour? We'll talk some more."

"Okay," Rona said. His teeth lined up perfectly. Rona watched the mail truck and for a long moment, she didn't think her legs would work, like the bones had been sneaked out of them. She climbed the porch steps, her heart pounding. All she could think was, He wants to talk with me, he wants to talk with me, though she knew what he really meant wasn't talk at all.

And he forgot to leave the mail, she thought, then she got up and walked towards the woods.

As usual, the park was almost empty, but Rona couldn't find Burke anywhere. She stayed until it was almost dark, walking along the edges of the woods and watching the parking lot for him. She wasn't sure if he would show up in his mail truck or his own car, and she thought he wasn't going to show up at all, but then a rusty brown car pulled into the gravel parking lot and Burke got out. He went and stood by the playground. Rona ducked behind a tree. The air was cool and she could see her own breath. She took very small, very short breaths.

He stayed for about fifteen minutes and then he went back to the car and drove off. Rona made her way through the woods; the air seemed gauzy, a gray curtain coming down on the world and Rona told herself over and over again how stupid she was, how she was a chicken and she'd just missed her chance, how she was just a little girl and not even a woman at all.

The next day when Burke pulled up at the house, Rona was waiting.

He was later than usual, and the sun was already low in the sky. Burke handed her two days worth of mail and said, "I knew you didn't really know so much."

"Well, I was there," Rona said, "but I didn't see you."

"Look, it's okay. You're too young to know about that stuff anyway."

"I'm not too young," Rona said. Burke wouldn't look at her. Rona never thought such a simple thing could make her so mad. "I know everything."

"Listen. Let's just drop it." He flipped through some letters in his lap. "I wish there was some way I could make it up to you, though. I feel bad about that whole thing with the magazine."

Where he couldn't see, Rona ground the toe of her boot into the ground. She said, "No thanks."

"Want to ride in the truck? You can finish my route with me."

Rona laughed, in spite of herself. There was only one seat. "Where would I sit?"

"In the back. You can sit on the mail pouch."

He was serious. He was looking at her again. Rona glanced at the house. All the windows were dark, and her fingers were numb inside the gloves. Burke said, "You want to go tell Mom and Dad first?"

She hated the way he said that. Mom and Dad; as if they were his parents, too. She said, "Nobody's home."

"Well, you could leave them a note."

"That's okay," Rona said. "They won't care."

Burke opened the sliding door and Rona hurried in. She had to climb over him and then past his seat, and she was careful not to touch him too much as she did. Once she was in the back, he slammed the door shut and she started to laugh. The sound was so strange coming from her that it made her stop. Then Burke started to laugh, too.

From the back of the truck, all Rona could see was the road coming towards her over Burke's broad shoulders. He had his hair pulled into a pony tail, and he told her some things about his route, but Rona wasn't really listening. She was watching the way his neck disappeared into the collar of his uniform.

After a few more stops, Burke pulled into the park. Rona moved around in the truck so she could see his face. He leaned back in his seat and closed his eyes.

"I always come here to catch my breath," he said. "Once my route is done."

"It's very beautiful here," Rona said. Her voice sounded grown-up, like it didn't belong to her.

"Did you ever see that big rock back in the woods? The one with all the names carved on it?"

Rona shook her head, but Burke's eyes were still closed, so he didn't even know she answered. She felt like it might be better not to say anything. Burke said, "It's down by the creek, a little ways from here. It's a bit of a walk." He opened his eyes and Rona saw how pale blue they were. Almost white. He said, "Want me to show you?"

They climbed out of the truck. The parking lot was empty. Heading for the edge of the woods, they walked down a narrow dirt path rutted with foot prints and the slim treads of bicycle tires. All the low trees had already lost their leaves, but they hadn't been down long enough to lose their color yet. The tops of the high oaks were bright orange and yellow and the sun came down through the branches and made the wide trunks into dark, heavy lines. Winding around the path, Rona kept her eyes on Burke's feet, the thick black soles of his shoes, kicking through all the yellow and orange. Up ahead of them, there was a rock the size of a small car, hunched like the back of some ancient animal, slowly rising out of the ground.

"Where's the names?"

"On the other side."

Rona went around. Burke was already there.

"You're a smart girl, Rona," he said. "But you don't really know anything."

"I do," Rona said. Her voice disappeared as it went out into the woods.

"No, you don't." He stared down at her. She hadn't realized he was so tall. "Do you know anything?"

She couldn't lie to him anymore. She tried to nod her head, but the movement was so slight he might not have noticed. She said, "I'm a good kisser."

"Are you now?" It took forever for him to lean down towards her. She felt his lips first, not pressing too hard, and then a little harder. She inhaled and his tongue touched hers. There was the points of his whiskers and then the softness inside her mouth. He pulled back and said, "That's not so bad."

He kissed her again, and this time he put his hand on her waist, gripping harder, leaning over her to reach. Burke could have lifted her in the air, if he wanted; he could have pinched her in half. She started to pull away, like the women in the romance novels sometimes did, but Burke squeezed tighter. She felt each one of his fingers jabbed against the small of her back, his thumb at her waist, his weight hovering over her. She felt like she couldn't breathe, like he was going to suffocate her.

Finally, he stopped. He looked like something hurt inside his chest. He said, "Do you want me to show you something else?"

Again, Rona tried but failed to nod. The light, silver and sharp, sliced over his shoulders, and his hands moved towards the front of his pants. It was hard to see, at first, in the shadow of his body, but then her eyes found it. It wasn't at all what she expected. She felt like she should move away. He caught her by the wrist. Her forearm disappeared in his hand, which was too tight, and she saw her fingers open crookedly, a line of pain up her arm, the orange glove, the black stripe. His mouth opened and he lunged towards her face and she thought he was going to bite her. She jerked away, trying to fall, but he still had a hold of her, twisting, dangling in the air.

Then she was on the ground. She scooted backwards, through the damp leaves and collided with the rock, suddenly right behind her and he was on top of her, pressing down. He pulled hard on her legs so that she was looking up into the trees and all that color and the wind was like a terrible sound coming out of her. She couldn't move, everything far away and at the same time she saw the wind stealing leaves off the high branches. They spiraled slowly towards her. His weight was crushing her, pushing against her again and again, his hands fumbling, tugging at her clothes, his breath rising off his body, his hands. She was going into the ground. He was pushing her into the dirt, shoving the cold earth over top of her.

Why aren't you screaming, she thought? Why aren't you doing something? She tried to call for someone. Merrilee, Merrilee. No one would save her. She had come here knowing, thinking she knew, she hadn't known. Merrilee! Merrilee, and then the weight was gone and there was a shadow in the woods. Huge and black, it had a hold of Burke and it was throwing him into the air. It slammed him into trees and the big rock and its arms swung down into Burke's body as he lay on the ground. Burke's pants were still half down and he struggled to get to his feet but the shape was on top of him.

Head was there. Rona pushed herself up, pulled at her clothes. Head was picking up Burke and knocking him down. Burke had pulled his pants up, and he tried to fight back. Rona screamed and Head turned to look and then Burke had somehow pulled the knife out of the sheath on Head's belt. He came running forward and Head grabbed him by the wrist and spun him towards the rock. There was a dull, wet sound.

Burke's hands went up to his head and his legs went out and he fell straight down. Head came towards Rona and picked her up with one hand and said, Run! and the branches whipped against her as she went. She held her hands over her face and she was tripping and stumbling, but she made it to the creek and then there was only the sound of her feet splashing into the water, the sound of her feet trampling all the fallen leaves.

V.

When Stella finally had her puppies, there were four of them. Rona thought they would never come, and she spent most of her time following the dog around, waiting for something to happen. All Stella seemed to want to do was sleep on the floor of David's pick-up truck; two or three times a day, he would come up with an excuse to take her for a ride, and she would heave herself into the passenger seat and stick her head out of the window, watching the world with that same judgmental expression she wore when David first brought her home. Even the half-hearted barks she occasionally offered to people on the sidewalks seemed to say, I knew it. I knew I'd see you walking there.

Rona would ride along on those drives, and David would talk about the class he was teaching at the community college, filling in for one of his friends who'd had to go on leave. It was a literature class, like David had taught in California, and Rona had never seen him so genuinely happy before. He even stopped drinking so much. The last time Agnes' had one of her committee meetings at the house, Rona sat in the next room where she could hear everything and even peek around the corner if she wanted to see what was going on. One of the ladies, Mavis Tuttle, said in that politely impolite way, "I didn't realize David was qualified to teach anyone anything."

Mavis had a plateful of cake resting on her plump belly and it bobbed up and down as she spoke. Agnes said, "Well, he may not be completely qualified, but at least he's trying."

It was the nicest thing Rona had ever heard her mother say about her father. At any other time, David's return to teaching would have been huge news, but Rona couldn't find a way to concentrate on it. She told herself it was because she was so worried about the puppies, though nothing in her head sounded right.

"I guess maybe I've been drifting," David said, as they rode in the truck with Stella, "but it was the principle of the thing, Rona."

"The principle of what thing?"

Then David laughed and talked about all the books he wanted to assign to his class, how there was never enough time to cover everything. He rambled about titles and authors and time periods, social significance and reasons the authors wrote what they did.

"Not that the reasons matter," he said.

As Stella got closer to having the puppies, David was afraid to take her too far from the house and so he would drive her around the farm, over the grass and down the gravel drive, through the orchard and around the old foundation of the barn and along the bank over-top the gully. The lamb seemed glad for the rest; she would watch the truck making its slow circles and solemnly chew, never taking its eyes off the dog, as if Stella might come bounding out at any moment, pregnant or not pregnant.

Rona didn't go along on those rides, because she didn't like the idea of being seen, riding around in the yard, her father occasionally hollering out of the window to the lamb. I should be hiding, Rona told herself. No one should ever see me again.

As soon as it was time for David to leave for his class, Rona would go up to her bedroom for the night and Stella would follow, swaying her slow way up the steps. The days had turned hot again, and Rona's room seemed to hold the last heat, as if the memory of August hid there, waiting for its season to return. There was a box fan in the window, but even with it turned on Rona had to sleep with only the sheets on the bed. She had the worst dreams every night, all flashing silver and shadows and the sound of things crunching under her feet. She would wake up, disoriented, and see Stella, sitting in front of the fan, pushing her nose into the artificial breeze. It must have been the next best thing to a car ride, and Rona was willing to go along with the idea. She'd pretend the sound of the fan was really the wind coming through a car's window, and the dull vibration she felt always on the edges of her body only the wheels on the road, rolling away as fast as they could.

One afternoon with Agnes at work and David nowhere to be found, Rona put her books in a bag and carried them down to the book store. She looked everywhere but at the old man as he thumbed through them, one by one, raising his eyebrows at Rona as he studied the covers, as if she hadn't bought them from him. He gave Rona some money; she didn't bother to hear how much it was, just stuffed the bills in her pocket. When she got home, she left it all in the laundry for Agnes to find.

What had she ever liked about the books, anyway? She thought of how Agnes had found them, and how she hadn't even looked at them since, and she felt ashamed of herself. For awhile, Rona tried to draw with Irene, but all her pictures looked like they had been drawn by someone who was pretending they knew how to draw.

Rona and Irene watched Stella as if she were some kind of present that might unwrap itself at any moment. The two girls spent a lot of time together; Rona liked the distraction of having someone around, and Irene liked to get away from her brothers. She had been babysitting them for two weeks, ever since Head went back to West Virginia in the middle of the night without bothering to tell her exactly when he was coming home.

If Irene sensed that anything was wrong with Rona, she never let on; she talked and talked and was so nice that not even Rona could hold it against her. Irene drew city scenes, real three dimensional streets vanishing off in the distance, and Rona would color and tack the pictures to the walls in the corner where the dog slept. David had piled some blankets into a bed for her, and Stella laid on her side, sometimes letting out a miserable little growl that would cause both the girls to look up expectantly.

Irene made up two long lists of possible names for the pups, and this was all despite the fact that she had to cook and clean for her brothers and make sure they really went to school and did their homework and their chores. The only one Head took with him was the youngest, Aubrey, and it was up to Irene to make sure no one found out her father was gone, not Agnes or David and especially not anyone at school.

"Daddy told me to beat them if I had to," Irene said, laughing. She was putting the final touches on a poster; there was a row of buildings and a dog standing on the sidewalk, wagging its tail. "Momma left us this way once, when Daddy was gone off to work somewhere and Dewey was just a baby. I was only eight, but I did okay until Daddy came back." She leaned close to Rona, as if what she was about to say would make all the difference. "Twenty three days, I had the boys that time."

The girls were adding rock stars to the list of puppy names when Irene said, "Why don't we name one after Mr. Van Meter? In honor and all?"

"In honor's only for someone who's dead. We don't know he's dead." What else could Rona say? What else could she do but cry? These thoughts were around her all the time, and Irene gave her a long hug, and Rona accepted it even though she knew that Irene probably thought she was crying because Burke liked her so much and they were such good friends.

The puppies were born in Rona's room, and Rona was glad because now that she had seen them, she could stop wondering what they would look like. That question had become her favorite distraction, but it had been starting to fail her, as if by thinking it so much she had worn it out. It had been the same way with Merrilee, only then she had imagined women and men in love, in lust, willing to do anything for each other, or to each other. Even while she watched the paramedics wheel Merrilee out of the house, her body huge and overflowing the edges of the stretcher, those thoughts had been with her. David helped them lift Merrilee into the back of the ambulance, barely awake, her head lolling towards Rona, who was right there, who had been alone with Merrilee when she stopped talking and slowly lifted her hand to her throat.

"Call David," she said, her voice like the last of her breath, and when David got there, Merrilee smiled at Rona and closed her eyes and wouldn't wake up, even with David screaming at her. In the hospital, the doctors took her other foot. She was in a coma. Agnes came to Rona and said, "Do you want to go see your grandmother?"

They were in the kitchen. Rona pretended to do her math homework, her mother's gaze like a doctor's hands examining her. Agnes, too skinny at Merrilee's stove. "She's going to die," Agnes said, and then almost started to cry, which seemed so false to Rona, so untrue, her mother who had done nothing but argue and bicker with Merrilee. Rona tapped her pencil on the columns of numbers, afraid to look up. She imagined adding, or subtracting. She imagined being on the back of a horse, galloping towards some lover, across a field that between the rise and fall of hooves turned into a forest and then even the ground was gone, falling away into the darkness.

Now, whenever anyone around her started talking about how the mailman disappeared somewhere in the park beside her house, Rona would be able to think about Stella and the puppies and how they were all like a little family, how they all needed each other.

◇ ◇ ◇

"Did you know he was only twenty-three years old?"

"I knew he was trouble."

"How could you know that? You didn't know a thing about him."

"Something seemed off."

"But twenty-three?"

Rona woke up in the dark hallway outside her parent's bedroom, listening to David and Agnes talk. She blinked her eyes hard; it felt as though she'd just been sleepwalking, and she couldn't remember getting out of bed or even going to sleep.

"That's how old we were when we left," David said.

"But at least we told someone where we were going. His poor mother."

"His poor mother? No one said anything about my poor mother."

"Including you. And what makes you think he was so much trouble?"

"I could tell by looking at him, by how he looked."

Agnes laughed once, short and sharp, like a needle in the ears. It was the way she laughed when she thought someone was being ridiculous.

"Laugh if you want. I'm not the one with my picture on the front page of the paper. He probably looked down the line and saw another thirty years of civil service coming his way. Thanks, but no thanks."

"They found marijuana in his mail truck. And the police were all over the woods. Maybe it was some kind of drug deal."

David laughed. "Then maybe they ought to talk to Head."

"I don't even want to know," Agnes said. "There's more of a problem around here than you think."

"They always make things seem worse than they are."

"Rona was out there all the time. What if he was trying to sell some of it to her?"

"She's got more sense than that." They were both quiet. "Doesn't she?"

Rona closed her eyes and saw black shoes kicking through the leaves, a dark shape with silver teeth flying through the woods.

After awhile, David said, "Anyway, when's the last time you saw Head around?"

Rona went back to her room and lay on her bed. She couldn't stand to have even the weight of the sheet on top of her. She could hear the wind and it sounded like the hooly-hoo, chasing itself around the house.

◇ ◇ ◇

The day after she followed Burke into the woods, Rona walked past Head's house on her way to school and saw that his pick-up was gone. The night before, she had gone home and right to her room. She thought that maybe she cried, that maybe she went to sleep. Leaves were falling on her, burying her; she tried to lie still but she couldn't stop them from rustling.

In the morning, there were bruises on both her arms, thirteen of them, shaped like fingers. She put on a long sleeve shirt. The zipper on her pants was torn from the seam. She put the pants at the very bottom of a drawer. Around her waist, there were red marks that looked like rope burns. At breakfast, Agnes asked if she was feeling okay and Rona said she was fine. She tried to eat. The room warped around the edges, as though she were inside a bubble looking out, and she thought she saw the vague shapes of people pushing against the surface, leaning in with their hands and faces, stretching towards her, mouths opening and closing, tongues writhing. But as soon as she saw that Head's truck was gone, the bubble didn't so much pop as begin to fade, the world becoming real again.

Irene came out of the house, her eyes puffy and red. She didn't yet seem as brave as she would later in Rona's room. The cousins trailed after her, all of them upset except for Hack, who had his chest puffed out like he was the man of the house. They gave Wyatt and Rona the whole story, how Head had kissed them all in the night, telling them to be good and he would be back soon. He told them how important it was to just act like he wasn't even gone, and not to let anyone know, and how if there was an emergency to go get Agnes or David, but only then if someone was going to bleed to death or something.

Rona flinched at that part of the story, thinking of Burke getting a hold of Head's knife, then Head getting it back.

"Then he just left," Dewey said.

"And he took Aubrey with him," Fulton said.

"Just like Momma left," Clay said. "Except she didn't take anyone with her."

All the young ones started to cry, and Hack said, "Knock it off or I'll beat all you all until you got something to cry about."

"You aren't beating anyone," Irene said, and she held the hands of the littlest ones for awhile as they walked towards the school. Wyatt listened to the whole story, but he didn't say anything, and Rona tried to make the bubble come back. She couldn't make her mind shut down, though that was all she wanted to do; against everything, she kept trying to figure out what happened after she ran. At school, she stayed in for recess by herself, thinking, not wanting to get home until after the mail came. She imagined Burke showing up, his face bruised and bloody, but then she heard again that sound he made when Head threw him into the rock. And Head was gone. Head left in the night, like one of the characters in her books.

At home, Rona came into the kitchen and found Wyatt and Agnes sitting together at the table. Agnes had a look on her face like she'd been waiting around all day. She stood up and handed Rona an envelope. It was the last of the letters she mailed to herself from Burke. "We had a new mailman today," Agnes said. Rona felt like she was twisting on the end of a pin. She looked down at the little hearts over the i's and her hands started to shake, the writing so obviously her own, and Agnes said, "So where'd you get the stamp?"

When Rona didn't answer, the lecture began, Agnes' anger feeding upon itself in that awful way, her voice getting louder and louder until finally she sent Rona up to her room, as though she would kill Rona if she had to look at her for even one more moment.

My mother, Rona thought, sitting by herself on her bed. Furious about a stamp. Think if she'd opened the letter.

She tried to imagine telling Agnes what had happened and started to laugh. Then she couldn't stop. She jammed her face into the pillow, afraid that Agnes would come stomping up the stairs, and she wished that Stella was there, so she could rub the sides of the dog's belly and tell her everything was going to be okay.

That night, Agnes made TV dinners and everyone sat in front of the television, eating off trays. Rona figured the meal was supposed to be some kind of apology, but all she could do was push her food around the little foil plate. It didn't even look like food; it looked like dirt, dirt with leaves and bones in it. There was a knock on the door, and through the white curtains she could see a policeman standing there. He had a big, square chest and a flat face that moved around like a rotating camera. David stepped out on the porch and closed the door, then he came back and called Agnes out.

Rona and Wyatt almost fell over each other to get to either side of the door so they could hear what was happening, but everyone spoke too low to be understood. When David turned to come back into the house, the two of them scrambled back to their TV trays. David said, "The policeman wants to ask you two some questions."

Rona's composure was a testament to both the way she could keep a secret and her promise as a witch. She didn't say much, nodding whenever she could, or shaking her head, or shrugging. The policeman talked to Wyatt first; between his flat face and the way Wyatt just stared back at him, the two of them looked like a pair of walls glaring across an alleyway at each other. The policeman turned to Rona and asked her the very same questions, as if she hadn't just been standing there, listening to everything he said. He kneeled, bringing his face level with Rona's. It was the kind of thing adults only did when they wanted to act like nothing serious was about to happen.

"What's your name, sweetheart?" Sweetheart? The policeman had great, bushy eyebrows that went up and down like curtains at the beginning and end of each question. She told him and he said, "Rona, your mom and dad tell me you liked to talk with the mailman. Is that true?"

She nodded.

"What kind of things did you talk about?"

"The mail."

"Did you two talk a lot?"

Agnes said, "They talked almost everyday."

The policeman gave Agnes a look, then said, "You talked about the mail?"

Rona nodded.

"Did you ever talk about anything else?"

Rona shook her head, then she said, "Sometimes he would talk about his route. He asked how I was doing in school."

"That's good." The policeman gave her the kind of smile that looked like it was hiding an extra row of teeth. "Did you talk yesterday?"

Rona turned the question over in her head. She thought she should tell the truth as much as possible, so she said, "Yes."

"Did Mr. Van Meter say or do anything unusual?"

"No."

"Did he say he was going anywhere, or did he seem worried or anything?"

"I guess he seemed worried. Maybe."

There was a quiver in her voice and Rona couldn't make it go away. Watching the policeman, Rona tried to gauge if anyone had noticed. She could feel Agnes and David looking at her like she might be coming down with a cold.

"Do you and your brother ever go to the woods by the creek?"

"That's where I got my arm broke," Wyatt said.

"Sometimes they play there," Agnes said. The policeman looked at her again. "Did you see anything unusual in the woods yesterday? Anyone you've never seen around before? Any noises like someone having a fight?"

Only my uncle trying to kill the man I thought I would . . .

Rona stopped the words before they could come out. She shook her head firmly, as if to answer all three questions at once. The policeman groaned as he got to his feet and handed a card to David. "If anyone thinks of anything, give me a call."

He smiled at Rona, and he looked like such a nice man all of a sudden. He looked like he wanted to believe her. He even touched the top of the head, then turned to do the same to Wyatt, awkwardly stopping himself before he did, then made his way down the steps, walking towards the next house down the street, moving away from the park.

When Rona came down to breakfast the next day, Agnes and David were hovering over the newspaper, unfolded on one end of the table. Rona almost turned around before she reached them, but they looked up at her and she had to keep going. The headline read, MAILMAN MISSING. That was slightly better than MAILMAN MURDERED, which is what Rona had been expecting. She tried not to laugh, afraid that she wouldn't be able to stop herself again.

On the front page, there was a picture of Burke that looked like it might have been taken for his high school graduation. His hair was shorter, his mouth a parody of the smile, only a twist at the corners. His eyes were dark and flat, almost no white showing around the edges. In Rudy Edson's class that day, all anyone wanted to talk about was the mailman. Irene spent the whole class in tears, until finally Rudy sent her down to the counselor. Once Hack saw how his sister got out of class, he started to cry, too, and soon the whole class was bawling, except for Rudy and Rona, who thought her own lack of tears must have looked like a sure sign of guilt.

The newspaper either added new details everyday or repeated things that everybody already knew, and every article gave Rona something else to worry about. What if they found evidence that she had been in the mail truck? What if someone else was in the park? What if they found some blood on the side of that rock and followed her footprints back to the house? Head didn't strike Rona as a master criminal. She couldn't imagine him hiding a body someplace where it couldn't be found, especially not in those woods. They just weren't that big, and even though the park seemed empty, people did go there. They went hiking. There had been bike tracks on the trail.

Maybe Head had only scared him enough to make him run off, Rona thought. She heard the noise, the dull thump, something split open. Some people, people who didn't know the whole story, would blame Burke for what was happening when Head had found them, but Rona knew differently.

All of Agnes' friends and acquaintances kept calling the house, as if Rona's family should somehow know more than anyone else just because they lived so close to where the mail truck had been found. Mavis Tuttle stopped Agnes in the grocery store and they traded rumors, Agnes acting like she was above it all, but Rona could see how much she enjoyed the attention. She would make little dismissive sounds, as though it was all old news to her. Rona stood there the whole time; all the secrets she had tried to learn came to this, and how terrible it was to be the only one who knew the truth.

Irene kept insisting they name one of the puppies after Burke. "It only seems right," she would say, her voice as heavy as the air in Rona's room.

The cousins had all come down to the house at dinner time. They were running out of their own food. Irene was starting to wonder what she was going to feed her brothers, so Rona smuggled out as much as she could, a box of cereal or a bag of chips or some cans of pop in her backpack, but Agnes was catching on. She grudgingly made enough macaroni and cheese to feed everyone, and then right in front of all the cousins, she said to David, "That brother of yours has to pay his rent by the end of the week."

"Half-brother," David said, giving the cousins a wink, all of them trying their best to wink back. It was already Wednesday. David looked at Agnes like he didn't want to talk about it, but when Agnes didn't look away, he said, "He'll pay soon as he can."

"As soon as he can is Friday," Agnes said. "If we can't pay our bills, then we can't pay his. I'd hate to see the bank come and take that house away."

Agnes looked at Irene. The other cousins were too busy stuffing food in their mouths to notice, but Irene looked down at her plate and stopped eating. David slammed down his glass and milk splashed onto the tablecloth and Agnes started asking each of the cousins how they liked school and if they were getting along okay. Most of them answered with food in their mouths.

In Rona's room, Irene held two of the puppies in her lap. Rona held the other two and tried to make Irene believe Burke wasn't dead.

"Who says he can't be missing?"

"Everyone says he's dead."

"He could have run off."

"Dead. We have to face it. They'll probably never catch who did it."

"Did you ever think maybe Head isn't coming back?"

Irene let a puppy chew on her finger. She said, "Of course he's coming back."

"Your momma never came back," Rona said, which came out worse than she meant it, especially the way she'd said momma.

"Daddy's different. He always comes back."

"What if I told you I saw him kill Burke?" Irene took her finger out of the puppy's mouth. Rona said, "What if I told you he killed him because he found us in the woods and Burke was trying to rape me?"

It was as close to the truth as Rona could come. Irene stood up and almost threw the puppies off her lap. She said, "You say the meanest things and you say them just to see how much they hurt."

"But that's what happened," Rona said.

"It is not," Irene said, her voice that same shriek she had used on her brothers at the parade. "I know all about you, sneaking around, spying on everybody. You tore my poster. That's just like you to make up something like that. You're awful. You're the worst person I ever knew. You're worse than Hack. You're worse than Wyatt!"

Irene looked like she could have gone on naming people forever; instead she turned and left without saying anything else. Rona listened to her go down the steps and heard the sound of the door slamming. For a while, maybe even hours, Rona just sat. She was sinking into the floorboards. She laid down beside Stella and the puppies, and closed her eyes, and her mind began to leap from place to place; the door opened and her father came into the room, carrying Merrilee's tooth in a box filled with leaves. Merrilee was there, the liniment smell, the way her body moved the air, but Rona didn't open her eyes. She didn't want to see Merrilee. Rona was standing in the basement beside the well, watching napkins embroidered with orange and red as they floated on the cold water. She was floating. The puppies nuzzled against her, nipping at her stomach with their still toothless mouths.

Rona woke the next morning to Agnes and David arguing about the rent. Agnes was making breakfast and slamming things around. She said, "You think that job of yours makes you some kind of hero. Who do you think's been paying the bills while you drive around and talk, for God's sake, to a sheep?"

"I can't ask him to pay with money he doesn't have."

"We finally have a chance to get ahead and look how you waste it."

David started cursing them. Rona listened to the two of them and tried to imagine a time when they were in love. There was a picture of them at the house in California, a house Rona remembered only distantly, and they were smiling, genuinely smiling, as if everything would always be perfect. She had gone through her mother's diary once, but it was only filled with the kind of entries Rona refused to write; meetings, what she made for supper, movies they had gone to see. Wyatt broke his arm today playing with Rona. The doctors want to do some more tests tomorrow, and the last time Rona checked, her mother hadn't written anything new. There was never anything as interesting as Merrilee's letters; Rona had found six of them in the old boxes in the basement, and the last one had read:

Dear Momma;

The things I shouldn't have done I'm sure I don't have to tell you. You and Pop probably wonder all the time how you raised a daughter like Noreen and then one like me. You probably wish things worked out opposite and I don't blame you.

I keep writing you these letters and only getting half way through, but it's like that preacher of yours used to say, it's the trying that counts. All this stuff you don't want to hear anyway, and already I'm losing steam. This one won't make the mail, ha! Just let me say I didn't want to hurt you or Pop and someday I know you'll forgive me, you all are too nice not to, probably though I don't deserve it. Remember you used to say the heart sounds just like footsteps and it wants what it wants. Please don't take that as me blaming you, I'm just saying I remember you said that and it meant something to me. Oh, hell.

In the middle of the argument, David stomped out of the house and Agnes slammed up the stairs and Rona crept down to the kitchen, disappointed to find Wyatt creeping in from the other direction. He watched her eat like he was counting how many bites she took, like there was a right number and a wrong number.

"You don't look so great," he said.

Rona wished, though she never would have admitted it, that she could tell Wyatt the whole story. He would know what to do next; he would be able to figure out what was going to happen when Agnes and David found out Head was gone. He might even be able to stop it from happening, but Rona knew she couldn't ask for Wyatt's help, not even about the rent, because he would want to know why she cared about Head all of a sudden. She could hear him saying, You can't even get along with Irene, and she likes everybody. You must be worse than Hack. Worse than me.

Rona didn't figure out what to do about the rent until she got to school and discovered her history book was missing. She looked in her backpack and her desk and over by the bookshelf where she usually liked to read. Rudy took lost books very seriously. In front of the whole class, he gave Rona a lecture about how the books belonged to the school and how hard they were to replace and how she would have to take a letter home to her parents if she didn't find it and they would have to send the money to buy a new one.

None of which meant much to Rona, although the lecture part bothered her because the whole class turned and stared at her, except for Irene, who hadn't so much as looked at her since their argument. Hack snickered through the whole thing, and he walked behind Rona and teased her the whole way home, until finally she turned around and tried to repeat her kick from the basement. He kept running his mouth, but at least he kept his distance.

As for the letter and the money, those were no problem. When she got home, she opened the letter and found out that the book cost twenty-two dollars, then she signed her mother's name at the bottom. As usual, it looked just like Agnes' handwriting. Then she went out on the porch to make sure Wyatt wasn't around; she saw him going towards the creek with Hack. Rona ran up the stairs to Wyatt's room, and as she took the jar out from under the bed, she saw all the crumpled bills crammed inside and, as Head himself would have said, Damn if they didn't look just like rent money.

She took the jar to her room and uncrumpled the bills. There were five hundred and fifty-six dollars there, all of it in fives and ones except for eight crisp tens and six twenties that looked like something someone had chewed up and spit back out. She left the change uncounted. The rent was four hundred dollars, which she knew because Agnes said it twenty times that morning, so Rona took that much plus the money to pay for her lost book. She found an envelope and wrote RENT in big block letters like she imagined Head might do. She was going to put it in the mailbox, but just as she got to the front door, the mail truck pulled up and stopped.

Rona stopped, too. Her legs felt like someone had driven an iron bar down through them. The man behind the wheel, balding, pot-bellied, a goatee straggly on his chin, didn't even look up at the house, and Rona decided it was best to just leave the envelope on the counter.

Back in Wyatt's room, she couldn't make the jar look full again, no matter how many ways she crumpled and uncrumpled the remaining money. Somehow, she was going to have to get the money back. Until then, though, she took the jar down to the basement, down to the room with the old canned food. There on the shelves the jar looked like it might float back up the stairs and through the house to wherever Wyatt was, opening itself like a laugh, showing him how much was missing. Rona twirled the lid and slammed one of other jars inside, hard enough that she thought she might have broken them both. It was all a terrible mistake, she was sure, but she had no idea what else she could have done, other than find some spell of Merrilee's that would let her go back and start all over.

◇ ◇ ◇

Finally, Head came back. He didn't stay long.

He was waiting in the driveway beside the little house as Rona and Wyatt and the cousins came walking home from school. The cousins ran to him like he was a parade incarnate, and they were so happy that they managed to knock him down, or maybe Head let them take him to the ground just so he could feel them climbing all over him. They screamed and laughed and pounded on him with their fists. It was an odd kind of love. No one laughed louder that Head.

Only Hack looked disappointed; it wasn't long before the younger brothers started telling Head about all the things that Hack had done while he was away. Head did his best to seem angry, but he couldn't keep it up. In all, he had been away for eight days, ("Short by this family's standard," he said), and he told them now that he was back for good. He said, "It's a clean slate, starting right now. Right now."

He clapped his hands for emphasis. The cousins nodded like a congregation. Head turned to Wyatt and said, "Say, boy, you ever going to cheer up?" to which Wyatt simply turned his back and started walking home. Head winked at his kids, then said, "Go get yourselves cleaned up. We're going to your aunt and uncle's for dinner."

Screaming like they hadn't eaten at Agnes and David's in years, the cousins tumbled over each other as they ran into the house. Head tried to smile at Rona and said, "Let me walk you home."

Neither of them said anything until they were halfway to Merrilee's house. Rona felt like her throat was trying to swallow her throat, and her voice choked as she said, "What happened, Head? What happened to him?"

"It's better if you don't know." He asked how things looked up here, what people had been saying, if the police had come around. Rona told him everything she knew, and he listened carefully, sometimes nodding or grunting. He said, "All right."

They made it down to the driveway and stood by the fire pit. Rona said, "Did you kill him? Because you did, didn't you?"

Head looked down at her. With just the slightest movement, he nodded. Rona cried out once; she would not have believed she could make such a sound, and then she hit him, slamming her fists into his legs and stomach and he just stood there, taking it all. Rona didn't think she would ever stop hitting him, and then she had stopped and his huge hands held her shoulders and she cried against his belly, the denim of his overalls pressing into her cheeks. I wanted it, she said. I made him do it, and Head said, That's not true. You think you did, but you didn't.

"I don't know how I was out there," Head said. "I just wandered around all morning, feeling like I should be somewhere else, and then I was there. There's no sense to it. I closed my eyes and then I saw you."

Rona felt him raise his hands off her shoulders. He set them back down. He said, "You know I didn't mean to, right?" Rona didn't answer. "It was how he hit that rock. He hit it and I could see everything that was going to happen. I drug his body down the creek and when it got dark I put him in the truck. There's places in West by God no one'll ever find him."

Rona put her hand over her mouth and backed away. She wanted to run, back to the woods, back down to the creek and the sound of the water.

"Some people get exactly what's coming," Head said. Rona kept backing up and he said, "I won't tell anybody."

Rona turned away and didn't look back at him until she heard his footsteps going towards the house. He moved slow, swaying side to side, moon-shaped and just as heavy. Above him, Rona saw Wyatt's face in the window. He had been watching the whole thing.

For dinner, Head went out and bought the buckets of chicken. Agnes picked at hers, as if waiting for some rude punch line to be delivered, but David seemed overjoyed. Everyone was in great spirits; Agnes and David because they were the ones eating for free for once, and the cousins because they knew they got away with one, and Head because he made it back to his children. Wyatt spent the whole meal staring at Rona.

Rona waited for a chance to tell Head not to say anything about the rent, but as soon as dinner was over, he went out with David to start a fire. They took with them a cooler of beer to chase down the fresh moonshine Head had brought back north with him.

"Don't worry, it fermented along the way," he said, and even Agnes had to laugh. She sat with all of them by the fire, and stayed after Head sent the cousins home and David told Wyatt and Rona to go to bed. Rona watched from the porch, too far away to hear, waiting for some sign that Head had told them what had really happened. There was a noise behind her. Wyatt stood at the end of the hall. He looked at her for a moment, then turned and went back to his room.

The next morning as they walked past the little house, Head was sitting in the pick-up waiting for them. Irene and Aubrey were in the front seat. Head said, "I told your folks last night. We're going back to West by God."

He smiled like he had just said paradise instead. The other cousins opened a flap on the side of the cap and waved like crazy.

"Surprise!" they shouted. Head pointed with his thumb toward the back.

"They didn't want to leave without saying so long," he said. He looked especially at Rona. "Me either."

Rona came over close to the cab. She looked past Head and said, "Bye, Irene."

Irene looked out of her window. Head said to Wyatt, "Boy, it can't be all that bad." Then he gave Rona a slow grin and backed down the driveway. As the truck started down the street, Hack hung his head out of the side flap and yelled, "See you later, losers! No school for us!"

And all Rona could do was watch them go.

The week before Halloween was quiet. Rona hadn't realized how much space Head and the cousins had occupied in her life, and the stillness in the house and around the farm took some getting used to. She spent most of her time with the puppies, trying to help Stella keep track of them all because they were so active, but it wasn't the same without Irene. David seemed lonely and maybe even Agnes was, too, despite everything. The house was finally beginning to seem more like theirs and less like Merrilee's.

Wyatt was devastated by the loss of his work force; he didn't seem to have the ambition to do it all by himself, which Rona knew was good news for her. As soon as he started trying to make money again, he would discover the missing four hundred and twenty-two dollars. It had seemed impossible to ask Head for the rent, on top of everything, though she knew he would have given it to her. But to ask? She couldn't.

Then one day she watched Wyatt go walking across the yard with his rake, headed for the subdivision and she knew it was over. Wyatt came home and didn't say a word to anyone. He went straight upstairs and in a little while, she heard him slamming things around, and she heard his foot steps all over the upstairs. Then there was nothing but quiet. Rona stayed downstairs by her parents; she offered to help Agnes with dinner, but she was only calling out for a pizza since it was time to start the swing shift again. Rona tried to help David work on the little shed he was making for the sheep, but as soon as she went outside, her father went in to change his clothes for class.

❖ ❖ ❖

There was no sign of Wyatt until after their parents left. He came down the stairs and said, "Where's my money?"

"What money?" Rona asked

"You know what money."

"Sorry," Rona said.

"You used it to pay Head's rent, didn't you?"

"Like I care enough about Head to steal for him."

"Stop lying to me," he said. Rona could see how upset he was, and how he was trying not to let her know how angry he really was, and with his anger that same calmness, that sense of calculation.

"You went through my stuff," he said. "So I went through yours."

He took a handful of envelopes from behind his back. There were little hearts all over them. He unfolded one of the letters, letting the envelope fall to the floor, and he started to read. "Dear Burke, I think you are the most handsome mailman in the world. I want to marry you and . . ."

Rona ran towards him, but he balled up the letter with one quick motion and threw it over her head. She turned around to get it and Wyatt started to read again. "Dear Burke, I wonder what it will be like the first time we . . ."

She yelled for him to stop but he just kept reading, he kept going, reading louder to be heard over her yelling. "Dear Burke, please don't be angry and don't just drive past anymore. I'd do anything for you, even let you . . ."

Rona came running towards him and Wyatt said, "Even if you get these back, I've hidden all the other ones. I'll give them to Mom and Dad and then what'll you do?" Rona was trying not to cry and she said, "Please Wyatt, don't. I'll get the money."

"I don't want the money anymore," he said. "This is better than money. You're going to do whatever I want."

"Okay," she said, "just give them back."

"Tell me what was going on with you and Head the other day and why he left and don't lie to me because I'll know. Your a terrible liar, you can't fool anybody."

Rona shook her head, crying.

"You might as well tell me because I already know," Wyatt said.

"Then why do I have to tell you," Rona said, but the words came out so mangled by her crying that she didn't think he could understand her.

But he did. He said, "Because I want to hear you say it."

There was no choice, really; she had to tell him, and when she was done he sat there, studying her. He listened through the whole thing, patient and still, only his eyes moving occasionally from place to place on her body. "I should tell the police," he said. Rona shook her head as hard as she could. "I should tell them. It's my duty, and I have to tell Mom and Dad. They should know what you did."

Rona cried without making any sound at all. Then Wyatt said, "You have to do some penance." He made her wait, and then he said, "Go get one of the puppies."

◆ ◆ ◆

The dog squirmed in Rona's arms as she followed Wyatt down into the basement. He told her what they were going to do and why they had to do it but Rona could hardly keep the thoughts in her head. Wyatt knew, he knew, he would tell. He took her into the room with the cold spring, turned on the light and said, "We'll do it in here."

Rona felt the room lean against her like her own hands, tight on the puppy. She held the dog closer. Wyatt was going to tell, he was going to tell, and then everyone would know, they would put Head in jail, they would all know what she had wanted to do, what she had done.

Wyatt said, "You want to be saved, don't you?"

The water looked black, dark as oil, gleaming. Rona could feel the coldness seep out of it and she said, "It's too cold. That water'll kill it."

Wyatt shrugged. Rona went over and knelt on the blocks that formed a lip for the water. Instantly, her knees ached. They would all know. She lifted the puppy away from her body.

"Do it," Wyatt said.

Rona closed her eyes and dunked the puppy as quickly as she could. It thrashed in her hands and she was afraid she would drop it as she brought it back out. She held it tight and soaking wet against her chest.

"Again," Wyatt said. Rona shook her head and he came up behind her and kicked her in the back. "Again."

His voice was so calm. The puppy went down and came back up.

The coldness was like metal in the joints of her hands. Wyatt said, "Longer. It's not baptized yet. You aren't sorry yet."

She put the puppy under and he said, "Don't bring it out until I say so."

Rona couldn't stand it. She brought the puppy out and set it down and screamed at Wyatt, hoping that the dog would run, but it didn't. It shook itself and snorted and trembled and Wyatt went over and grabbed it.

"I'll show you," he said, and he plunged the puppy into the water and held it under. "You have to be forgiven, and to be forgiven you have to be sorry."

The puppy went still in his hands and she grabbed Wyatt by the arms and tried to pull his hands out of the water, but he was too strong. She could feel his thin muscles locking and even as she scratched at him, he held on.

"You just watch," he said. He cursed at her through his teeth and said, "You just stand there and watch," but Rona ran out of the room and went to the shelves where she'd hidden the jar full of money, reaching stupidly for the knob that turned on the light and there was Merrilee again, and gone as quick as the light filled the room, so that she was never really there at all. Rona grabbed the jar and ran back to the spring.

"Here," she said. "Here, you want it so bad."

Wyatt turned and he was that ghost white again as he brought the puppy out of the water. It hung limp as a dishrag in his hand, and he let it flop to the floor. Its body made a spongy sound, already water logged. Wyatt came towards her.

"Give me that," he said.

The jar trembled in Rona's hands as she started to take the lid off, and Wyatt came towards her. She kept the well between them and when Wyatt ran around the side she dropped to her knees and thrust the jar sideways into the water. Instantly, it filled, freezing cold, and then Wyatt slammed into her side. Rona lost her grip and tumbled over, holding her side. Wyatt knelt down, reaching into the deep end of the water. She crawled towards him and he swung his fist, catching her in the mouth, his knuckles slamming into her front teeth. The room went bright and then dark, then bright again.

Wyatt laid down on his stomach beside the well, his arm in the water up to his shoulder, the puppy limp in a puddle beside him. You have to be sorry, Rona thought, as she came up behind him. You have to want forgiveness. She came down with all her weight on Wyatt's back. The air burst out of him and when he tried to arch up out of the water, her hands grabbed a hold of his neck and shoved his head back below the surface. She no longer felt the fighting of his body, she felt only the coldness of the water, working into the joints between her knuckles like ice. She felt everything seize, her brother's body nothing more than water flowing slowly through her fingers, a chunk of ice between her hands. Wyatt was ice, hard and smooth, and Rona was surprised to see her grandmother's tooth gleaming beneath the dark water, just past where the rippling reflections of her hands closed on something that was trying to escape. In her hands she had Merrilee's tooth. The body beneath her went still and she tried to squeeze harder, tried to hold onto the tooth as it tried at the same time to slip from her grasp, like something that hated the touch of hands, something that did not want to be found, and then Rona felt a tremendous pain where Wyatt had hit her on the mouth and she fell backwards, pulling the motionless thing beneath her out of the water as she did and she brought her numb hand up to her tooth, which was throbbing as if someone had reached into her mouth and snapped it like an icicle and everything made sense.

Rona could sit there in the cold beside the well and see what the rest of her life would look like. The rest of her days reflected across the surface of water, and she cried because she didn't want to see anything that terrible or that beautiful. No one will ever know what Head did in the woods, he never leaves his family again and Irene always draws those beautiful pictures, all the cousins on farms of their own, skinny dipping in creeks, watching parades. And David finds whatever California took away or whatever the Dangers left behind and Agnes understands, her whole life becomes parties and true love and they see how important it is that Rona has been listening the whole time, that she has heard and understood all the awful things that people say to each other when they think no one is paying attention. Everyone's life settles into an easy grace, Wyatt's hair grows back, long and white and beautiful. He wears a pony tail until the day he dies, which is not today. Today his darkness becomes a kind of light. He is again the boy who didn't want anyone to know his sister broke his arm, and there is no disease for him, no death but the death he is willing to accept and even Merrilee could be there. She could come back and sit on the porch and rock, she could stare out over the land that David bought back for her, the houses and the subdivision gone. She could go back to the mountains and Rona could go with her, Rona with her front tooth gone black where Wyatt hit her, like black lightning in her smile and it was all going to happen. Rona could feel it as she watched Wyatt's body, limp as the ruined puppy, one hand still in the cold, cold water. All will be forgiven, as soon as Wyatt's body begins to move.

Upcoming in 2008
Duo: Novellas, Volume 2

Winners of the 2006 Ruthanne Wiley Memorial Novella Contest as selected by finalist judge Tom Barbash:

A Martyr for Suzy Kosasovich
by Patrick Michael Finn
of Asheville, NC

A Momentary Jokebook
by Jayson Iwen
of Madison, WI

Contest submission period: April, through October, 1 annually. For complete guidelines, visit us at **www.csuohio.edu/poetrycenter** or send S.A.S.E to:

Cleveland State University Poetry Center
Novella Contest
Department of English
2121 Euclid Avenue
Cleveland, OH 44115-2214